JOSÉ DONOSO

A Novel

Edited by Julio Ortega

Translated from the Spanish by
Suzanne Jill Levine

NORTHWESTERN UNIVERSITY PRESS
EVANSTON, ILLINOIS

Northwestern University Press
www.nupress.northwestern.edu

Printed in the United States of America

10 9 8 7 6 5 4 3 2 1

Library of Congress Cataloging-in-Publication Data

Donoso, José, 1924–1996.
    [Lagartija sin cola. English]
    The lizard's tale : a novel / José Donoso ; edited by Julio Ortega ;
translated from the Spanish by Suzanne Jill Levine.
        p. cm.
    "Originally published in Spanish under the title Lagartija sin cola in
2007."
    ISBN 978-0-8101-2702-9 (cloth : alk. paper)
    1. Artists—Spain—Fiction. 2. Art movements—Spain—Fiction.
I. Ortega, Julio, 1942– II. Levine, Suzanne Jill. III. Title.
PQ8097.D617L3413 2011
863.64—dc22

                                     2011017409

Contents

TRANSLATOR'S NOTE

Translation is a creative act, we have been reminded time and again, and sometimes even a leap into reincarnation. Jorge Luis Borges contemplated the latter when he considered the enigma of Edward FitzGerald's efforts to resurrect and give a larger life to an unfinished Persian poem from many centuries back. In the light of Borges's often illuminating views, and thinking of the reader of this posthumous novel by José Donoso, I would like to add a few words to Julio Ortega's eloquent sketch of the challenge he faced as the editor charged with bringing this manuscript into print. Having known Pepe, as Donoso was called by his friends, and having translated two of his novels (*Hell Has No Limits* and *A House in the Country*), I also visited the Firestone Library retracing Julio's pilgrimage, where I found some answers to the initial enigma of how to approach this unique project. One of the answers concerns the title: among his original titles was *The Lizard's Tail* (*La cola de la lagartija*). Because another 1970s novel from Latin America (by Luisa Valenzuela) bears this title, Julio made a slight change, giving the title a more explicit image related to a significant motif in the novel.

This work in progress actually consisted of three related unfinished manuscripts; the titles of the other two were, respectively, *Pap Test* and *The Visa*. In a notebook, dated 1973, corresponding to the project at hand, Donoso spoke of wanting to achieve a "classical effect" stylistically—for the book to be written in a complex way but to flow for the reader. Julio Ortega rightly suggests that, in its most brilliant passages, this novel has achieved a powerful effect of both flow and complexity. As the translator I have tried to stay close to certain eccentricities, for example, of punctuation—the colon is more pervasive in Spanish than in English prose, and certainly in this manuscript—but I have also taken liberties where I deemed that the text's unfinished nature (almost like the castle of which it speaks) was undermining its own effect and underlying clarity.

Donoso, who learned English in a private school in Chile where one of his classmates was Carlos Fuentes, spoke English fluently with a somewhat British accent, and in the novel he includes phrases or words in French, Italian, and especially English. What most stood out to me in his notes was a comment he made in the midst of complaining that Spanish wasn't easy to "conquer": "I would give my life to write in English." Often, in the course of working on this translation, I have heard Pepe's voice as if it were in English. In any case, I have tried to honor his wish in giving his book a life in English he hopefully would have welcomed, and, in this spirit, I have given his title another "turn of the screw"—to cite his beloved Henry James—*The Lizard's Tale.*

Suzanne Jill Levine, 2010

Editor's Note on the Spanish Edition

José Donoso (1924–96) began to write *Lagartija sin cola* (*Lizard Without a Tail*) in January 1973 in the Aragonese village of Calaceite, where he had bought an old house, whose renovation would be more costly than the buying price. His daughter, Pilar, discovered the manuscript of the novel among her father's papers at the Firestone Library at Princeton University. He appeared to have given up revising the novel and literally had abandoned it. He only managed to revise the first chapter or part, which he later made into the third.* He eliminated several pages in the beginning, erased some paragraphs, noted some indications of plans, revised a few sentences, and corrected a word here and there. A good part of the book was left uncorrected, in its state as a first draft. Perhaps because he distanced himself from the text, he tried to imagine it as a book, ordering it in alternating sequences, dividing it into parts, tracing the route of its reading. In a notebook he acknowledged the difficulty of discovering its final form: "It's so difficult to grab the end of the skein to be able to unravel it." He plans, he says, "to join it all together quickly in order (or disorder)" and the idea of "beginning with year seven, and returning to year

---

*And what is now part 4 was originally the second chapter. —Translator

one" doesn't seem like a bad one to him. However, he never got to complete that articulation and left several threads at loose ends. A decision I had to make, for example, was to put at the end, as an epilogue, the loose pages on the protagonists' childhood. And so this is a recovered edition of the novel: it was necessary for me to revise the manuscript somewhat, especially the prosody, so as to reduce repetitions or clumsy wordings and thus facilitate its extraordinary fluidity. Donoso's distinctive prose here frequently flows at its best—his clear and transparent style reverberating in the light and shadow of his obsessions. Donoso was proposing here a tale both ironic and melancholic about the loss of Spain under the hordes of tourism, a story parallel to that of an artist who renounces his art, disillusioned by its commercialization. The protagonist's abandonment of art, because of its devaluation by the marketplace which turns it into refuse, perhaps made it impossible for the author to resolve the project of this novel. Seldom have readers had the privilege, however, of witnessing the pleasurable intimacy of a work which, as its promise unfolds, cannot find its way out in a world that no longer recognizes value without a price.

Julio Ortega, 2007

THE LIZARD'S TALE

Part One

THIS MORNING LUISA CALLED TO SAY THAT WHEN SHE came over this afternoon she would bring some good news. But for me, at this point, what could be good news? That Bartolo came back to life, that the whole Dors thing never happened? That Lidia isn't a mess, adrift somewhere in the megalopolis of Los Angeles? That the critics and the *marchands* have finally banished Cuixart and Tàpies and Saura and Millares as impostors or imitators, and that of all them I was the only real painter who had any worth? That somehow, inconceivably, I am going to get rich, come into loads of money? Poor Luisa, incurable optimist that she is, must rid herself of these illusions: there is no good news for me, no possible joy. Luisa tells me, as does my son, to leave the apartment on sunny mornings, to take walks with my cane, to go to a bookstore, to a supermarket to buy something I like, and to stretch my legs a bit. But of course it's impossible. It would mean breaking the necessary cycle beginning in the morning and being conscious of waking up in the hell of this apartment, which is how I want it, isolated from everything, where nothing can happen, until the day passes and night falls, in a state of anxiety, fear, terror: fighting, at light's end, shoulder to shoulder, against dusk for nothing to happen, to prevent darkness from taking over, that darkness they spoke of there as the real beginning

5

of life, night falling that was the portal of death, the hour of human sacrifice and the blood with which they celebrated the death of day and the coming of night, because what happens at night after the death of day is what happens in the other life, the true life, the life that doesn't happen here, on this street, among these cars, among these ladies who have given birth and therefore believe that they can no longer know the darkness which makes everything possible and dare to enter it via the portal of dusk . . . Bruno—the Italian, sitting at the table in his café on the Dors plaza facing San Hilario Church and its bell tower with the arched Romanesque two-light windows rising higher and higher—would explain it all to me, and I would simply smile, telling myself that this wise guy was trying to take advantage of the situation and of their innocence to lord it over all the young men and become, as he did, in two years, the center, the dominant and most powerful man in Dors. I, of course, never had that quasi-religious fear and love of sunset that the young men in Dors had. But here this strange phenomenon has happened to me—in Barcelona, two blocks from Via Augusta, a block from Muntaner, not too far from where I was born and went to school and where I had my painter's studio when we all were discovering "informalism" as a religion, as a passion. Here, precisely, is where I understand what the Italian was talking about and my daily struggle is not to cross into the world of night and of sleep which, they said, was and is the real life, the prolongation of death.

Sometimes I do feel like going out: I feel, sometimes, that what would give me back my capacity to feel pleasure, my potential for excitement and for enthusiasm, would be not so much a date with a woman, or with a friend, but rather, a relationship with the city; I think of those I've known—Madrid, Paris, Buenos Aires, New York, Munich, Rome—but Barcelona is here and I am from here and I'd like to go out for a walk, in the morning, and without fear in the evenings, and rebuild that old relationship.

It's absurd, of course: I no longer belonged to the group by the time their faces started to appear in the magazines and newspapers, when they did that group exhibit which produced shock and scandal and for several years they were admired on all continents. No, I had already abandoned them. My face is not known. But going outside is exposing myself, nonetheless, to someone saying, "That's him, the poor guy," to being pitied by someone who might recognize my face from back then, who might by chance make the connection between my face and those paintings I did, and who will then come up to me and tell me that he feels so bad that I had abandoned painting at the very moment the informalists triumphed, that I was the best of the whole lot, the most talented, that I alone held the school up and that when I risked it all, the whole thing fell apart and became commercial, vulgar, impoverished . . . *Señor Muñoz-Roa, please, don't run away, I have a painting of yours, it would be such a great honor, you should have never stopped* . . . And it would be, of course, as if they were skinning me alive and applying salt and hot pepper to my raw naked flesh. It would be horrible to be remembered and told, for example, that they are hoping I will return . . . "Hope" is a hellish word, the threshold to horror, to the impossible.

And how is it, then, that Luisa has hope, survives on hope, and that hope doesn't destroy her completely? I don't understand how she doesn't see life as hell, or perhaps it's because she does accept that life is hell that she doesn't fear death. Perhaps I fear death so much—when the sun sets, that threshold, real life after dark, the time of sacrifice, of love, of dreams, of orgies, of bodies—precisely because, though I don't know it, life doesn't seem like hell to me, but rather the opposite. And I sit here waiting, in the artificial light after night has fallen outside, and I sleep as little as I can, and I sleep with all the lights on in the apartment. But I always think of myself, never of her. And of course, I now realize, the good news she is going to bring me tonight is that if she passes this Pap test it means, finally, that she's free of cancer and will not die, will never die, and there will always be light and always day for her. That's the good news she's bringing me.

But, thinking it over clearly, no, that isn't the news. Never, not even in a case like this would she make such a hullabaloo about herself, and not out of generosity—her marriage failed because of her incredible selfishness and cruelty—but because of her vitality, because it really doesn't matter to her and she doesn't consider it "news." It's something else, something having to do with me, though I can't think of anything good having to do with me. After all, if I'm so afraid of death, it's because I already know what it is and how horrible it is because I've committed suicide. Yes, I was brave once, and committed suicide. What else could you call it, then, the shock I produced six years ago when I publicly snubbed everyone, saying in an open letter published in *Destino* that Spanish informalism was a rip-off that had turned into a dirty business arrangement between the artists, their *marchands,* and their critics. I swore, also publicly, that I'd never paint or draw again, and here I am doing nothing, with Tàpies, the big gelded black cat sitting in my lap purring, with the lights in this strange apartment turned on around me, waiting for the hours to slip by, knowing that I could be painting, that perhaps I should be painting, because it would give me pleasure, that pleasure . . . Oh how I've left it behind, how difficult it is to touch it in some way and how easy it would be to take again in my hands that blank paper in my desk, and a pencil—or perhaps I would like even more some black ink and a pen, and a brush—and do a fabulous sketch . . . Pleasure, do it all for pleasure. But no, hope would rear its head again, giving birth to fear, another fear different from this one I know so well, and don't like. Perhaps it was heroic to criticize myself in public, to declare myself mediocre and impoverished when responding to the angry letters of the other painters and *marchands* and journalists. Envy, they said, naturally, because Muñoz-Roa is the least brilliant of the whole group, the name that has received the least attention, something I must immediately state was completely incorrect. Envy. I committed suicide out of envy? I withdrew from the circle, hung up the habit, castrated myself, really, out of envy, for fear of competition? I don't think so. Luisa knows it isn't true. In my whole life I never envied anything or anyone. Frankly it was out of disgust. To see informalism—so passionate, so virile, so strong in its first moment—later decline into an unmistakably fake imitation of itself, without any character, until it was just a school that produced easy merchandise to sell here and in other countries, furniture for the pretentious bourgeoisie, some awful thing without engagement, without vitality . . . And, of course, history has proved me right, because the lights went down completely, and then Pop and Op arrived, and *zap!* It showed its greatest relationship as much with life as with intelligence and then left them all exposed, useless, all of them except, maybe, Tàpies—or rather, except perhaps me if I had kept painting, but I didn't want to, I preferred not to, and I committed suicide out of disgust. Disgusted, I was not about to produce lifeless furniture for rich people, lithographs for books, for millionaires: I was a painter, a real painter—though I had never had any academic training and couldn't sketch a portrait, a still life, a cat to save my life . . . Yes, I was a painter, I created paintings, produced works of art, not raw material to keep in motion the grand middle class and philistine machinery of the galleries, *marchands,* exhibitions, vernissages, aficionados, collectors, decorators, that whole inferior race, all the bloodsuckers who ended up prostituting and liquidating those who at one moment were painters but who today, to continue painting, have to deny their concepts and *change,* and change means not evolving but rather adhering to other ideas and schools they did not invent as we invented informalism, and lie, falsify in order to be able to sell names . . . It's been six years since I've seen my name in print anywhere, which gives me pleasure. First my grand public act of self-criticism, then, for a couple of months, polemical letters, protests, insults, my name and my photo everywhere, for good or for bad, and generally more for bad, and then total silence, hunkering down in the attic, erasing oneself as a public figure to grow as a private individual brewing in the broth of my confronted fears, and thus recovering myself without turning my back on my essence, thus resurrecting myself from everything, even the insults of the friends I lost. Perhaps remembering—or rather feeling myself marked forever by what I did then and living out its harsh consequences in this solitude and this poverty and this disconnected present—is my great, my good consolation: I did something, although it meant killing a whole half of myself, which was probably a good thing.

The Dors experience, which began immediately after that, of course led me to fool myself into thinking this wasn't a partial suicide whose wound still hurts, a mutilation, so that at the beginning I didn't realize I had actually lost a whole part of my being—as when the lizard, faced with terror and a threat, willingly sheds its tail. Dors made me believe for the first time that within my reach was the possibility of a full life. Luisa was with me all the time, night and day, during that whole bitter time which followed my public act of self-criticism, my dismissal of the others' values, and my demand that they also criticize themselves publicly. One night, leaving a movie theater with Luisa and Alberto Mármol, her then lover, some young painters attacked me, cursing and throwing stones from the other side of the street. Luisa did not leave my side, nor did Alberto, but it didn't matter. Like all Luisa's lovers he was an appendage, one of her ephemeral objects. Very soon after this Luisa needed an operation and they removed her left breast—we are, the two of us, mutilated beings. This unites us in a kind of conspiracy and so I confined myself indoors with her, to watch over her day and night as she had watched over me, because her daughter didn't want to have anything to do with her, as she was married, living a very bourgeois life in Madrid, and hated everything her mother represented. Also, Luisa felt somewhat humiliated by the operation: losing one of her beautiful breasts was like losing part of her femininity—no longer Luisa de Noyà, powerful, olive-skinned, gypsy-like, who at forty, in a Dior miniskirt with a branch of basil behind her ear, could drive any guy crazy, any man, dancing with him in any nightclub in Cadaqués or Marbella. Now, she said, all that was over. It was necessary to find another existence, which I too had to find, and no one, I had to clearly understand—hence one reason why I alone took care of her and only I knew of her operation—that no one should know about her shame so that they wouldn't feel sorry for her. By the time she had convalesced "the sound and the fury signifying nothing" that raged around me and the scandal I had staged had already passed. People no longer recognized me in the café or on the street. Or did they pretend not to recognize me? Oh well, what does it matter? I felt so alone that I dialed the phone number of Ramón and Raimunda Roig as if to take the temperature of what they—so affectionate at one time and such admirers of my work, and those they saw, who had been my world in Barcelona—were feeling now with respect to me. I dialed the number, listened two seconds, and hung up. No, I couldn't expose myself to cheap shots like that. I had to do something, not close down but open up. And though I knew the tide against me was not unanimous in its direction, that perhaps I had found experts that even congratulated me for my attitude, I preferred to isolate myself. I told Luisa:

"I'd like to travel."

"Let's do it."

"You're not too weak?"

"I'm in great shape."

"I'm very poor, as you already know."

"I don't care, I'll invite you."

"But not a complicated trip, with languages I don't understand."

"No, a trip near here . . . long . . . leisurely."

"Well, a slow trip, to be able to look at things."

We packed our bags and left in Luisa's car for the coast heading south, toward Tarragona. Without planning it, both Luisa and I had envisioned lonely beaches in sleepy fishing villages where we could take long walks. But as we got closer to the south we realized that our fantasy was only a memory of the Mediterranean coast ten or fifteen years ago, not the base commercialization of tourism which brings in foreign currency but destroys all identity. Total prostitution: billboards announcing hotels obliterated the landscape; campgrounds with Dutch and French names followed one after the other; if the tourists came in summer, and then left with the horribly vulgar and superfluous equipment which has been built to shelter them, well, perhaps things wouldn't be so bad; but this commercial assault of the most vulgar taste on the landscape, on the natural environment, which the natives think signifies "progress," well, it was disgusting, simply repulsive. The bad quality of the food, the sculpture parks, the invasion of the masses from the north which the natives, even the middle class, which should have some discrimination, take as an aesthetic, moral, and intellectual model . . . The water pollution, everything, all of it, as we got farther south got worse, so bad, that we no longer spoke about ourselves, our problems and our struggles and our suffering and our fears, but about that, about what we were seeing—the insult of not seeing a single bull, except the Osborne bull, and the awful possibility that a child, for example, would see an Osborne bull, aggressively disfiguring the shape of every hill, before knowing what a real bull looked like. We asked one of the friendly waiters serving us in some restaurant:

"Where are you from?"

"From Horta de San Juan."

"Horta?"

"You know it?"

"No, but Picasso lived there."

"I don't know that man."

"And you like this?"

"Yes, a lot."

"And you wouldn't like to return to your hometown?"

"No, it's very backwards."

"And here you're very happy?"

"Yes, here you can see the progress. They say farther south, in Benidorm and Alicante, it's much better; let's see if I go there next year, it's even more modern. Lots of Belgians around here, they're good the Belgians. Not the Germans though. The Dutch are, and the French, but the Germans aren't. Even worse are the Spaniards. Uf!"

And he turned up his nose. This was in Salou, heading south a little past Tarragona, where we had lunch. His promise that the coast was "more modern" and filled with condominiums toward the south seemed horrible to us. Nevertheless, we got in the car and continued on. Cambrils, campgrounds, billboards, and the oil-slicked Mediterranean sea: at the gas station they told us oil had been discovered in Sant Carles de la Ràpita, and that the whole coast, in a few more years, would be a factory of refineries, with all those iron structures—vast refineries lit by torches, by lights like enchanted cities gushing poisonous gases. Progress, and people disguised as what they are not, and the condos, and the fast-food concessions, and the discotheques, and as you got farther and farther away from Barcelona, they got poorer and smaller and uglier until we were so angry and frustrated we didn't even utter one word about ourselves—because those condos and all that fast food were merely a more base extension of the art galleries and *marchands* and painters who fabricated informalist paintings and the prostitution which the whole thing signified. And all this ugliness was stealing our souls away, keeping us from confronting our own and very real problems and that our memories—of how Masnou was ten years ago, how Tossa was twenty years ago, how Calella de Palafrugell or L'Estartit were ten years ago—were useless, impotent, that this, this human mass descending from the north seeking the sun and bargains and absolutely nothing else, was what took over and imposed its shape upon this poor Mediterranean that was selling itself

13

so cheaply, and was eliminating human beings, even us, we who were, after all, an elite.

We continued on to L'Hospitalet de l'Infante where we felt a violent repulsion: on the awful beaches in this month of July, the air smelled not of salt or fresh fish, but of olive oil for suntanning. We got back on the highway to Valencia. I tried all the wines in the places we stopped, ordering the local wine, and drinking a half bottle, or a whole bottle: tannins, artificial coloring, sediment, all of them the same, some more harsh than others, and all of them brought from someplace else. I was a little drunk, perhaps, and when we returned to the Valencia highway, we sat for a while, indecisively, in front of a stop sign waiting for the long caravan of cars to pass: should we go on to Valencia, or return, in disgust, to Barcelona, to seclude ourselves in the apartment.

Suddenly a third possibility opened before us. Across the road from the car, a small sign said: MORA LA NUEVA, TIVISA, DORS. Luisa and I looked at each other, she, who was driving at this point, as if consulting me. I shrugged my shoulders and went along with her, almost before knowing what I had agreed upon. After looking both ways Luisa stepped on the gas and the car set off straight ahead, on the narrow road indicating the way to Mora, Dors, and Tivisa, toward the mountains. Right after the excitement of crossing the highway, we looked at each other and laughed. Not Barcelona nor Valencia, nor Sitges, nor Peñíscola. Something else. Perhaps ten minutes' driving already showed us that this was something completely different, that we were breaking new ground. We left behind a monstrous development with its frescos of Don Quixote painted on white walls for the benefit of Belgian workers hungry for sun and exoticism for twenty days in the summer, and we were already beginning to climb, higher and higher, into the canyons of the mountain, to see stone-fenced terraces scaling the slopes that fed a few olive trees, perhaps a thousand years old, and small tactile velvety green hazelnut bushes with their blue shadows and shapes like spurting springs. Here and there a

14

massive golden rock charted the mountain, but nothing more, nothing, except an occasional farmer on his motorbike, or on a *tartana* with his dog tied underneath, smiling at us, scooting out of our way. Ten kilometers from the coast there were no signs of the "progress" the fellow in the Salou bar had spoken about, and what we saw was so simple and direct that we almost didn't see it, and without commenting on the beauty of the panorama revealed by each curve of the road, we returned to ourselves, to deal with our own issues, as if a lock had risen and closed us off.

She discarded her handsome cousin who was jaded like her, a horseman who rode "English" saddle. How we laughed at him, so corny—Manuel Ibáñez was too much, and besides from Madrid . . . and so her marriage with Manuel Ibáñez, disowning and rejecting me and all that I wanted and was, because I wanted to be and was, despite my family's incredulity, no, I couldn't be, a painter. I should finish school and as I didn't finish, *off you go to a bank, yes sir, a bank clerk and that's it,* and years and years at the bank while Luisa was in Madrid for years and years with her husband who also worked at a bank, but as branch manager of the bank belonging to some uncles of his who were nobility on his father's side, while I, in shirtsleeves, was a bank teller, gradually "making my career" in Barcelona, hating my career. Until I couldn't stand it any longer, and I rebelled and said, *I'm going home, I'm leaving the bank, I'm going to be a laborer in London, in Paris,* and I lived there, and worked only enough to survive, and I lived, and in living I completely forgot about Luisa, transforming her into a caricature, young love, a laughable romantic vignette, a mere trifle, forgotten, and a new life among painters and bars and new women, and Hardy's majestic granddaughter, or great-granddaughter, a nonconformist and a rebel without a cause because her family had rebelled a long time ago and had won their revolution, and we lived together, and we had Miles. And then her parents advised us that it would be better if we married and then we

15

had Miguel, and then something broke, no, it didn't break, only the need to return to Spain—but impossible for her to live in Spain because she hated Spain, a dirty backwards country, fat women filled with children, or shrouded in black mourning, housewives, no one to talk to, *they'll think I'm crazy because I want to study, because I study despite their considering me crazy. And you do nothing, living somewhat off my money, don't you, we all live somewhat off my money but that's OK,* but as we're living off her money I seek and do not find, and get bored and my friends are no longer the same, all they talk about is the war, and only about the war, and I was very young and I spent the hard years in Paris and London out of pure chance, but that's where I spent them, and Diana says "that's it": no more sex, no more living together, nothing, why deceive ourselves, *it's better to separate now so that I can have a life,* she says, *and so that the children aren't fatherless,* and she takes them with her and I really don't care, let her take them away; the worst is she doesn't care really whether she takes them or not but it's better for them to be with her because she can give them more, not only materially, but also emotionally and intellectually. If they stay with me, on the other hand, how awful: going to school in Spain, with religious problems at a time when nobody in the world is having religious problems, and sexual problems when nobody is dealing with sexual problems, and especially *the great danger that they will be a burden for you: thirty-two years old and you've accomplished nothing, a dilettante, embellishments here and there, a bit of self-promotion, and trying to find yourself underneath all that, yes, I know it's the worst sort of cliché, but what can we do, the things that are on everyone's mind, the problems today in Spain are even worse clichés seen from the outside but that's how it is, with your searching for yourself. That's it. And if I leave the children with you—I would regret leaving them with you, but if that would help you I would, absolutely—they'd be a burden.* It was so peaceful when they left. Living on others in a city that wasn't mine, wandering the streets and meeting up with friends and women I knew, and knowing that in Barcelona, even if I wanted to, I couldn't die of hunger, not even if I tried, because they all knew me and had always loved me. And I painted, a little, not much; I had seen Soulages and Bram van Velde, and the School of Paris, and Mimieux, and the New York School in Paris, and I knew I didn't need to know how in order to paint, that you didn't need the academy to be an artist, and during that time I painted quite a bit, a lot. And I met up with Luisa at a film club to see *Forbidden Games* from ages ago, and we had coffee at an outdoor café, where I don't remember, near Plaza de Cataluña in any case, and she was no longer living with Manuel . . . jeez . . . it had been years since she lived with Manuel. Their daughter had stayed with him. She was a little bourgeois chick, completely Ibáñez, with none of our genes, the Garriga madness—like the monsters in Bomarzo inhabiting the park, half in ruins, with run-down balustrades adorned by the occasional amphora and broken lightning rods—from great-grandparents, and dead grandparents, and parents dying goodness knows when, probably soon. And we'd never gone to La Garriga, why not, the house was for sale, and so we went, and found it all devoured by weeds, and a porcelain doll left lying in the labyrinth of boxwood; we couldn't find the caretaker, and so we climbed over the gate and broke a window: inside nothing was left, space, nothing more, faded bits of walls where wardrobes and paintings had been, and a pile of books rotting in a corner—we looked for *The Borgias* but couldn't find it—and chipped living room furniture, covered with white sheets that protected nothing, nothing, because everything was rotting from within, worm-eaten to the very core of the wood, and all falling to pieces, and all that remained were the dirty sheets, once white, only ruins that would last a bit longer. We stayed only a little while. We didn't even go up to the second floor, or to the attic rooms under the mansard roof. We went in and came out: they wanted to sell it, the house and the park, to make a new neighborhood, like those now called Miami that we saw along the coast, condominiums like those in Salou perhaps, townhouses with frescos, doubtlessly like those Don Quixotes in Cambrils. And they haven't sold it yet, waiting for the price to keep going up, so says my cousin, who knows a lot about business, who's been saying the same thing for years—that it's better to wait a few more years, that the value of everything is increasing incredibly, and that we twenty-two cousins who have a right to all this, all except Luisa and myself, are in agreement about waiting, Luisa too, really. Now that her husband and her lover—the owner of another bank, I don't remember which, a rival of the husband's—have abandoned her, she's become a decorator and specialist in renovations, and it's been going well for her and a little extra money never does any harm, although they wouldn't hire her for urban development because her taste is too refined, too pure, and she'd surely want to preserve things—hundred-year-old trees, grown from seeds originally brought by her great-grandfather from Cuba along with his overflowing pockets—and as it was noncommercial, Luisa had no illusions about making a fast buck. She said to me on the train that took us back that evening from La Garriga to Barcelona:

"I can get by. I lived with Tenreiro for five years, and am proud to say that when I got fed up and left him, I walked out of his house with absolutely nothing other than what I had on."

I expressed my admiration. But she added, so that the whole thing didn't turn into some tacky romanticism:

"Of course, among the things I was wearing that day of our final fight, when I left the house forever, was a huge diamond ring, worthy of an exclusive call girl and of course, since then, I've been living off of that ring I happened to be wearing on my finger . . . Of course I've increased its value many times over . . ."

I showed her my things, putting one painting after the other on the easel under the light, as she sat on the fringed and faded green velvet armchair, which she got such a kick out of, which I placed in front of the easel. She made no comments. She didn't even seem to blink as I changed one painting after the other on the easel, following her indications. As I did it, I felt the atmosphere in the room change, the relationship between us changing, I remembered La Garriga and my studio in the hot attics in the summer, she suddenly becoming a cat— she with her aggressive "chic," so un-catlike—curled up on the corduroy armchair, and enjoying the heat emanating from me, and the fire my paintings imparted, but not only the fire from my paintings, but rather, as when we were children but with a different power, my fire, from my body that enveloped and transformed her, revealing that embraceable body of hers, her triangular face, all that emanated from her, enveloping me, desiring—not to repeat a secret act in the secure garden of childhood, in which the experience had only the quality of an unguarded moment—this present that I had and was having the capacity to forge, in this present we both were occupying, now not like accomplices, but like two beings enveloped, as in the warm hollow of two hands intertwined in love. But of course, one couldn't speak of love. There were too many other things to speak about first. Nevertheless, I came over, behind her chair, drawn by this mutual, reflected heat, and touched her hair with my hand. She took my hand and, without pushing it away, said:

"No, wait."

I asked her what we were waiting for. She answered that, unfortunately, she was only attracted to successful men, and I wasn't, that is, yes, she saw my power inscribed in all my paintings, my personal vision, my world tinged with bitterness, anger, it was all there, expressed in those different layers of thick enamel (Kiko Zañartu), and my rage and rancor had a positive value that was power, expressed in those acid greens, in those distances engendered by the different layers of enamel, dripping over one another, some wrought arduously over others, creating an atmosphere like rain in the hills, separating them, leaving only the distances like reality between the hills, cruelly eliminating details and life and, on top of this, stained with a jab, sometimes black, sometimes brown, the hermetic

19

calligraphy of my meanings impossible to unravel, the mystery, the secret remaining on the canvas, veiled.

Now she was the heat, I the purring cat, and I purred not only from the pleasure of hearing someone analyze so freely and appreciate my painting, but because her body itself radiated, as if she were feeling not with her intelligence but rather with her skin, so swarthy, so soft, so close to mine, so snug in the beautiful knit brown dress she was wearing. For the first time, making the effort to tear myself away from the balm emanating from her presence connecting us as one, I looked at her: she was all one color, brown face, brown dress, her skin brown all over, her enormous almond-shaped eyes an intelligent, shining brown. Only her thick lashes, not curved but as straight as eaves, and her straight hair, thick, heavy, smooth, metallic, parted in the middle and falling on her shoulders, were black, like the pupil around the luminous center of her brown eyes. Sitting at her feet—she was smoking—I asked if such a power weren't sufficient, the power of the thing itself which had evidently moved her so, the power that meant having the drive to create a world that moved her, and she answered no, that I was wrong. Naïve like most artists, I believed this was enough. It wasn't. It was, truthfully, an important ingredient, but not everything, not everything, another power was needed, negative power, contemptible, abject power was needed to translate that power of pure artistic creation into power in the world and for the world and for and about human beings. She's a woman of the world and what was missing was the incredible, terrible power that is success, the success that elevates man not only in her eyes, as a private woman, but in everyone's eyes. It was necessary, therefore, to acquire success. Of course I had the main thing, talent—why did she not say genius, why not? She knew. She knew galleries, she knew Juana Mordó in Madrid, who owed her plenty in terms of public relations, and she knew Gaspar in Barcelona, who owed her nothing, only having introduced her to Tàpies, and many galleries in most of the capitals of the world. Success? Easy to achieve. It was something that could be artificial—she recognized—but something artificial that she needed in a man. Manolo Ibáñez had it from the beginning . . . how he jumped the hurdles on his white horse, for example, how he did the dressage, something that did not interest her in the slightest, but which made him a winner, doubtlessly the most handsome and most successful boy from her youth, and this was what attracted her so much so that she let herself be dragged into a marriage she knew was doomed from the very first night, and even before, to failure. And then the other guy, the other banker, was simply a matter of money, millions, simple, of course, but also complicated; he was ugly, and a bit overweight, but seeing him enter his bank and how surreptitiously the tellers and the managers raised their heads and how the directors stood up on his Persian rugs and beneath his abstract French paintings—the Spaniards weren't big yet—and his mahogany desks buzzing with telephones and dictaphones . . . He didn't need any of these external signs of power; he was himself, and that sufficed, and, of course, like her relationship with Manolo, this one too was doomed from the beginning. But us . . .

Then the party really began: Luisa organized my first show at Gaspar's, attended by *tout* Barcelona that had anything to do with painting, with invitations to the big shots from Madrid, critics from Paris, and coordinating the exhibit so that it would take place the exact same time the director of the Museum of Modern Art in New York was passing through town. The whole thing perfect: even Tàpies, who never left his house, attended, which everyone took note of, and also the minor ones, Cuixart, Tharrats, the Madrid artists, everyone, and by the day after the launch, the whole show was sold. A runaway success, the magazines and newspapers declared, a revelation, a self-taught painter is now leader of the Spanish informalists. I was something now, not much yet because the Spanish informalists weren't much yet. But my paintings formed part, in very little time, of the big exhibit that traveled to all the capitals of Europe, that went to America, to Mexico, to Buenos Aires. And the reviews were superb: Tàpies descended from Dubuffet; I, on the other hand, had roots in a much more distant past, with my golden varnishes and my slides, as if some member of the international school, of Gothic Flemish or Catalan painting, had gone crazy, and had been resurrected in our time. It was fabulous. So fabulous that Luisa and I became lovers. And it could have lasted a long and happy time right up until now but instead it was short and sweet. *No*, said Luisa after some time, *all this is false, all that I've demanded in order to love you is false, artificial, has nothing to do with your essence. I'm the one who invented and demanded it of you, and you did it all to win me over, to please me. It doesn't work. It's been a great year, but I can't, I can't; I don't think there's anyone in the world whom I could have a stronger or more definitive relationship with than you, not even with my own daughter (who doesn't love me), no one in this world of people drifting from one country to the next, from one class to another, from one house to another, from one neighborhood to another, from one profession to another, in this world of improvisations I hate and of which nonetheless I form part, with my urban designs, which after all are only improvisations, but I can live with them as long as they're mine, but not when the reputation of the man I'm with is improvised. Yours is a false power, your fame is false, just as your talent is not false. Your talent interests me but does not make me love you: your power in the world—if it were real, as was Manolo's power to dominate his white horse, or my banker lover's to dominate his empire, their power that was part and parcel of their personalities—is what would make me fall in love. I admire your talent, however it is neither here nor there, does nothing inside me, where love lives; it's been a good year, but the love I have for you isn't true. What is true is something else that's between us . . .*

Yes, I knew it. And Luisa went to America for a time and I stayed here. I stayed in the position she left me in, enjoying it as king of my false and spurious success. False. Artificial. Not belonging to the essence of my personality, as in the pure and odious case of Tàpies, whose quality you couldn't help recognizing as hand in hand with his success and that one was the complex flip side of the other and both were one and the same, but yes, now that Luisa had introduced me to his work, it was necessary, indeed impossible to live without him, reading hysterically the reviews, the articles, to see if someone had excluded me, to see if someone had forgotten to name me, intentionally, or out of carelessness or because my paintings were insignificant, fostering all the infinite possibilities of paranoia that lay dormant in me, hungry for power, to be able to change the trends, to prescribe and to control, for them to look up at me with admiration, to see if I could sell my paintings at a higher price than the others, to see if the museum in Amsterdam called me for a one-man show, if São Paolo invited me to an exhibit in a space just for me, if Kassel were interested, if Amsterdam, if California. I never understood why Cuixart and not me for the Grand Prize at the São Paolo Biennial. Curious, yes, I agreed with Luisa: these things, this hunger for power did not belong to my essence, but it was as if having touched upon them, as if knowing them had literally skinned me alive and left me completely vulnerable to that whole side of things. Yes, it was as if I were certain that my painting was not vulnerable, but was solid, good, each day wiser but, unfortunately, each day more secondary to the vulnerability of fame, of success and of power.

The disaster was short and definitive. I can't believe it all happened a mere six years ago, when informalism had been defined as a group but did not succeed in forming a school, rather each one of us continued using, in his particular way, the newly gained techniques. I, then, seeking new formulas, began to paint works that, despite following the informalist model, had a figurative aspect. A huge international exhibition of Spanish formalists in New York, which was to be like a battle cry, wanted to bring formalism up-to-date after so much pop and so much op, and so much poor art and so much constructivism, and at this moment of such infinite emptiness in the pictorial arts, again propose Spanish informalism as the most serious as well as the most coherent of the last decades. Señor Gaspar, the gallery owner, made the selection, and when it came to considering my paintings he flatly rejected them. He spoke at length: it was a matter of presenting a "school," of redefining once again a theory of the plastic arts to revive criticism and the world. "Don't lie, Señor Gaspar, your proposal is too transparent, you, the *marchand* of all the Spanish informalists, want to give them again the weight they had fifteen years ago, yes, that's it, and especially to raise the price of the paintings so that once again they will have the international fame they once had; it's a dirty commercial gambit, and has nothing to do with reviving and defining a school as you profess," *and this is why you, Muñoz-Roa, with what you're doing, have to be excluded.* The voices of the other painters— all those who were my friends and my comrades in former times—agree with Gaspar: *yes, Muñoz-Roa, our salvation is constraint, and if we want to revive the market—yes, the market!—for our paintings, well, we have no choice but to be strict; we're dealing with a revival, and a revival with your apples and your hands floating in a sea of informalism, really, let's face it, would defeat us from the get-go, we would no longer have any limits, try to understand . . .* But I didn't understand. And while the Spanish informalist exhibition caused a revival in the USA, and renewed interest in its concepts after fifteen years of more than partial defeat, I organized a show in Barcelona. The critics attacked me, unanimously, when they didn't laugh at me, saying what they had never said before, that, essentially, my failure was inevitable, that, after all, I had always been the weakest, the most insignificant painter in the group. But fifteen years ago it was the critics themselves who had praised me to the skies, practically calling me a genius, raising me to the same level as Tàpies! In view of which, I wrote a letter to *Destino* magazine where I say precisely that the same critics who now attack me as the weakest, placed me fifteen years ago in the highest echelon. I give names, quote paragraphs; in a restaurant I confront one of the critics, and curse words pass from table to table until we come to blows and fistfights, and amidst the scandalous uproar and paparazzi cameras flashing, they haul us off to jail. The next day the papers flashed the photo of the critic grabbing me by the beard and me with my fist in his eye, a cause célèbre in the grand tradition of painters, from Romanticism until today. But I am convinced that what they want is not a revival, not a conceptual principle that justifies a position in painting, but rather something artificial fabricated by the *marchands*—those pigs, yes, pigs who falsify everything for the marketplace. This year it's informalism, so one must paint in the informal style; next year it will be poor painting; the following: little electric machines that color the wall; after that . . . whatever. And to sell our paintings to those fine middle-class buyers who want to "invest" money, who want their "invested" money not to lose its value because if they spent a hundred thousand on a Tàpies, and informalist painting loses its prestige, then their investment in the Tàpies hanging over their fireplace certainly will lose its value . . . yes or no? That was the game, and one had to say it straight, and now that I had been attacked and was on the first page of the newspapers, well, this was the moment . . . and I wrote my great exposé, my terrible act of self-criticism in *Destino:* No, I would no longer paint, I said, because painting was over, because it was only an instrument of the commercial bourgeoisie, because it was all lies, because I refused to lend myself to such filth any longer, this fraud that mystified the world about the essence of painting, of art. And I killed myself willingly, artistically speaking, to remain pure, to seek other forms of creation, so as not to sell myself. I reprimanded the young painters—whom I attacked in this article for following recipes and not seeking their essence—and they assaulted me coming out of a movie theater, the latest bearded hipsters, who should quit being hippies already, pot smokers, idiots, illiterates . . . and the newspapers also picked up on this stoning outside the theater, this time laughing at me pitilessly, and for the last time. Afterwards, I was forgotten . . . a necessary oblivion, really, because at that moment Luisa had the tumor in her breast, and day and night, for months, I remained at her side with that horrible mutilation, that humiliation she suffered upon seeing that her body that she loved so much, that all of us had loved so much, had been left so horrendously mutilated . . . that crater, red at the beginning, which little by little closed and faded, which she showed me, which at times she made me caress to see if that crater still had sensitivity like her nipple, to see if it would serve her for love, that I shouldn't mention to anyone—she cried this time, upon asking me this, the only time in my life I saw her cry, and she didn't cry, on the contrary, when she told me that she wouldn't be completely free of the danger of cancer for five years, not until she did the fifth Pap test in five years; there was always the possibility that the cancer might regenerate in some other part of her body with a monstrous metastasis that would kill her—because she didn't want the humiliation of her body to be public, she still wanted to be able to function for love; yes, she was still good for love, I would soon see how well she worked for love, how despite everything the most seductive men would fall for her, even boys, even though she didn't like them and still, despite everything, she would be the beloved and not the lover . . . because she didn't want the humiliation of being the lover.

After those months of seclusion, of course, people no longer remembered me or the scandal surrounding me, and the informalist "school" of Barcelona fell apart as a school, but individual values persisted, though not supported by the publicity machine of the school in fashion. There was no faction, then, that would attack me, since the individuals, now dispersed, could not attack in the name of nothing—and I, of course, with my minimal good sense, realized I couldn't attack individuals the way one could attack them when they were all lined up, assuming a position and forming a school. Each one entered his own individual world to continue painting, or to stop painting completely, like me, mutilating myself, or better, killing myself. Someone once said, "One commits suicide out of respect for life, when life ceases to be worth it." Life, which was painting, which was the *marchands* who wanted op and pop and poor art now, was no longer worth it: hence the death of one as a painter, the voluntary act, the choice, the moral position of the strong man who says no to that and yes to this, even if it kills. That's why, perhaps—even though after I abandoned painting the pain and confusion were horrible—I had triumphed because it was not humiliating, but simply like the paralysis of some part of my body, an important part of course, a paralysis that would end by killing the rest of my being.

Part Two

WE THEN CROSSED THE TARRAGONA–VALENCIA HIGHWAY, and entered the Serra de Pàndols or its foothills. Soon the sordid urban developments disappeared, along with their perfunctory chalets—with their painted Quixotes and agaves, and their token bougainvilleas to attract tourists from latitudes where the color of the bougainvillea is impossible—and we were now entering an older landscape, the sudden hills covered with pines where deep little valleys were home, along the river, the stream, the thread of fresh water, to rows of green vegetables, and when these little valleys were larger, to hazelnut plantations and naturally molded velvet foliage casting blue shadows, and stone terraces marking the slopes, not too large, cultivating two, four, ten olive trees perhaps a thousand years old, and farmers dressed in black, also primordial, cleaning the terrain around them, scrutinizing their silvery leaves to assess this year's, this winter's, olive crop. That farmer's look at the foliage made me think that winter was probably not too far off, and I felt afraid. Where to go, what to do, how to live? I note this down now as my thoughts, but I should clarify that it all came out, then, in the form of a dialogue with Luisa, interweaving our thoughts and our intimate words: I proposed going to live with her. She was driving and stopped the car at the beginning of an avenue of plane trees receding behind a curve.

"You know very well that we can't."

"Why?"

"You know very well that I'm not in love with you."

"Yes."

"Nor you with me."

"No."

"And that what you're looking for is a refuge, beside someone you feel is as mutilated as you are."

"Yes."

"You can sleep and live as much as you want in my house, you know that. As long as there is no deception about a love that doesn't exist between you and me. You and me, we've turned a corner now . . . that's how I see it . . . and we have to look for something new . . ."

I held her hand on the car seat, as if wanting to grab on to something, to feel or recover something of my faculty to feel emotion and pleasure. But no, the hand was inert, familiar, as if I were touching not a different hand that could give me things I didn't have, but my own . . . Yes, that hand gave me comfort and support but no pleasure, no emotion. To continue with the experiment, I leaned over to Luisa and kissed her on the mouth as if I loved her, as if I desired her, and she let me, but I didn't love or desire her, nor did she love or desire me. Missing was intimate passion, a different feeling, a feeling of passion bringing me close to that difference without ever feeling at one with it, and I felt, upon holding her in my arms and while she gently caressed the back of my neck, that no, no, that I wanted someone young, someone different, a stranger . . . I didn't want to go back, which is what I realized I was doing, trying to do, but rather move ahead so as not to die and I wanted youth, horribly, passionately, something new, something that wasn't La Garriga, that wasn't painting, that wasn't flattened from so much use.

When we released each other from our prolonged embrace, calmly, gently, perhaps even serenely, the sun was setting. A conventionally reddish twilight tinted the baroque clouds, exposing the V of the canyon in the hills as we advanced along the avenue of plane trees, and the sky turned completely red for a moment, just before what (we knew) would fall, a penumbra announcing the night. I said:

"I had a lover who, at any sunset, would oblige me to kiss her while she closed her eyes and sighed."

"And when there was a full moon too?"

"Yes."

"And by the sea?"

"Yes."

"I too have had such lovers; I'd get rid of them immediately because it was a pain in the ass."

We were moving ahead fast as it got darker and darker, and the clouds, not threatening, all looked the color of live coals in the fireplace when you let them go out. I followed the avenue of the old plane trees until, after rounding a hill, we came out of the canyon and saw—dimly lit and bunched together, encircling the slopes of a cone-shaped hill—a village crowned by a castle and a cathedral.

"It looks Gothic."

"Yes, Catalan Gothic."

"Yes, notice how ample the arches are . . ."

"Lovely."

"Very lovely."

"Particularly because it all gives the impression of being so alive, surrounded by its orchards with its farmers dressed in black or shiny blue, look how they move about, it's the hour, entering the village in their *tartanas* and tractors, on their mules, sometimes on foot, followed by their dogs . . . The return of the farmers to the village is much prettier, I'd say, than the return of the fisherman to the beach or the port . . ."

"And similar."

"Yes."

"Shall we enter the village?"

"Let's."

We didn't need to detour since the road lined with plane trees was leading directly to the village—it was clear that the old road passed through the very center of town—while the new highway, which led to Mora, abandoned the plane-tree road. We slowly continued, so as not to disturb the farmers who greeted us as they were returning to their homes after a day's work—all very *Angelus* by Millet but different to see when one believed this no longer existed and that only the condos of Tarragona and Salou existed and the boys and girls who during the season migrate there to serve, look, here enter all the people who walk toward the town, boys with their hoes upon their shoulders, incredible, it makes one feel like preserving them as certain governments preserve the primitive tribes of the Stone Age to study how they lived five thousand years ago, and now these too should be preserved as survivors of another era to be studied—and to eat their supper and off to bed.

The road between the two rows of plane trees straightened as it headed toward the river, and, framed by the huge arch of leaves, we now saw the perfectly cone-shaped village that hugged the hill like a compact hard fist, and higher up, the castle and the cathedral, and these, illuminated by floodlights that animated, as if they were vital living flesh, their building blocks blushing gold. Before us the bridge—the river passes through the two eyes of its arch, irrigating the orchard—and beyond the bridge a narrow gate, then the perched houses with covered or open porches, with clothes hanging out to dry, old women leaning on railings right over the river where at twilight children play amid the heather and tall reeds on pebbly islands. We moved slowly ahead, in awe, as if we were about to enter or return to another completely different time. Two weather-beaten stone lions, with their front paws raised, held up two coats of arms, and in a shell-shaped niche Saint Roque and his dog—the pilgrim with his dog and his staff and the shell on his hat—blessing all those who entered the narrow gate. Upon crossing its threshold, we went downhill a few meters and reached the square, which seemed to be the main square. We stooped to look at the Renaissance buildings and the thirteenth-century inn, and we decided to leave the car there, get out and visit the village on foot. We were awestruck: the village glimpsed through the trees, with its cone shape and crowned by the castle, had been a dreamlike vision: things like this, one thought, no longer existed.

The square was narrow and could only be viewed through the arch opening on to the bridge, which confirmed its authentic antiquity: in those eras clear notions of perspectives and panoramas inside towns did not exist. To defend a village from the elements and its enemies, everything would be bunched tightly together; this square, so little, surrounded by buildings that seemed very tall, was like an open-air hall with a roof of stars. And if you twisted your neck toward one side, amid the dark heaps of medieval houses climbing the steep slope of the craggy hill you could see the illuminated human carnal tip of the castle—or the church. The square, with its Renaissance trim of eaves wrought in wood and portals adorned with coats of arms, was closed off. On the other side the inn, a building made of golden stone like the castle, but dark because of poor lighting, crenellated on top with a great stone fan over the main door. On the other side was another similar building with portals only, which, according to what we could see, continued downhill along a dark street, and sheltered countless little tables where a waiter, a white cloth rolled around his waist, served coffee and liqueurs. Luisa exclaimed:

"This is extraordinary."

We looked at it all, not with archeological fervor, not trying to identify the coats of arms nor dating the eras of the façades and craftsmanship, but rather enjoying it, enjoying every little detail. The children pedaled their bicycles around the square shouting and scrambling up the iron grates of a window, so thick that they must have belonged to a medieval prison, and a group of children with castanets in their hands awaited their flamenco teacher. We asked why flamenco, why not *sardana:*

"Because it's on television."

This was a small blemish in the perfect surface of the atmosphere. Then, over the arcades, between two stone gargoyles and on a medieval façade, we were horrified to see a walk-on balcony, glass enclosed, adorned with bits of ceramic, modern, awful, like those we'd seen on the coast. I pointed it out to Luisa, and she closed her eyes in horror, covering them with her hand.

"Salou, at its worst . . ."

"Or Torredembarra . . . Come, let's sit here under the arches, at one of these tables. From here at least we won't see that horrible balcony."

We ordered our liqueurs from the owner of La Flor del Ebro bar and he served us. There was a lot of chatter on the square, but not like big-city noise since—despite the cars passing and the television that boomed from La Flor del Ebro where numerous customers with their backs to the street watched it from the bar—the place had a peaceful feel, supremely provincial, beautiful, with the two dead-end slopes descending the hill into the middle of the square, populated by children sliding on the smooth stones. From where we sat, along a street sloping uphill, one could see the façade of the church with its enormous stained-glass window right in the middle like a European, Spanish, Christian mandala, inviting one to meditate. Luisa said:

"Tomorrow we must visit the church and the castle."

"So we'll stay here?"

"Hadn't we decided to?"

"We haven't even mentioned the matter. But let's stay. I'm happy here, and also curious."

We asked the owner of La Flor del Ebro if he thought we'd find a bed at the inn.

"Yes, but it's not very good."

We said it looked fine.

"Why would you go there!? On the other side of the village— in the modern part you folks didn't see because you came in on the bridge of Santiago the Apostle, from the mountainside, and not on the good modern highway that comes from Tivisa and Mora—there's a good modern hotel, and it's better, I think, for you to look for a room there . . ."

We congratulated each other on our luck that we had not seen the "modern" town of Dors, across an iron bridge on the other bank of the river, according to what we were told later by the owner of the inn—that didn't have a name, not "Miami," "Copacabana," or "Monaco," but was simply "the inn"—as he showed us our two rooms on the third floor of this thirteenth-century edifice, which were next to each other with a connecting balcony facing the river. It's not that the rooms looked thirteenth century, or noble or anything, but their framed color prints and their clean starched sheets and their vanities with marble tops and water jars indicated a way of life, or rudimentary needs that at least now, while the summer heat lasted, were sufficient. We were tired. The trip from La Garriga in the morning—all across the nasty and ugly corniness of the coast prostituted for the most vulgar tourism, to here, to the tranquility of this balcony over the river that scarcely moved—was a lot, and we asked what time they could serve us supper. They said in an hour. We took our creaking wicker chairs out onto the balcony, and we took out our books (I had a volume of letters, Luisa, one of the latest Latin American novels) and we began to read because, until we finally got to Dors, we had talked too much during the trip.

I felt, in some way, that we had really "arrived," that the whole structure of the day had been planned by "someone" for "something." As we both sat with our books on our laps, looking at the slow lights of tractors moving along the road across the river, Luisa said:

"The kind of thing your son Miles believes, in London, and that he brings about by playing the flute and smoking marijuana."

"Perhaps in some way he's right."

"Perhaps there is 'something' and 'someone' and perhaps, finally a form or structure . . . the mandala . . . look where we came upon it, there right on the front of a church lost in a tiny village in southern Cataluña . . . That's the kind of thing young people talk about nowadays. I feel very marginal to all that. Sometimes I feel glad that my daughter likes to read

Hola to see how many of her girlfriends show up in the magazine, and to play golf with her husband . . . Until she begins, I suppose, to play golf with her husband's friends, and then takes on one of them as her lover, out of sheer boredom, as in those American novels that are all alike which we used to read before, remember . . . ?"

But the landscape was bewitching in a special way, as if that big beauty mark on the middle of the vast façade we saw from the café on the square was, somehow, the end of a long voyage. We read a while longer. But I wasn't reading. After a long time, after years and years, perhaps from the moment I began to paint, I felt that I had "arrived" at some definitive place. In some way, spending all my days here outside on this balcony, all my sunsets contemplating the thick row of plane trees on the other side of the river, and beyond the orchard, the hills with their terraces where man, for perhaps millennia, cultivated the same olive tree passed down from generation to generation; all this gave me an enormous sensation of peace, washed away my envy, my need to have a cat named Tàpies, the anguish that all things ended ignobly, in failure, like my painting, like my fatherhood, like my ability to feel pleasure—now gone, or so it had seemed until this moment, eternally vulnerable to Salous, to the commercial world, to my own incapacity to take any action that wouldn't be totally castrating for me. And what if—perhaps—I again felt the capacity to fall in love? With something . . . or someone? Luisa, her feet resting on the railing, leaned her chair on its two back legs, holding the book up, her profile lifted against what remained of the now-dim light in the sky. Friendship was something, something that enveloped us both; we were accomplices, allies, we were partners. In the end this was what remained of love, and it wasn't bad, and one couldn't really complain, but of course it had nothing to do with pleasure . . . with that completely oxygenated blood which suddenly, without rhyme nor reason, I would feel pulsing and coursing through my veins, nourishing me . . . painting . . . someone once, yes, someone, but it was indisputable that fidelity, and love for something, for a city, for example, a passion for something would last much longer than the passion one can feel for someone. I sensed her body, almost smelled Luisa's body beside me in the delicious but not magical twilight; I felt her presence, now, as a dog feels the rug in front of the fireplace upon which it has the habit of resting. I compare that innocent sunset, clear as a bell, on the terrace facing the river in the inn at Dors, that first sunset of my new life, with the sunsets now, after so much water has passed under the eyes of the bridge—and so much blood in Dors, in the shadow of the castle, and now that I am here in the apartment Luisa has left me, waiting for more blood to flow—while the intrepid farmers returned from work with their carts and goats and dogs and sacks, in a single file under the plane trees, celebrating the rites of laying the first stone with which, under the direction of Bruno the Italian, that damn filthy dago who launched Onassis in La Flor del Ebro bar, as the day turned into night, the unreality of the light into the reality of darkness, the clarity of consciousness scribbled on an unconsciousness stained with myths, with a sort of fricassee of Jung and Zen and hippy philosophy only half-understood, of Nietzsche never read (in reality you don't need to read Nietzsche to understand him, so filled is he with platitudes and universal clichés), with a desire for power, such a huge hunger to dominate, that I can only compare it, in another sense, to what emerged in me when I saw that first innocent calm sunset, when I thought I had finally arrived, had settled—and was not yet persecuted by the cries, the screams of pleasure and pain in languages one could understand inside the ruins of the old castle as night came down, which I thought I heard—contemplating from my terrace the face blushing in the light, the golden stone marked with two-light windows, semidetached to the church, to religion, the church whose unsoiled façade bore on its very center the mandala of the stained-glass window.

The first thing we did, upon getting up the next day, was to take a walk around the village. We climbed the medieval cobblestone streets rising abruptly from the square—the Old Plaza, as I later learned it was called—narrow rough slopes to the top of the hill. The houses were modest, windows and here and there a façade tinted blue, applied directly to the rosy-golden stone of the region, that living sandstone which, afterwards I knew, lives and dies like a human being, and like flesh itself, deteriorates. Piles of wood tied into enormous cords, log-laden donkeys we would encounter, from time to time, entering a very low arched doorway wrought into a sumptuous stone fan. The balconies of carved wood, on the top floors, made it feel like an alpine village. One sensed the abundance of wood on all the façades, the wood on the balconies, or next to doors the piles of firewood, upon which some cat was dozing, in the thick rustic beams which through some open window we'd glimpse in the interiors, supporting the arched Catalan roofs—this was the rudimentary way of supporting the top floor. But the sensation of narrowness, of streets where a mule could barely squeeze through, of balcony touching balcony, of tortuous tight spaces, of density, overwhelmed and exhilarated us as we made our way up the hill. If the streets were dark and the houses narrow, high up, from the second story and the garrets, the sun was boisterous and yellow. Luisa said:

"Good houses to live in."

"And how do you get up here by car?"

I resisted her because I was already thinking it. We continued uphill until the streets suddenly opened out, and there at the top a long wide staircase ended at the church entrance, a pointed Gothic portico with the statues of the four evangelists, and above, a stained-glass window—white glass as the original pieces had fallen during the war—and from the base of the extended flight of stairs the pointed Gothic arch looked like two hands joined in prayer or meditation, under that mandala, solitary on the front of the church, inviting prayer or meditation. When we finished climbing, Luisa said:

"Let's go in."

"Wait."

"Why?"

"Not yet."

"Why? I want to see, it's marvelous . . ."

"Let's go to the very top of the hill first to see everything."

She understood, and she followed me. It was only a little stretch more, stepping among bushes surrounding the crumbling walls around the castle, and then the castle itself, set upon the highest plateau of the hill, a rosy-golden hunk of sandstone so worn down by time that some of its corners had worn edges, and other blocks, the weakest, eaten away by time, exposing the inner ribbing, the bones as it were, the skeletal structures of building blocks which could not endure. The hulk was immense, square, with several Gothic two-light windows, and on the crest, arches extended along all sides of the castle. But for the moment this wasn't what interested me, though later, it did; for the moment, scrambling up to the highest remains of a wall, where they hid the floodlight that illuminated the façade at night, I contemplated the whole valley.

The village was situated in a strategic position, nestled in the bosom shaped by the river surrounding us on three sides. We, I noted, had arrived from the mountains—I saw them, green and ocher, gray with olive trees and blue with hazelnuts, abrupt, opening upon the orchard, an enclave in the midst of which stood the hill of Dors. I saw the row of plane trees and the arched back of the bridge ending in the square I couldn't see, so steep was the slope to the village. Then I looked toward the other side, toward the road leading to Mora, where, around an evidently principal road, the new town clustered with its modern three- and four-story buildings, a street with very few shops, a "modernish" square, where I noticed a pond in the shape of a liver, decorative bushes that had nothing to do with the region, a monument to the Rotary Clubs—or so it appeared, something looking like a wheel—and all of it disconnected, a life alien to the life of this medieval cloistered Dors clustering around the castle. That other life had gas stations and pigsties and expanding factories; this life, on a donkey's back, slow,

41

vertical. In any case, if the square where we had sipped our liqueurs the night before existed, if the stone bridge, the hill and the river that defended it all existed, one could be content. Three-fourths of the landscape was and remained pure . . . one minuscule part, the new Dors, was ruined. I thought, nevertheless, of the balcony facing the medieval structure of La Flor del Ebro café in the square and felt a knot in my stomach, a repulsion equal to the one I had felt when I realized that the *marchands* were marketing the painters who were letting it happen, when I committed suicide and broke with everything, abandoned it all because I didn't want to be involved, because the fight I put up ended in failure. And here the rudiments of another battle were now presenting themselves. Returning from her walk, Luisa said:

"Warrior's castle, monk's castle, certainly not a feudal lord's castle . . . How strange . . . I don't get it."

"Did you go in?"

"No. There's only one door and it's sealed with lock and chain."

"The church was open. Let's go . . ."

We clambered down among the plants and rubble, and reached the church door. We had already heard the banging of stonecutters, and upon entering the church we realized that some place, nearby, they were working inside the enclosure. The nave was simple, pure, and had suffered, or enjoyed, a discreet and recent restoration which had left the structure Gothic but without a thirteenth-century elevation—naked, and with a totally contemporary look. We had already wondered about that immense castle, looking rather institutional, whether private or governmental, crowning that insignificant village which, nevertheless, displayed certain noble features. This church, next to the castle as if it belonged to it and were its necessary extension, also seemed disproportionate to the village. And even more so when we realized the central nave had been cut by a stone wall a little beyond the entrance. In that rough stone wall, different from the polished stone walls of the rest of the church, there was a little door. Since the church had been stripped of any ornamentation worth examining, and offered only its structure for the enjoyment and admiration of the eyes of men and the eyes of God, there wasn't much to detain us there, and we opened the small door in the improvised stone wall—if it's possible to improvise anything with stone—and we entered, or exited. Outside was a courtyard, or so it seemed at first, replete with broken capitals, bits and pieces of gargoyles, coats of arms and medieval leaf-adorned arches, and of virgin stone upon which two men worked, at one end of the "courtyard," their hammers and chisels resounding in the enclosure; looking up, however, we saw the transept of the original church, ending in two naves, in a cross, with a piece of the wall at the end holding up—oh prodigious—a stained-glass window. Only the skeleton of stone, apparently, miraculously raised like a communion wafer in the air, remained of the high wall. On one side an almost completed chapel, with its ribs and piers, gave the model for the other one, identical but in ruins, on the other side, which these stonemasons, aided by the models and the pieces that remained after the war, were reconstructing, with intricate scaffolds upon which they lifted up the stones. We went over to them. They didn't raise their eyes from their work; I saw a row of winged demons, all alike, which were going to be used on capitals for the subtle ribbings of their bat wings. We stood there watching them work for a long time— perhaps a father with his son to whom he had passed down this forgotten, almost extinct profession—and as they worked, to the sound of the hammer and the chisel, as the hours passed, I saw that the father's mustache and hair got whiter and whiter, turning him into an old man, as if the space of five minutes during which we stood there watching had stretched to a great length, until making room for the transition from youth to a man's old age: he seemed stooped over to me now, weak, old, defeated. He had finished a gargoyle and placed it next to the others. We took advantage of the pause in work to greet him.

He answered "hello" but his greeting did not invite further conversation. Nevertheless that wizard, that magician, seemed to hold in his hands the secret of time and of all these ruins: from those hands, again, the recreated reality of this castle and this church half in ruins would emerge. We offered him a cigarette, which suddenly dissolved the doleful crease in his brow, and he put aside his hammer and chisel, now of a mind to chat. He didn't wipe away the dust that covered his face, or his hair, giving the curious impression that one was talking to God the Almighty Father. Nevertheless, in his crinkly eyes—not because of age, as he was a man my age at the very most, but because he had to squint against the dust, which left clear traces in his wrinkles—diminished in defense from something, there was humor, a precise focus, that seemed to recognize us.

We chatted awhile with Salvador, from Horta de San Juan, where everyone's name is Salvador, who would later become such a good friend to us; he explained that he was restoring and rebuilding the church of Dors, where we were now: under the enormous skeletal stained-glass window, the altar from another time rose with its two wings, one of which he was reconstructing, as the church originally had the form of a cross. Now, while the reconstruction was being finished, the cross was upside down in the lower apse, and the head of Christ, the Mass, the sacrifice, remained at the foot of the church. He looked at us as if seeking our reaction, but scarcely affected by matters of occultism and religion, we apparently did not react as was perhaps expected. Salvador continued:

"Something having to do with witchcraft, yes, those priests have become sorcerers, black magic, and with the Christ upside down anything can happen in this town."

"And you believe in all that?"

Then he began to shake, and from beneath the dust emerged a vigorous young man, realistic and well dressed, who replied:

"No, I don't believe in anything. But it's amusing to think about it, especially because it serves me as a tool . . ."

"A tool for what?"

He sat on a capital in the grass to finish smoking his cigarette. Luisa sat on his wooden bench, crossing one leg over the other, with the rays of sunlight piercing the skeleton of the stained-glass window and falling upon her face, and I leaned against the wall.

"Bartolomé, the bumpkin who has the most work in town, is very Catholic. He was on the other side during the war. I have him convinced that as long as the church is like this, upside down, there will be poverty and there will be no progress in the village. He wants progress; he wants hotels and he wants tourists to come. He built that horrendous hotel on the Mora highway where no one goes, and he wants to make condos and to destroy the ancient houses from here, Castillo—this hill is called the Castillo—to transform them into horrendous condominiums. Since the olive and hazelnut harvests have not been good during recent times, the new town, with its new square, has been held back a bit, and nobody is building condos, so that, at the most, there's someone who asks him to fix the façade of the houses here in the castle and he rebuilds, or destroys them, modernizing them . . ."

Climbing up to the castle we had in fact noticed, with despair, two or three modern-looking houses, and had closed our eyes so as not to see them.

"He hates me because I prefer to remain poor as I am, living in my grandparents' house here next to the castle, than do the things he's doing. I'm alone. I don't have any needs. And I like working with stone, which was the same work as my grandfather and my great-grandfather, who always lived in the house next to the elm tree, a block away from here. He thinks that what one should do is raze the castle of the lords of Calatrava to the ground, and this church too, and fill the hills with condos for tourists . . . as if tourists came here. What would they come for? Sometimes there are elite tours for members of that club you must know—but not tourists—and they stroll around and talk about this castle of Calatrava . . ."

I asked:

"Did the Calatravas get this far?"

"Yes, this is the principal castle of the region. Montsegur, it was called . . ."

"Montsegur . . . the Holy Grail . . ."

"I don't know: Montsegur is how it's remembered in the region. They say that the coats of arms with castles in each of the entranceways to the castle are from the Segura family, since the Great Master who built the castle in the twelfth century was a lord in the Segura family . . ."

"But the similarity is too great: Montsegur . . ."

Luisa, who had been watching me attentively, broke out laughing:

"You fell for it. I know you as if I'd given birth to you. You're already making connections to the Templar Knights, Sir Galahad and the Roundtable, and God knows what other strange rituals . . ."

"But those things don't interest me."

"No, but they amuse you."

"Well of course they amuse me. And you too! I mean, finding Montsegur and the Holy Grail and all that . . ."

"Fun stuff."

"Definitely."

And addressing the stonecutter, I asked:

"And can one visit the castle?"

A cloud darkened the worker's face, as if he had once again used his chisel and covered himself in dust, futility, and time. He replied:

"No, sir. You need to have permission from the head of the province. It's in a bad state, and they fear stones may fall and it might deteriorate even more. I've known it, from the time before they closed it down. It's not really that badly deteriorated . . . The floors and ceilings are missing, but the stone is in good shape. Bartolomé, who's the mayor's friend, succeeded in having it closed so that no one can see it, because he feels such a ruin is a shame for a village like this which should be progressive. He even wants to get the mayor to build a horrible brick wall to 'hide' this shame, since of course the church is different, because it's a church."

Luisa and I showed our enormous disappointment at the fact that it would be impossible to visit the interior of the castle of the lords of Calatrava . . . this Montsegur transplanted from its native Pyrenees to this Catalan mountain, beside the Ebro river, in this strange little town of Dors. Anyway, there was a lot to see in the village, strolling around the streets, looking at mules and macho goats and donkeys loaded with cargo, and sitting down, finally, after the wonderful lunch at the inn, to have coffee under the arches of the square in La Flor del Ebro café. We spoke very little, as if the principal language of the moment—contrary to what usually happened between us, as we verbalized everything—was that of things, of the light, of the spring warmth, of the sun caressing the stones, of the worn-down gargoyles whose smiles, suddenly, became less diabolical and were merely decorative. We took a walk by the bridge, along the river, went up the hill again, peering at the aborted project of new Dors with its closed, deserted hotel and we returned to the café, and then, tired, to our rooms overlooking the river, and took out our books to read awhile at sunset. We did not speak of going, of leaving. It was as if we had established ourselves there forever. And I heard Luisa's voice—as if echoing my thoughts that weren't even thoughts but just feelings, sensations, still reading the book on her lap upon which her profile was fixed, without lowering her legs from the railing—ask me gently, as if her voice were coming from inside me:

"And if you stayed here?"

I put down my book, not looking at her but rather at the river, the green hazelnut trees, mesmerizing against the ocher of the terraces of the hills facing us, the peaceful transparent twilight of that summer that was beginning.

"What do you mean?"

Now she did look up from her book, but not at me. I knew exactly what she was going to say, because during our first

47

walks that afternoon in the village I had already seen houses, doors, windows I liked in a way that was different than how an outsider likes things, without any connection other than an aesthetic one to those things.

"Why don't you just stay and live here?"

I didn't interrupt her, so that I could formulate my whole theory, because if I did stay, I wanted it to be logical, without any doubt the right thing.

"Buy a house . . . Salvador said that all the owners of these marvelous houses from the Middle Ages, or from whenever, all stone houses with arches over the entrances, the only thing these owners want is to sell, sell so that they can build little houses on the main road, with glass-enclosed balconies like the café's, with disgusting metallic-painted iron railings, or to buy a unit in one of the four or five apartment buildings constructed indiscriminately and which have been selling little by little . . . A noble old stone house, with whitewashed walls and thick wooden beams as if from the whole trunk of a tree . . . for nothing . . . and it's not as if this were thousands of kilometers from Barcelona, in three hours you're here . . . or they're here . . ."

"Who?"

"I don't know . . . whoever wants to come see you . . . me, your friends . . . , Miles . . ."

"Miles . . . he would like it."

"He'd go nuts here."

"Can you imagine what would go on with crazy Miles here, with his farcical Spanish, his long hair . . . Did you see those kids slyly shouting *Fidel* at me because of my beard? They don't know from hippies here, him with his sandals and playing Mozart on his flute . . . ?"

"And his marijuana."

"Yes, his marijuana."

"What's he up to now I wonder? Does he ever write to you?"

"He never writes. When I get to see him, every six months or so, he's up to something new, and is a completely different person. What would happen if Miles came to Dors and moved in with me?"

"It would be a nightmare!"

"I don't know . . . He is my son and I do love him."

"I don't love my daughter."

"She's exactly like Manolo, how could you love her?"

"And she plays golf."

After dinner we decided to go out. It was ten thirty and the whole town was silent, deserted, swept clean; inside every other window you could see a face leaning over the sewing on the brazier table, or the napes of three or four necks outlined against a television's blue screen. A donkey smell permeated the fresh air and was sharp as the blade of a knife, and then suddenly we sought to touch things with our own hands, which were still enjoying the warmth from the fine food and wine we had at dinner. Seen from the old plaza on the promontory above, stood the heavy ever-present swollen mass of pink stone, weighing down upon the squat, tortuous yet stately village, ending at the top illuminated by the church and castle of the lords of Calatrava. Our path and plan was obvious: go all the way up, now that the town was asleep, follow the twists and turns of the narrow streets, climbing amidst the frozen silence of those narrow slopes until coming out onto the wide staircase leading to the cathedral, and finally to the castle.

At that hour, against a sky as clear as blue glass, the rosy mass of the church and the castle emerged strikingly carnal, more like flesh than when seen in daylight, and one got the impression that this stone was capable of responding like the body of a lover, resisting, recoiling, or quivering if touched sweetly or if you caressed her with your fingertips. Luisa was silent beside me and because we hadn't yet reached the stone I wanted to touch, I took her arm. She reacted, looked at me with surprise, but did not delay our ascent; beneath my fingertips I felt the resistance of her bare forearm and then felt it merge with my own skin. It's curious that, seemingly by mutual agreement, intoxicated by our embrace, we did not approach the church, the portal of two hands joined in prayer below the mysterious stained-glass mandala, but rather we turned left and ascended the slope, climbed past the fallen leaves and crumbling capitals up to the terraced entrance of the castle. There the floodlights cast our joined shadows onto the blank screen of the vast wall—the empty wall of the main floor of the castle—which got smaller and smaller as we came closer to the main door, to the wall, until those shadows almost became one. And Luisa and I, as if seeking the same thing, touching the surface of the pink stone that did not react to our touch, mute and frustrated we held each other in a tighter embrace until my arm circled her shoulder and her hand clung to my waist and we felt our bodies joining, reacting, feeling as we had not felt like feeling in many years. I said:

"But there must be a way in."

"We must look for it, I'd love to see inside the castle at night, especially a clear night like this . . ."

"We must look . . ."

Without parting ways, as if in separating we would lose each other, or get lost forever, we went around the castle, passing pits, ruins, and rubble, looking for the entrance, an entrance it seemed not to have. The whole bottom floor was impregnably closed, hermetic, stone masonry without a hole anywhere, nowhere was it possible to climb into the enormous empty two-winged windows through which, here and there, one could see branches of a tree growing inside, amongst the broken arches and truncated columns. Nonetheless we kept going all around the castle, as if each time we went around it would be easier to enter, to get a reaction out of that dead, inert, and yet forceful-looking castle that still did not react. From time to time I saw her touch the wall, as if pleading with it, as if to see if it would somehow melt or react, and for my part I, without her seeing, also touched the stone from time to time, and each time I did, each time the stone rejected us, it brought us closer together. Seeking intimacy more and more, emotion

50

reflected, the dialogue of the animate seeking footing until, as I helped her cross a moat in one leap, Luisa fell into my arms, and against the pink and golden wall that didn't respond to what we were seeking, our silhouettes, reflected, joined in an embrace that had not united us for a long time—years, maybe eight—and in a kiss we gave each other, giving each other all the heat and vulnerability we were not finding anywhere else, we made love right there, over the flat grass at the entrance of the castle, in the light cast by the floodlight, and each of our movements was reflected, magnified by the light onto the castle wall which had given us no answers. We said nothing, as if we wanted to protect this episode from our words and our analysis, but it had to happen there, and not ten minutes later, after descending the hill, in our rooms at the inn. We stood up, and the embrace that connected us, after shaking the dust off, was tighter than before—but no kiss now—and we remained entwined, as before, I with my arm on her shoulder, she with her arm around my waist.

We sat thus entwined on one of the buttresses of the wall, the lights jumbled like the lights on a Christmas pine tree in the village, falling from the castle, then lining up in an orderly way as the streets became the straight numbered blocks of the new part of town. We ran to the other side, so as not to see the new town's square blocks of streets, to see, instead, the untamed landscape of the mountain, the river, the Old Plaza, which was ours. A breeze, becoming cooler, touched our faces. Yes, I thought, I must stay here. I must have said this aloud, because Luisa said:

"I would stay here forever."

I let some minutes pass so she wouldn't think that what I was going to tell her had anything to do with her desire to stay in Dors, which was only, anyway, I already knew, a passing fancy because Luisa was a woman for whom the fast worldly Barcelona life was preferable to the centuries-old peace of Dors. Then I said:

"I would buy a house."

51

Now she didn't respond, perhaps most probably because she realized that her wish expressed out loud was only a rhetorical proclamation of the happiness to which she didn't have access because it simply no longer amused her. But I wanted her to react and I continued:

"And you could remodel it and decorate it . . ."

She replied:

"No. The things I do are very whorish . . ."

"What do you mean 'whorish'?"

"Well, very *House and Garden,* what rich and ignorant people see in the good North American magazines, and want to immediately apply it here . . . Or in the magazines of Italian design, you know, like the house of Marina Agnelli, like the house of the duchess of Windsor . . . that's what I do: adaptations to our price bracket, and to our cultural level, of the houses of the duchess of Windsor, of Jacqueline Kennedy, of Agnelli . . . These wouldn't have anything to do with this village."

"No."

And after a while I said:

"Besides, I'd like to be alone."

"Do you want me to go?"

I thought for a moment, looking at the landscape, mining all its possibilities and touching with my hand the skin hidden under her collar:

"Yes."

"When?"

Again I thought. The possibility was a possibility, but it was necessary to resolve it immediately, and with urgency:

"Now."

"Tonight?"

"Are you too tired to drive the car?"

She thought for a moment.

"No."

Our lovemaking hadn't tired her, had not left a trace in her whatsoever. I had not made love with her, then, but rather with the stones of the castle, of the whole village, of the immense night. I had taken possession because she declared that it wouldn't matter at all if she left right away and drove— it was eleven o'clock—three hours through the night back to Barcelona. Perhaps she'd want to at least meditate on the meaning of what we had done, and so I asked her:

"Won't the trip be too boring for you?"

"Yes, but, anyway . . ."

She could have said "no"; she could have said "I have a lot to think about"; after all, after her operation, it wasn't strange to rethink life a bit. But she did say she'd be bored, which left me alone, and at ease. But I felt I had to explain:

"I want to stay here alone. I want to think. I'd like to see some houses to buy, to choose one . . . If you stayed, probably you, who have more sense and better taste than I do, would dominate me and if I bought a house suggested by you, it would never be mine . . . I want to make my own mistakes, not yours . . . And then, it's possible that tomorrow you'll find this town horrible and the people intolerable and brutish . . . I don't want you to stay."

She let go of me almost with hostility.

"I already told you I don't want to stay."

"Well, then."

"Shall we go down?"

"Let's go down."

We went down together, but this time without touching each other, completely distanced, as if to erase what had happened up above. I remained sitting on the curbstone of the bridge while she went up to her room to look for her case of toiletries and the keys to her car, and when she came down, I opened the door for her and put her case on the backseat. She sat at the wheel and asked me the way out, since we both were well aware of the fact that she had no sense of direction, and I had to indicate, on each road, which way to go. I told her to make a turn on the river side and take the new road, along the new city, where the castle and the old town were not separated from the earth by the river, and to continue toward Tivisa and Mora where she would find signs that would show her the way to Reus, Tarragona, Barcelona, and the known world. I looked at her in the driver's seat. She was occupied turning on the dashboard buttons one by one, as if making sure that all the parts worked, as if she hoped—I thought—that something in the car wasn't working right and she would have to stay, at least until morning. But I realized I could not bear the fact of her possessing the town in her body, her staying here a minute longer. This was now mine. She was redundant, a disturbance: she was the past and this was the present, the future, and perhaps, even another past.

"Good-bye, then. Good luck."

That's what she said to me.

And I said to her:

"Be careful . . . it's night . . ."

Starting the engine, she laughed a little. And in her laughter I realized that perhaps she had realized, upon my telling her to drive carefully at night, that I had felt, without formulating it further, the wish for her to have an accident and die. Yes, why not admit it: now that the car disappeared along the street and left me alone in the village whence I did not know how or when I would return, my solitude in Dors would be total and definitive, and at least she wouldn't share with me and infect the day tomorrow, devaluing the experience with all her memories of La Garriga, of our love, of the inadequate informalists I had now left far behind; it would be a complete and totally new day.

I waited for the red lights, blinking along the narrow medieval street, to disappear. Then I went up to my room, and sitting for a while on the rocker on the terrace, I looked at the landscape, that landscape I would not fully recognize until the next day, and which tonight, together with closing my book to go into my room to sleep, was closing, closed until tomorrow—which wouldn't have occurred if Luisa had stayed with me—to look at it with eyes as innocent as the first eyes that saw the world.

But I didn't enter my room, nor did I read, but rather I closed my book and lay there thinking that having Luisa in my arms that night had had the almost official, institutional quality which, despite attraction and even despite love, had ruined my love for my wife. Something in the touch of the flesh in both cases, something of the expected responses . . . But no, I couldn't deceive myself, telling myself the story that my marriage failed because of sexual dissatisfaction, even, so to speak, a romantic dissatisfaction. It was the irrefutable proof that love is not what holds marriages together. Diana was the granddaughter of Thomas Hardy and belonged to a sophisticated world, and indeed liberated for many generations already: Her grandmother had fought for women's rights and had been imprisoned. Her mother had been one of the bright young things who in the pages of Huxley and Evelyn Waugh dance the shimmy, cut their hair à la page boy, and get drunk on gin. She no longer had anything to liberate herself from, and she married me after Miles, our first son, was born, and her suffragette grandmother discharged her duty as our godmother holding our son in her arms during the intimate wedding ceremony, which took place because my father, dying in Puigcerdá, wrote to me asking me to, that he wanted to see me married by both laws before dying. We married and he died. And Miles grew up and I lived in England four years maintained by Diana's money, as she said: "But why are you such a Puritan, why do you have to work if I have money? Enjoy the peace and the leisure which many would like to enjoy having the luck of being married to a woman with money and without prejudices," starting to paint, but without Diana taking my painting very seriously, as she didn't take seriously any artistic expression unless it produced pleasure and then it was worth the trouble and was effective, and for me painting did not produce pleasure, it was a rather poor way to justify myself, and after four years of marriage, of justifying my frequent trips to Paris to see the paintings of the informalist school in Paris, because even though our union worked in terms of sex and friendship, there was something dry. Diana always said, and said to Miles, who was six years old, and to Miguel, who was four:

"Passion for one thing, for something, is much more important than passion for someone, for a person, and lasts much longer . . ."

She was beautiful, Diana was, with her pre-Raphaelite head, her slightly thick neck, her mane that fashion and lack of fashion never managed to tame, and her slow-moving body, which only functioned beneath another body—mine—and for her sons. She'd say: "What am I to do? I thought I was a modern woman and all that interests me are my sons and being a mother; I'm trapped by the age-old vice of women: maternity. I know it's bad, what can I do . . . ? I suppose I am going to spoil these two kids horribly and they'll never be anything . . ." And that's precisely how it was. We separated when the moment came that we realized it was totally useless to continue living together. I didn't take the boys because it was obvious—we decided in mutual agreement—that it was absurd to educate the children in Spain if it could be done in England, and besides, she didn't want me to feel burdened by any economic obligation to them. I was charming, she'd say, but like a slightly retarded child who had not developed spiritually in a total way yet. I hadn't found myself, no, the children would stay with her. And they did, especially because the experiences Diana and I lived in Spain were brief, and for her atrocious, as she couldn't see herself reduced to "mistress of the house" dressed in black, a conformist going to Mass, and the other cliché also gave her the creeps, the "free" woman who has a love affair one day and the next day with someone else, who doesn't have sex unless she feels like it, and all this transformed into material that had to be justified and explained, and she had no desire to fall into any cliché that needed an explanation or justification in any way. She was herself, and could only be herself in London, where nobody asked any questions and the supply of conversation was endless because, as she got older, she was more interested in conversation, with free, ironic, daring people, than in love. Miguel grew up hating England, and he transferred in order to live with me at the age of sixteen, finishing high school here. Upon entering the university to study architecture—afterwards he left to enter the Massana School of Design—he said he wanted to live alone, as people did in civilized countries, and that with the money his mother sent him he could manage very well. He had had everything since he was very young so that it was easy for him to do without everything, and in fact he did without, and lived very modestly but very organized until he finished his studies, always accompanied by some sexy, modern girl—seasonably interchangeable and whom I never recognized—who kept him company in bed, and while he studied helped him keep the house clean and orderly. He visits me from time to time, we speak often on the phone, and after the Dors affair he has been a good sport, never throwing it back in my face that he had "told me so" with his forthright and realistic criteria. Miles, the handsome one, the romantic, my favorite perhaps because I saw him only every once in a great while, stayed in England with his mother, in that tremendously huge and messy house, always filled with people who were doing something, and he, in sandals with his haired tied back, and his long-haired friends, inundated with guitars and marijuana, and their children, all of whom were maintained by Diana in the role of universal mother, comic at her age with her frizzy hair, also in Afro style, ornamented with little wreaths of flowers, charming, interested in everything, always reclining in a chaise longue piled with newspapers she supported and subversive magazines she subscribed to, beside a window facing Regent's Park, with newborn babies vomiting and peeing all over her, and then screaming until the corresponding mother came to take the baby away for a while, reading, reading endlessly while the others, Miles's girlfriends who now occupied the house, cleaned the big house when they thought it was time to clean, which wasn't very frequently, and made something to eat when someone was hungry and asked for eggs or something or went shopping, when someone remembered . . . And meanwhile he played the flute, Mozart endlessly, almost always, with the guitars and guitar-playing friends coming and going, Mozart and pop stuff, the Rolling Stones, and on the walls papered with gray silk they had tacked posters of Mick Jagger, beside the great golden Adam mirror in the small sitting room where Diana directed the operations, read, and received an endless rosary of friends and friends of friends and children of friends who came to keep her company because she almost never left her house, and she liked the windows tight shut, winter and summer, watching the people run into Regent's Park, two floors below, toward the river where the black poplars grew—their new leaves looked reddish to me in the twilight, in the reflected light, vermillion red—and the water and time transpired in a time so different from Diana's. But I didn't miss her. We'd write to each other frequently— she had the English flair for endless letters—and at the time of my written resignation from the informalists, she phoned to congratulate me and to tell me she was proud of me, and if I wanted anything, money or whatever, and I told her no, despite the fact that I needed it so desperately, and that same evening Miles called me, without having spoken to his mother, that he had seen it in the newspaper and was so proud; no, he didn't know that Mama had phoned that same day, he almost never saw Mama now, he ate at different hours, and as he spent the whole day playing the flute with his friends in a back room so as not to disturb the neighbors and at night, yes, at night they'd go out anywhere to listen to music; no, Mama didn't stay alone, there was always someone in the house, too many people really, staying there keeping her amused and busy . . . no, he saw very little of her, and that's why Mama had called early, and now him, but anyway, *congratulations, Dad, you did well.*

Did I do well? Have I done anything right my whole life? I doubt it. Probably the only good I could do would be, I thought then, to just keep looking at the river flow in the twilight forever, from this window, in this village lost in the Sierra of Caballa, without doing anything to justify myself, after all, existence is free, given to us gratis, and I also knew it would cost nothing for it to be taken away. This, living here—totally hidden away here, doing without the most desired pleasures of civilization, without contact with friends on the same level, with the movies, with exhibits, with beautiful and sophisticated women—was, in a certain way, taking life away gratis, a form of suicide. Deep down wasn't having renounced painting taking this semi-suicide to its ultimate consequences? If my renunciation of painting had some meaning beyond the gesture, shouldn't I simply disappear, and wasn't Dors the ideal place to disappear?

The next morning I got up early and went to have breakfast at La Flor del Ebro café. Despite not seeing it because it was right over my head, under the portals where I sat, I sensed that the balcony on that beautiful thirteenth-century façade weighed upon my conscience. I looked around the narrow square. The Renaissance trim also had something sticking to it that had nothing to do with the essence or atmosphere of the square. And why did the electricity cables cross, absurdly—very *Feininger*—like senseless scribblings in the little sky over the square, blue on this early summer morning, instead of being buried under the pavement? In some way this little square, this noble space, or with possibilities of nobility, was presenting itself to me as living matter in which to sink my hands in order to animate it, like Diana's flesh, years ago, and Luisa's, more recently, and like painting; and I, as if in contact with this material, was getting erect, emerging, arming myself, coming back to life. Yes, there was something to do, pleasure is doing something, connecting me with this space, with this town, doing something. What? Climbing the winding streets, and counting the ruined façades which were, finally, many more than had appeared on an initial visit, the answer was clear: buy a house here, restore it, speak to the people here, make them conscious of the jewel they possessed, teach them, and help them recover its original purity and nobility. The task I set out for myself, upon reaching the summit, the castle, was simple and noble. Around the esplanade that surrounded the castle I took a slow stroll, with a slight breeze in my face, and the whole map of the city and region became clear in my mind. People, after all, had the right to live as they wished. The new town was horrible, very poor, wretched with its little red brick church and shapeless tower, its four or five developments surrounded by gardens, its main commercial street in which two-story businesses alternated with vacant lots, and the two or three apartment buildings. If that's what they wanted, people could live there, they had the right to choose, and fortunately the new town—with its tiny square, and pond shaped like a kidney—did not disturb or deform in any way the solid old town made of stone, nestled on the hill in the bend of the sheltering river. From one side, looking over the orchard and new town toward the highway to Mora, the view was lamentable. But over three-fourths of the view was magnificent, almost untouched from here, with the stupendous panorama of the mountain, with its unexpected cliffs suddenly opening on to olive groves, vineyards, orchards of hazelnut trees, until reaching the plane-tree road and the old arched bridge where we had arrived. One could say that it was perfect, almost perfect, as everything in life is almost something, but sufficient, more in reality than what I ever dared expect of a place. Not that I ever expected much of a "place." I've never had a very refined sensibility—neither particularly acute nor well trained—to submerge myself like D. H. Lawrence in the beauty of places and things, unless those things had been made by man. My sensibility is too engaged with the world of design, of city streets, shop windows, artificial lights, than that of the great outdoors and landscapes that expand and ascend. Here, nonetheless, as if it had been beaten out of me, all that old sensibility seemed exhausted in one fell swoop, and replaced by this violent love of the landscape I was seeing, which did not signify a "preference" for a special kind of landscape, since that was a problem I had never proposed to myself, but rather a newly born consciousness that yes, landscape really did exist—and with this admission, from here, from the plateau which on the summit of the hill supported the castle and the church, upon receiving the ample and vibrant landscape I was seeing, I recovered suddenly all the other landscapes of my past, for which my sensibility had not left a place; this place, then, this site, was all my locations, all my places, and this present incorporated my whole past. How to leave, then? Impossible: the very idea of separating from this landscape, abandoning even for a short time Dors with its golden stone houses, its narrow streets, standing high over the landscape and against the wind, suddenly frightened me as if it were the worst threat against my individuality as a human being.

I was so lost in thought—curiously the typical phrase of the Romantics facing a landscape when they are suddenly torn from their contemplation—that I didn't realize that behind me, on the terrace at the foot of the castle, a group of boys had brought in a cart loaded with rosemary bushes and pine branches, and were piling them up: the fragrance added, then, to other weak perceptions of the landscape which came to life with that revived sense. I approached the boys to ask what they were doing.

"Tonight, the night of San Juan, is the bonfire of the recruits who are going away this year to enlist. And at night, in the square, is a dance . . ."

They had already asked me for money, in the square, to contribute to the celebration of the recruits going away this year, and I gladly gave. This was the night. How would the face of the castle look animated by a bonfire, like an immense torch there at the summit of the town? I slowly descended the streets scrutinizing almost house by house, portal by portal, promising myself to attend the festive *verbena* and bonfire that night, though noise, or crowds, was what I least wanted at those moments, nevertheless being able to attend felt like a fiesta. I felt liberated from my whole previous self, which of course would not have enjoyed a celebration like the one they were preparing for this night. My new self, a landscapist—I felt it to be a bit absurd and inadmissible—on the other hand could at least contemplate, if not participate in, the celebration planned for tonight. On one of the hills I saw a cart laboriously climbing, filled . . . with what? I drew near to find out. They were columns of carved wood from one thick log with the remains of golden paint, torsos of saints or angels without arms, or perhaps headless: they were carved beams, parts of altarpieces made of gold or with remains of gold, and a boy guiding the donkey sang happily while another, sitting on top of the wood, urged him onward. I asked them where they were taking all that.

"To the bonfire."

"Where did you get it?"

"We found it in the cellars of city hall."

"And they gave it to you?"

"Yes, for the recruits . . ."

I came closer to look. The Barcelona antique dealers—why even mention the Italian antique dealers—would have given me millions for these pieces, these torsos, these Solomonic columns, these golden beams, the raw material with which many precious antiquities have been "fabricated": a cornice, a *dessu de porte,* a golden organ loft, a torso on a stone wall, a hand laboriously wrought of wood in the *L'Oeil* collection of the *New York Review of Books* on the coffee table, the most used clichés of decoration of the upper middle class and sometimes, with splendid results, the type of things Luisa sought desperately, no longer finding them now, desperate to find them, and if she found them, they were very expensive and highly valued. And, who knows, if among all they had taken one wouldn't find something that had an exceptional value, a Martínez Montañés torso for example, burnt at the stake of the drafted recruits from this miserable village of Dors, hidden from civil society and far away in history? How many villages in the world, how about recruit bonfires, must have burnt carvings by Martínez Montañés, or Berruguete? Suddenly, realizing that these remains of churches and convents destroyed during the Civil War had fed the bonfires of the recruits for thirty-six years, awakened my fear, my terror of ignorance, and my realization that if I remained in the margins of history it was not only a danger that could destroy the future, but also, as in this case, the past. Like the towns of the Costa Brava devoured by the voracious worms of tourism, like the road to L'Hospitalet populated with Osborne bulls, like the condos of Salou, here it was dangerously, as it now seemed to me, the façades on houses ruined by Bartolomé's poor taste, about which the stonecutter of the church had spoken to me this morning. And, on the other hand, it was also the informalists vassals of the galleries against whom I had rebelled, and it was also Luisa looking for things in the Encants . . . it was everything and it had to be prevented.

I spoke to the boy who, perched on top of the pile of broken saints, was singing a song, who as I looked at him, seemed an extraordinary vision of beauty: long black hair, fair complexion, black eyes, and the whole delicate proportion with which he was made, made him appear like those saints and angels of wood going off to be sacrificed on the pyre, but with a joy and completeness so alien to them. I said to him:

"You're going to burn them?"

"Yes."

"Why don't you sell them to me?"

We had continued on up the hill to the flat summit, where their companions welcomed them. They were about twenty big fellows preparing the bonfire, the twenty who tomorrow would depart as recruits. I asked the archangel who crowned the cart that was filled with remains his name:

"Bartolomé."

"Son of . . . ?"

"Yes, how do you know? Aren't you a stranger here?"

". . . Well, I'm looking for someone to do work on a house . . . and they gave me Bartolomé's name."

I told him, then, that I'd buy the cartful of church remains. They all laughed. What did I want them for, what use were these worm-eaten images, truncated columns, pieces of saints

. . . was I crazy? No, I said, I knew what I was doing. That's why I would give them what two cartfuls of first-rate dry wood would cost them.

"Plus the hours of work?"

"Fine. Plus the hours of work."

They all laughed and Bartolomé replied:

"Done deal. Where should we leave . . . all this?"

"I don't know . . . I barely know this place."

"Well then, I'll leave it in the yard where my father keeps his materials, and you can get it from him. I'll also tell him you need it for a job . . ."

I paid him and asked for the address of Bartolomé's warehouse with the intention of claiming my precious possessions later on, and the boys, singing and laughing, returned beside their cart back down the hill. I waited for their laughter to fade away, and then went down to the town hall. I asked to speak with the secretary and proposed buying one of the houses of the Castillo—just like that, because I now realized this was what that neighborhood was called—an old house with interesting architectural details. The secretary was a sickly looking little bald man, whose eye was always tearing and who was eternally wiping that eye with a handkerchief of dubious hygiene. He had very polite manners, probably acquired as the sexton in some school for priests, and a nasal, saccharine tone of voice. The eye that did not tear, however, seemed tremendously penetrating, rapacious even, as if by projecting itself farther out than the other, it had a much more favorable angle than that of other mortals and supplemented, with interest, the obstruction of the other eye. He invited me to come sit under the portals, in La Flor del Ebro, to have a coffee while we spoke. I did not want to launch into questions about the origin of the pieces of lumber I had rescued that morning from the fire; I wanted to be cunning, and I began to speak about the town's extraordinary beauty, speaking with such enthusiasm, such passion, that the waiter, who already knew me, put the tray on the side table and stopped to listen to my heated and enthusiastic oration. As I spoke, I noticed that the waiter and the secretary exchanged somewhat ironic looks of complicity, of which I was the object. After hearing me out, he said:

"Yes, there are many houses to sell in the Castillo quarter. I don't think anyone would hesitate to sell and buy an apartment or house in the New Quarter. These Castillo houses are very big, very old, very uncomfortable . . . Why don't you buy, instead, a lot in the New Quarter, and have Bartolomé build you a chalet?"

When I heard this, all my fury, all the indignation building up inside me all day burst forth, and I almost shouted at him "no" that he must understand me, that I was turning my back on all that, and that Bartolomé was most clearly the culprit guilty of the destruction being wrought upon the village, his lack of discrimination, his falsification of what should have been declared a historical monument, at least of interest for tourists—but tourists shouldn't be allowed—to preserve it . . . Of course, this was all typical of Spanish villages: destroy everything, modernize everything with inferior criteria and no standards whatsoever. Of what barely remains after such architectural and aesthetic vandalism, they make postcards saying: *Typical picturesque corner of* . . . and it is those typical picturesque corners which, with greatest fury, they have destroyed. From what I had said Bartolomé was the principal culprit destroying Dors, and I added:

"This organ loft, for example, is doubtlessly the work of Bartolomé . . ."

A group, whose faces I didn't see, had gathered around us and greeted the secretary. He replied:

"Yes, Bartolomé, and mine too. It's my house . . ."

My fury was so enormous against these horrifying aesthetic blunders that I didn't even get flustered or shut down by my faux pas; it wasn't that terrible, and those sinners against aesthetics surrounding us didn't even blink, but rather looked at me ironically, their eyes filled with laughter as if I were crazy . . . and in fact, in the midst of my diatribe I heard one of them mutter: "He's the nut who this morning bought . . ." I could not manage to subdue myself because my enthusiasm was so immense, talking about the beauty of the Castillo's medieval streets, its marvelous porticos with their fans of stone, wooden balconies, corners, labyrinthine slopes ascending and descending, the sun terraces magnificently opened to a view of the valley . . . all of it, and the ferocity of my fury against the work of modernization going on in the castle. Until suddenly, when I was talking about the secretary's balcony which ruined the square, someone interrupted me, saying:

"It's his house, and where he was born, and he can do what he wants with it."

These words opened, it appeared, an enormous discussion among the men in their berets who hung around rolling their cigarettes, toothless, some of them young, all in their work clothes, some of them claiming it was necessary to modernize and that I was crazy, others stressing that what they needed was to conserve the picturesque qualities to attract tourists, none of them understanding, nevertheless, what I really meant, my love and admiration for the venerable stones of that village. The secretary said:

"Of course we're interested in tourism. This castle they say is very famous . . . and the church, well, those who understand find it very interesting and to fix it up the authorities from Madrid have indeed given money so it must be good, even though I like the modern church better, the brick one down below . . . But to attract tourists . . ."

I saw in all of them, without any doubt, a hostility toward my intrusion in their lives, but also in those vulgar rodent-sharp faces I saw greed, the wish to be like other villages enjoying the benefits of tourism and, since so few people came here to elevate the village from that point of view, I was opening a door, a hope: even if I was the madman who had bought the saints, I could also satisfy their avarice and small-town rapacity to bring tourists . . . Who knows . . . who knows if they would be able to free themselves and sell, finally, the old Castillo

66

manors to which they seemed moored, and make Bartolomé sell them one of his apartments in the New Quarter . . . a small apartment, without mice, without leaks, without spiders, easy to clean, manageable. All their wives sighed, they told me, for apartments instead of those big old houses; if only they could sell, if someone could buy . . . and of course contempt on the one hand but also greed and rapacity on the other, and the secretary at the head of the line, offering me another cognac, talking to me about houses they had available to sell: good, big, completely stone houses with stone-slab facings and carved-stone portals, with garrets, views, light . . . yes, all the facilities, let's go . . .

The secretary and I spent the rest of the afternoon looking at houses. Small and large, humble abodes and lordly mansions, totally abandoned for generations, houses with only one inhabitable room where an old lady in black lived with her cat curled up on the outskirts of the hearth, and others filled with screaming snot-nosed children playing amid the donkey dung and the sacks of feed, and the hay and the harnesses with their very particular smells, and the piles of knickknacks leaning against sacks next to barrels of rancid wine and almonds and hazelnuts . . .

At sunset I phoned Barcelona to speak to Luisa. I had seen too many houses, the prices were ridiculously low, these magnificent stone houses were being given away for nothing, but there were so many of them that I didn't know which to choose, which to decide on, which was the best for me . . . and could she lend the money to buy and fix it? I'd like to live permanently in Dors.

"Forever?"

I thought about it, and said:

"Yes, forever."

She answered:

"I can't come until the weekend but don't buy anything, wait for me, and if you push me I'll buy one too if they cost as little as you say."

"OK. I'll keep looking. I'll wait for you then . . ."

At nightfall, after all the chitchat with the secretary, after seeing so many houses, I felt completely exhausted. I would have wanted to order dinner immediately and get into bed, without even reading a line, and sleep until morning. But when I saw Bartolomé's son greeting me with an ironic smile, sitting at the top of a ladder, and hanging the square wreaths of colored paper and colored lights, I remembered that it was the night of the recruits' bonfire in the Castillo quarter, and that here in the square, later, would be the social dance to which people from all over town would come. I wouldn't be able to sleep. I had to take part in the social event, the first of many to be celebrated in my new town; I couldn't escape, as tired as I felt. Then I saw a group of boys, especially Bartolomé, gathering around a sporty white Fiat convertible with Italian license plates, parked on one corner of the square. Bartolomé came over to me and asked:

"Do you see how you're not the only tourist?"

"I do."

"Is it a friend of yours?"

"No . . . who is it?"

"We don't know; we haven't seen him."

"They must be wandering around the castle."

"Probably . . . yes: sometimes tourists come by, but they don't stay. From time to time they show up, look at the castle for a while, and then go . . . eat at the inn, have a glass of wine, and that's it, good-bye . . ."

I felt that Bartolomé was saying this somewhat bitterly, as if he wanted those tourists to stay and not to leave right away, as if he wanted them to bring fresh air from the outside. It wasn't in his case, however, a vulgar desire for money—the greedy shine in those little primitive eyes of peasants hoarding coins in a little trap door in the beams—but rather a desire for more ample worlds, for horizons, for something he himself didn't know what it was. He repeated:

"They go."

And I asked him:

"And they don't return?"

"No, never again."

That night after dinner I went up to the castle. I watched them light the bonfire, my firewood, and for a whole hour the logs paid for by me and the aroma of pine and rosemary perfumed the translucent early summer night. The faces intensified around the flames, the wine boot they passed from hand to hand, and we all drank—and the secretary, who didn't leave my side for a minute, offered me a chair, to sit and watch, more wine, until finally we went back down to the square, where everyone wanted to be when the dancing started. After all the boy was leaving for Zaragoza, and maybe for Melilla on the Moroccan coast two or three days later . . . No, they said to me, the next morning. And they asked me:

"And why do you want to live in this village that is so old and so poor, and so ugly, being able to live in Barcelona?"

"I am tired."

"Of what?"

It was difficult to explain, almost like explaining to a blind man what or how the color red is, for example, or how a Beethoven sonata is to a deaf person.

"This village is so old and so ugly . . ."

But I felt that if I spoke they would have jumped on me to tear me to pieces like lions. If they forgave me for the things I said it was because I was loving and respecting them, for the first time incarnated in the stones of that village they wanted to change, but, even so, they liked that someone loved and admired it, although it seemed to them that anyone capable of buying a cartful of garbage and exchanging it for two cartfuls of first-rate wood for the bonfire was crazy. Someone asked me:

"Are you an artist?"

I hesitated before answering:

"No."

They said:

"Ah, because sometimes artists come here, every once in a while, and paint . . . They paint the square, the church, the river . . . and then they leave . . ."

"They're strange, artists . . ."

"We thought you were an artist because they always talk, the few times they show up here, they talk about how pretty this ancient village is . . . They and you . . . You must be something, then, a journalist, or writer . . ."

No, no, no, I would have wanted to tell them, none of that, I'm nothing, I'm only a man who is tired of modern life and who's looking for a peaceful refuge in a place where not everything is for sale, where not everything has been destroyed for money, where there is tradition and beauty, and a firm structure in which I could participate. To form part of something, of course, you have to participate in that thing, but I couldn't form part of the village life, I was an outsider in fact and in spirit: my ethos wasn't theirs, it was even perhaps the opposite and opposed to theirs. Just as I had been incapable of forming part of anything in my whole life because sharing the experience of a community was alien to me, and yet I admired and envied the insiders as I envied those townspeople profoundly rooted in their world, and even envied my Catalan friends for belonging to a minority which had the privilege of feeling persecuted and hence protected by that community, enveloped and kept safe by that community; I hadn't even belonged to the school of informalist painting, which I had recently separated from as a lizard sheds its tail, so that, while the tail dies, she may continue to live. The only bad part was that I wasn't sure in this case if I were the lizard and the informalists who still formed part of a coherent school were the severed tail, or if on the contrary, I was the tail that would die and they the lizard that would soon grow another tail. My possible destiny as the abandoned tail of a lizard was something I couldn't know, as I didn't know the fate of those tails abandoned by lizards beyond those last rattles of death provoked by what little remains of life.

But the dance had already been organized in the square. Illuminated by colored lights, decorated with paper wreaths, the square wholly assumed its fate, its obscure remote provincial destiny as the stage setting for the trivial everyday event and destiny of the people who danced beneath the pink and green wreaths, awkwardly intermingling beneath the real height and magnification of the summer sky. Some fifteen or twenty young couples dancing awkwardly—I had seen them moving in their work and in their work clothes and they had seemed noble, not awkward but graceful, classical, eternal—dances I had seen danced with real pizzazz, real sophistication, but here, decked out in their Sunday best, even those with recent haircuts, they lamentably looked like what they were, country bumpkins, small-town provincials in their Sunday best, fatally destroying their classicism, their eternity. A band on a platform under the town hall portals, playing the current fashionable rhythms; groups of ugly girls, groups of shy girls prattling and laughing among themselves in the corners as if they didn't care if anyone asked them to dance; the eyes of the mothers watching without watching, the men in the bar pretending they weren't looking and inviting each other to glasses of wine or cognac, and the groups of boys in a corner who lorded it over the dance, who didn't dance because they—the real proprietors of the situation—didn't want to and preferred to drink and talk amongst themselves about the girls.

I saw Bartolomé dance with an insignificant-looking girl dressed in pink, obviously smitten with him. Of all the men he was the most lordly, and in his light blue shirt and dark pants he didn't look like a rube: he was a boy, boy personified, endowed with a grace and beauty seldom to be found in the village. Though transplanted and in another context, he was a boy (one thinks) who would continue knowing how to maintain that grace and beauty, that long black hair, but not exaggeratedly long and as if carelessly brushed, those shoulders not excessively athletic but strong and well proportioned, and his poise; in brief, his complexion, his features, his bearing

71

were all noteworthy, and not only to me, an intellectual and an outsider, but to everyone, in the way the girls looked at him, in the jokes of the other boys, in the invitations he received from the shouting men in the bar, which he answered with a broad smile.

It was impossible for me to conceive that all of them, who had known each other more or less all their lives, had been on opposite sides in the war—and that fathers, grandfathers, and brothers had killed one another—now forgotten by dint of its sheer force, or they hadn't forgotten and held on to bitterness for that very reason, and yet somehow these people who had all grown up and played together with such a background could produce this party atmosphere. But it wasn't really a party atmosphere, rather merely a muffled and ritual rhythmic shuffling of feet dancing, greeting or not greeting one another, eating cakes they'd been eating all their life, made the same as ever in the same bakery as ever on the occasion of some public or private festivity, merely drinking the same wine and then each of them going off to his or her bed, to sleep.

But my eyes, which from my table in La Flor del Ebro coldly looked over the crowd dancing in the square, suddenly fixed on a couple: a very dark tall man with a mangled mop of black hair and eyebrows and dark shining eyes, with a classical chin and Roman nose, dancing with another insignificant girl and doing so with a grace markedly different than Bartolomé's, like an animal that knew it was going to kill, consciously and with firm purpose, and one felt that the girl, who had surrendered to his arms, had really surrendered and was in danger. Yes, in a startled realization I felt the girl he was laughing with—so different from the way Bartolomé laughed and danced—was his victim and that he had come here to take her. He had come, because immediately after the sensation that he was an executioner and the others were victims, that he was the only executioner in the square, the following sensation was that he did not belong to this town, he didn't even belong to this region and my imagination gave a leap and I immediately connected this man who stretched and moved and had barely any flesh but at the same time just enough, like one of those long black cats whose anatomy is revealed entirely under the shine of their coat as they moved or walked, linking him to the Fiat I'd seen that morning in the square, showing off its foreign license plate, that of an Italian tourist. I felt someone touch my shoulder, I turned my head in fear, as if the cat man dancing in the square, the Italian, had instituted a reign of terror and everything, even the secretary's friendly pat on my back had turned into something dangerous. The secretary was inviting himself to my table and introducing me to Bartolomé the father, whom I also invited to sit at my table, and I ordered a cognac for him. He had none of his son's beauty; he was a middle-aged man, red-faced, rough, awkward, with a tie and collar that were too tight and made the flesh on his congested neck spill over—and with the bloodshot force exploding all over his face he spoke to me, spit flying:

"So you're the crazy guy wandering around here?"

There was hail-fellow-well-met humor in his words which could have been ironic but were, on the contrary, pure violence and ill intentions, and utter self-assurance. At the beginning of the sentence, his tone had irritated me, but I had calmed down by the time he finished because I understood that this was my enemy, the very incarnation of everything I hated. I didn't ask him what he meant, and he didn't bother to explain. The crazy guy wandering around was too trivial for a personage like himself, and while the secretary and I made plans to see houses tomorrow, he laughed, and he signaled to the bartender to serve a round of drinks to the boys laughing at one end of the bar. He heard part of what we were talking about and said to me:

"Why don't you build a chalet, there on the banks of the river?"

I explained to him that I hadn't come to this village to live in a condo but to live in another way. Then, ignoring me, Bartolomé addressed the secretary to comment:

"See, Eustaquio? These outsiders look down at us, laugh at us, that's why they come to 'this village . . .' Of course, why do they come if they consider themselves so big that we don't come up to their level? Why do they come?"

I tried to explain myself, that this hadn't been my intention, but no matter what I said, without looking at me, Bartolomé twisted my words around. He seemed to have an almost literary ability to do this, transforming each sentence one uttered into a weapon against the one saying it, so that the conversation stalled in a perpetual undoing of whatever I said, turning my sentences into a web in which Bartolomé entangled me, more and more, until, after one of my phrases showing my love for the region, referring to the land bordering the river with its orchards and to the plane trees, he said:

"The plane trees are planted, almost all of them, in land that belongs to me, and next year I am going to cut them down. I'm not leaving even one of them, so that the access road to the town will at least seem wider and more modern, not so woodsy. And as far as the land bordering the river is concerned, it's all my property, so as soon as I lay waste to the plane trees and it's all brought up-to-date, I'm going to partner with some Germans and build a development with fifty condominiums, those little ones with all the colors you don't like . . . yes, those."

Bartolomé stood up:

"I'm going."

But before going he told me:

"I'm warning you to be careful. We're the bosses here and we're in charge. We don't like to be criticized. You may have good taste, but that doesn't matter here, where the people want new houses, not old wrecks like whatever you're looking for, which is idiotic. Who is going to want to live in places like the ones you love? A madman like yourself, that's all, a madman capable of buying a cartful of broken saints and old beams. I'm warning you that already by doing that you've lost prestige in the town . . . I'm telling you so that you'll be careful.

We want progress. You're bringing us what you call good taste, but it isn't, it's madness, yes, sir, good taste is cleanliness and comfort, not the picturesque things that interest you . . . and this town's progress, because I own bigger lands in the region and province and am the major urban land owner and major contributor, this town's progress depends on me . . ."

I added:

"And the mayor, I suppose . . ."

Bartolomé split his sides laughing.

"The mayor . . . don't make me laugh. I appoint the mayor, and he serves me. A telephone call to the capital is all it takes and the mayor is replaced if he doesn't bow to my wishes . . . I already told you: we're the bosses here, those of us who have the right to park our cars in this here square—I've heard you criticize that which is why I'm warning you—and the life and the economy of the town depend on us. So you watch out. I'll help you with all you want as long as it serves the interests of what we consider the town's progress."

By the end of his speech he seemed to have calmed down as if realizing I wasn't an individual he needed to fear and that, perhaps, I could also be useful to him. Upon taking his leave he said to the secretary:

"Shall we go, Eustaquio?"

The secretary stood up. Bartolomé bent down toward me and asked:

"Shall we have the pleasure of seeing you tomorrow at Mass, the one given to send off the recruits that are going?"

"I never go to Mass."

"Ah, one of those."

"Yes, I'm an atheist."

"That's bad; you should talk to the priest."

I couldn't resist asking:

"And do you also appoint the priest?"

For a second he was struck dumb. Then he gave the secretary a hearty slap on the back; the secretary spit out the toothpick which during the evening he had been fiddling with in his uneven dentures, and, as the secretary stood up to follow him, Bartolomé responded:

"No, but I like people who go to Mass and follow the religion. Anyway, if I don't appoint the priest, I do appoint this fellow . . . I mean, not quite, but it's as if I appointed him, right, Eustaquio?"

Eustaquio preferred to laugh and the two of them, after a friendly farewell—perhaps too friendly—disappeared amid the crowd, greeting, slapping the backs of friends and of some boy who was leaving in two days with the recruits, joking with or sweet-talking some more or less good-looking girl who could barely keep her balance on high heels that were the latest fashion, even more exaggerated for having been bought at a store in the provincial capital.

Their departure left me uneasy. Uneasy, but nonetheless, curiously, antagonistic that war, declared so cynically by the boss, was a clear way for me to integrate myself into the life of the village. I had now created a relationship, a strong relationship of enemies, animosity, opposing positions in life and in (for me the most important) aesthetic vision, complete and total enemies; and I established a role, a battle to unleash in which I joined the villagers and became one of them, whether or not I wanted to, in order to find unity in my battle—in the battle I would doubtlessly have to unleash in order to preserve purity and beauty, to restore the unity and dignity of the town's architecture—a raison d'être, something to keep me alive and kicking, no longer the lizard's tail whose death rattle would lose energy gradually until becoming lifeless. I was the whole lizard, warm from the sun, with shiny colors, a dragon capable of breathing fire at the foot of the castle to free it from the roving forays of the enemy. I called over La Flor del Ebro waiter who had become my friend. He said to me:

"Don't pay any attention to him, sir."

His observation surprised me so much, that I didn't think I understood what he said for a moment and asked:

"What?"

"Don't pay any attention to him."

"To whom?"

"To Don Bartolomé."

"Why?"

"Nobody takes him seriously. He's just showing off . . ."

"The trees aren't his, then, and he's not going to cut them down?"

"No . . . they belong to his wife. And they say his wife beats him because the money is hers, and he does whatever she wants. She's one of those tiny little women, very pious, the ones who go to Mass and communion and say their novenas, who never say hello to anyone and never look anyone straight in the eye . . . but the money's hers . . ."

"How is she going to beat him if she's so little and he's such a big guy!"

"That's what they say . . . I don't know. He doesn't talk to anybody either, unless it serves him in some way. He's bad. Ask around in all the villages in the area who's the most evil man in the whole district, and they'll tell you: Bartolo."

"But his wife beats him . . ."

The waiter mused.

"Yes, poor guy . . . Perhaps he's not so bad. He was a country bumpkin with very little work when he married this rich old lady. She was from a better family than his, and rich, and he was handsome, like Bartolomé, his son, the one dancing in the square . . . Where is he . . . ?"

I told him not to bother to show me as I knew him, but we both stared at the square, and didn't find him, he was no longer there. The girl dressed in pink with whom he'd been dancing was sitting on the bumper of a car, talking to the other girls who weren't dancing. And the waiter continued talking:

"Poor Bartolomé. He's going into the army, now, a year before his time because he can't stand his father, they argue every day, and the father cries . . . that's what Bartolo says . . . he cries because Bartolo doesn't want to attend the Acción Católica school as his father did and Bartolomé the father

77

says his son is going to end up a communist or something like that . . ."

Above, crowning the village, from that table and that chair I always chose in La Flor del Ebro, I caught a glimpse of the castle, the mandala, the thick church tower and I waited a long while, watching it all—and watching the dance and the incredible sensation of feeling like a stranger which the people gathered in the square produced in me, and yet now we had a relationship because it was known that I had bought that morning a cartful of garbage. Up there was the pink façade of the castle all lit up, now fading, and the bonfire and songs were also fading, and what remained was the secure firm mass of the buildings, not lacking gravity because of the dancing fire gradually losing heat. I paid, said good night to the waiter, and slowly began to walk up to the church. In the dark narrow streets, here and there a couple descended silently in love, embracing or humming.

I remained for a moment in front of the church door, that portal of prayer with that pensive mandala in the very center of the façade, and then continued climbing up to the castle, to the bonfire. There only remained a pile of red-hot coals growing fainter at the foot of the castle that dominated the ample curve of the river and the vast panorama of hills wrought into terraces. No one was left on the esplanade, and I looked at that hermetic façade: one, two, three stories of enormous height . . . but this wasn't a castle, there were no fortifications . . . It was, rather, like a palace . . . On the first floor the two-light windows were enormous, four large windows on the front, very open, they wouldn't be so open if this had been in the slightest sense defensive: this was a castle, or palace, extremely sure of itself here on the top of the hill, a palace where the nobles, perhaps, would gather around a table to tell stories, not a defensive castle like the majority of those that crown the Spanish hills, with medieval terror written on their thick stone walls, on their battlements and in their portholes and reinforcements. None of that here, which was pure legend but not at all military: here is where the *provençal* troubadours might have come by to entertain an isolated but rich court complete with refinements, living on the hill, reigning over, and fed by the inhabitants of the thick knot of stone houses clustered tightly at the foot of the palace, working to feed the lords while the latter listened to legends of love and epic war poems sung by the troubadours. A kind of necessity or urgency to enter the castle assaulted me right then and there. I looked behind me. Nobody. I went over to the door, looked back once more: nobody. And I tried to open the lock that sealed it, shaking it, knowing this was useless, I shook it but no, naturally it didn't yield. Then I began to go around the castle, looking each time for some place where I could climb in. The keys are in Madrid, the mayor had told me; and then, Bartolomé: *They're thinking of restoring it, perhaps making it into a* parador. *But why a* parador *if nobody comes here? It will be a long time*—said the secretary, discouraged—*before they do anything: we'd have to declare ourselves a national monument or something like that. And that*—added Bartolomé—*wouldn't be so good, because then one wouldn't be able to paint a façade or fix a street without permission from Madrid, and the village would stagnate waiting for tourists who will never come.* I thought: I could do something. I know people; people know me, perhaps even Luisa who knows everyone . . . but this wasn't the problem. Now the problem was the imperious necessity to enter the castle (or the palace), the need to see what was inside, to walk inside . . . feel surrounded by those walls, feel enveloped in those ruins, part of the magic, not outside but inside and very inside and a part of everything; and there, perhaps, I could find a certain peace, a certain love that would connect me to what I was circling on the outside, to this pleasant thick-walled enormous structure, luxurious and mundane next to the church which I couldn't enter and would never enter, a fortress not impregnable to enemy hosts, whose walls and gallant windows said that it was because of me, my solitude, my lack of direction in the solitude of the ample Catalan night that I was excluded, like all the others—and this was a fact that suddenly comforted me and made me promise to myself to make the effort to enter, to be the only one who entered, distinguishing me and raising me to a level higher than others, who had never been inside the castle in ruins.

I soon realized that all attempts were useless, and decided to go back down. Upon passing in front of the church, however, I felt like going up the steps and I did, and pushed the door. It was open and I went in. Inside, still lit up by the Eucharist's purple lamps, and some candles, the Gothic arches of the ceiling danced. Advancing along one side, I approached the altar, where I stared at the crucified Christ—which the stonecutter said was hanging inversely—and I returned to the back on the other side. Just before I got to the temporary stone wall I saw a small door, also temporary, which something impelled me to push, and it opened. There, behind the door, began the access to the tower, worn-down steps inside a narrow passageway in which two-light windows lit the way, and I climbed up toward the night that became more and more immense. Larger and larger from here, from my position, even higher than all the other buildings in the town and the river flowing, and the square with its ugly colored lightbulbs and its garlands there below . . . and nearby, suddenly, near the top of the truncated tower I paused. Right next to me, the castle, the palace, so close one needed only to reach out a hand to touch its enormous two-light windows; from where I was I realized that whole immense wall, which from below seemed massive, was transformed into a lace-woven structure of light transparent stone. One could see everything inside. I was happy not to have lost the keys, because from the church tower the view inside, though static, was majestic: great halls with Gothic arches completely and elegantly curved but without a paneled ceiling, the halls opened to the sky, and the stone benches, where the lords would sit, in ruins like the worn grainy heraldries; trees grew among the ruins in the wondrous moonlight of the summer equinox, of the magical night of San Juan when anything can happen, animated by a slight breeze, the vegetation that bedecked the ruins as in a Salvator Rosa, as in a Piranesi, as in

Caravaggio. A castle born doubtlessly in the twelfth century, to be seen on a moonlit night by someone as I saw it now, as the incarnation of the poetic, with streams of moonlight between the arches and the two-light window and the foliage of the trees waving.

But, was it really only the breeze that was shaking the bushes and trees?

I had the curious sensation that a dog was wandering inside. But how did he get in? Impossible; I went up a few more stairs to look farther in from the two-light window; yes, someone was wandering around inside there where I thought no one could get in, some privileged being who was not revealing his name or his identity. I was afraid I would be seen and hid in the shadows of the shafts of columns. I heard voices, two voices. Two lovers, I said to myself, who somehow had gotten into the castle and, thanks to the shelter of the walls and their unseen entry, had taken advantage of the magical night and the magic of the privileged space, they, the privileged, to make love in a book-of-hours world, completely avoiding the vulgar reality of the colored-paper garlands and lights in the square. And I envied them.

Then I saw appear among the bushes the couple: she, wearing pants, thin, her hair short . . . and he, yes, yes, it was him, the cat man, the man exhibiting all those muscles, the man with the small face and triangular smile who danced in the square with that girl, as if he were about to devour her, yes, it was the Italian with the white Fiat—that stranger had managed to enter, and I hadn't. How? She perhaps had led him, and now as the stranger was leaving one of the halls of arms, overgrown with weeds, he descended the crumbling stone staircase invaded by branches of the common thyme of home-made stews, the fragrance of which one could get a whiff from where I stood in the hot night; now the stranger laughed, a quick laugh filled with cigarette smoke, alcohol, with having been everywhere and having done everything it's possible to do to a person without leaving a trace, without any commitment whatsoever. I saw him lithely descend the staircase without helping his fragile and well-proportioned companion, also in pants, coming down behind him. She was dressed just like the stranger, the cat man: dark pants and a light blue shirt, and as she suddenly leaned on the stranger's shoulder for help descending the steps, I suddenly realized it wasn't a woman, it was Bartolomé the son, the boy who was leaving the next day with the recruits, who was also laughing, whose head passed one of the windows for a moment, a ray from the floodlight illuminating the castle captured his face and revealed to me his unmistakable identity, outlined against a darkness made of trembling branches and stone Gothic arches under which ivy grew. Then both of them disappeared. Where did they exit, if they did indeed leave? Or didn't they leave and were they staying inside, in silence, performing, as it seemed to me would be the case, some esoteric, perverse ritual, whose meaning or content was as impregnable as the very walls of the castle. A perverse sensation of jealousy, of rage—as if my person were being plundered by the culpable cat man—came over me, feeling that the history of my life had led to my exclusion from the palace, from the mystery of the night which I could only observe in its everyday guise, from my usual spot at La Flor del Ebro, and in its magical aspect, from my place in the dark elevation of a Romanesque tower, without ever taking part in that adventure those two, who no doubt had just met casually, had undertaken, and which brought them together as one.

I waited a long time to hear, to sense again the presence of human bodies, of men, inside the empty void of that Gothic shell which was the enclosure, but my vigil was futile, because the hours passed—the bells of the modern brick church of the New Quarter were striking the hours, the half hours, every quarter of an hour relentlessly—and the bats flew around the lit floodlights, and the live coals of the recruits' bonfire gradually faded and grew ashen, and I began to feel a chill and stiffness, so that I started my descent.

I didn't want there to be a relationship between those two. Finally, I said to myself, Bartolomé leaves tomorrow for the army, in the morning, and as they said below in the square, the outsiders come, spend a day, and go. A bona fide relationship of the kind that would fix and mark these two gentlemen—it seemed to me that such a relationship could begin in the castle of Calatrava, in Montsegur—that is, the white young man and the dark stranger, cat man, could not continue. Inside of a week Bartolomé would be in the deserts of Melilla, and the Italian, no doubt, would be heading toward the Costa del Sol where guys like him not only belonged, but would be doubtlessly in certain demand.

The next day I got up late. Upon coming down for breakfast they told me in La Flor del Ebro that the boy had already gone with his fellow recruits, early in the morning, to get the train at Mora. I asked the waiter:

"And the Fiat?'

"It left too."

"In which direction?"

"The other way, to the coast road. He left early, when we were just opening."

"Where did he leave from?"

"The inn."

"He slept there?"

"Yes."

I had my breakfast calmly, unhurriedly, savoring the hot chocolate, the country bread, the fresh butter. Then I crossed back over to the inn, and asked the innkeeper:

"Did an Italian gentleman sleep here?"

"Yes, the stranger, he was very nice."

I assumed he had left a good tip. But then came the explanation:

"He's an actor, a movie actor. They say he worked in a movie, one they showed here years ago, *La Dolce Vita* it was called, and he played . . . I don't remember which role."

Barely an extra, I imagined. But no, the black cat was no extra, on the contrary, he was dreadfully central and horrifically the star of everything he did. *La Dolce Vita* was from twelve years ago. Let's suppose that at that time he was about twenty-five, so by now he would be about thirty-seven. He definitely didn't look this age from a distance; it just wasn't possible that he was only ten years younger than me—what part did he play? I felt anxious, almost desperate to see that film again and to find his face from fifteen years ago, and what role he played, in Fellini's masterpiece. I asked his name:

"Bruno Fantoni."

"Bruno Fantoni?"

"Bruno Fantoni."

I mentally reviewed the names of the actors in that film, so often shown and seen again, and so well known, and I couldn't remember. I thought for a moment that he was lying. But no, the black cat didn't lie; he could do many things, but not lie. He had doubtlessly worked in *La Dolce Vita,* in a minor role. But he didn't seem thirty-seven years old . . . He seemed so much more agile, so defined in his movements, intentions, and musculature, in the entire and aggressive sensuality of his person . . . Bruno Fantoni: an extra, no doubt, even if he didn't seem like one, one of those lowlifes who gained access to Cinecittà by sleeping their way up with whomever, to get somewhere . . . where they never got anyway. Like this Bruno, for example: scum of the consumer society, empty being, not a grain of pathos, without anything more than a shell. Why had he come to Dors, stayed a night, and left? If Bartolo hadn't gone, also, in another direction and on to something else, I would have been able perhaps to inquire, although I wouldn't have wanted to reveal the secret that I saw them together—if it was them—inside the palace. Anyway, flotsam and jetsam that end up forming a kind of seaweed where it should be, on the Costa Brava, on the Costa del Sol, and then vanish without a trace, taking away the memory of several conquests, a dozen, half dozen, two submissive women in love or not in love, in any case seeking something they'd never find, like a kind of Holy Grail which would make a whole population emigrate from north to south in search of the sun and its magic, of happiness, of Montsegur. It was necessary to take the trip to seek that satisfaction, that mystical realization of a happiness impossible within the world of sensuality and money, so intimately linked, so identified with each other. In any case, I thought with enormous satisfaction, Bruno Fantoni would not return here, this was not his landscape. I didn't know where he came from. He left no traces. I didn't know where he was going, perhaps alone, leaving some trace in Bartolo, but this was dubious. Bartolo must be in Melilla. That other guy, perhaps, on the Costa Brava. And he was a cornball, besides; a white convertible Fiat was corny. What a poor man who aspired to own an Alfa Romeo would settle for. When Bartolo returned from military service, and if he remembered, I would ask him about Bruno Fantoni. What was most certain, however, was that he wouldn't remember me.

I remember the two or three days that followed as the happiest, the most outwardly directed days of my life, when the call of life itself is so big that all of you is encapsulated in your actions and your decisions, and the inner self, to which one is usually bound like an executioner, loses its stranglehold, and you are free.

It was all about buying a house for myself. I first considered one which, like the inn, had a little terrace overlooking the river. They told me these would be the most expensive . . . one hundred, a hundred fifty thousand pesetas, and therefore they didn't recommend them; the price seemed ridiculously low to me, and I visited a few but I realized this wasn't what I wanted. While these revealed from their balconies a calm landscape, they also always had their backs to the village, to the Old Quarter, to everything that was urban and I didn't want that, because landscape, what was really called landscape, was not what I sought. I went up the hill, then, with the secretary and with Bartolomé, who really did seem to be the owner of almost all of Dors, he, or some relative, or some relative of his wife—ninety-year-old ladies curled up like oval black cockroaches beside a dying fire, houses with rotten roof tiles and families of gypsy squatters with their horses, dogs, cats, mules, rabbits, chickens running all over the floors under paneled ceilings with their noble beams, peeking out to cackle amid medieval "regalia." Houses with the remains of medieval paint on some stone roof, with indications of once having been a chapel or a sanctuary; houses completely made of stone on the top of the hill with garrets open to the valley, revealing an immense horizon, penetrating, as I wanted, the immense sky as if in a plane, an abstract vision, not incidental or anecdotal. Bartolomé spoke with the inhabitants, usually his relatives or lifetime friends, giving a magnificent, premeditated speech of how good it would be for them to sell that cold country house, of how, with what I'd pay them, they'd have enough for a down payment for an apartment he would build or had built, and what facilities he would provide to make their payments easy. We suddenly came upon one, and I said:

"This is the one."

It was a façade of stone masonry with a great stone doorway carved like a fan, two pairs of windows upstairs, the great opening of a grain loft that faced both sides, on one side toward the river and the village below and the landscape, and on the other—you entered the house in the back, from the church street which went around the castle, directly on to the second floor—you had a full view of the castle. Bartolomé asked me:

"Why this one?"

"I like it. The view . . ."

"But I've showed you houses that are so much better . . ."

"I like this one."

"You'd better think it over."

They left me the key and I wandered around the house for a whole day, opening dusty old trunks with rotting clothes inside, smashed Thonet chairs, paintings of first communions eaten by rats, bottles, imagining the house renovated and ready to be occupied, with its great hall filled with books on the sun terrace with the double view, its light-filled bedrooms with balconies, and the incredible silence. I also went alone to see other houses because the secretary and Bartolomé left me the keys. They said:

"So you can compare."

I compared, I got all covered in dust, I saw two days go by, two sunsets, two mornings in several of these houses and I always returned to the church street, the tranquility of the arched doorway, of the four windows, of the loft opening. This was the living space just right for me. There were other houses that perhaps offered greater advantages but somehow, for me, buying something larger seemed almost sinful, almost tainted, because it went beyond what I needed as a living space, and at the end of the second day, upon finding myself with a fistful of huge keys weighing down my pocket, now sitting with the secretary and Bartolomé in La Flor del Ebro, I said to them:

"The church street house."

Disillusionment was written all over Bartolomé's face; he wanted me to buy either the house on the river, or one house facing the inn on the square, enormous and closed since the war, a real palace, or another big house, also on the hill, also belonging to a sister or brother-in-law of his who wanted to get on his good side and thus he proposed the sale of their house as the best way to make peace. He said to the secretary:

"The house of the murder. This is your business deal, Eustaquio."

They told me that it was called "the house of the murder" because a few years after the war a mother and a son killed the father there and then buried him in pieces, in the wine cellar, but the Guardia Civil couldn't find him no matter how hard they looked for him, until months later the pigs, rooting around, uncovered the corpse and found the man in pieces. Bartolomé told the story, perhaps hoping to discourage my love affair with that living space that fit me like a glove. But I only laughed, and said:

"More picturesque: even better."

The price the secretary told me was ridiculously low. Nobody wanted to buy this house which had been empty for thirty years, because it was surrounded by the memory of that brutal murder.

I said:

"Done. When do we sign the agreement?"

"Tomorrow, as the notary is coming tomorrow afternoon."

I told Bartolomé to come up with an estimate, giving him the details of what I wanted done—heating, insulation, good bathrooms, and so on—in order to figure out how much the whole thing would cost. Three hundred thousand pesetas, he said after listening to me. Very cheap, but of course I didn't have it. Should I sell my apartment in Sitges, bought when it wasn't worth a thing? No, with the rental to tourists in Sitges during the summer I would be able to live in this house the whole year, without working, which is what I wanted. Diana. Diana always had money to spare. She always offered it to me, and considered the fact that I never asked her a demonstration of my limitations and macho prejudices as a Spanish male. Why not now? The project, of course, would amuse her to no end, the kind of thing she would understand completely and enthusiastically. I asked if the village had a public telephone. They said of course and accompanied me. When I told the operator that I wanted to call London, such and such number, I immediately noticed a change of expression on the faces of the secretary and especially Bartolomé: admiration, an unprecedented cordiality, filled them with satisfaction. The operator told me it was the first time they were making an international call from the village, and the telephone operators in the nearby villages, whom she doubtlessly informed or who had listened in, were alert and enthusiastic.

Bartolomé said:

"You're going to turn us into an international center."

I smiled, satisfied. I had won him over. He said:

"Why don't you sell houses to other friends of yours?"

He said this to me just when Diana's voice answered on the other end of the phone, and it was doubtlessly Bartolomé's question that pushed me to describe the village's beauty to

Diana, and then to Miles, and then my intentions. Diana said I should also buy a house for her and that I should fix it up according to my taste, that foreign styles were a bit heavy-handed for her but if it was like that, so primitive, as I said, perhaps it would be fun, and if they were asking for so little for what I called a palace, and well, so little for the renovation, well, and the peseta was so low . . . well, it was a gift, they were practically giving them away . . . definitely, what I was buying had to be good and in good taste, that I should buy according to my criteria, that tomorrow she would send the money order for my house and for hers to the bank in Dors, that not to worry, the only consideration was that her house should be big, very big, with a lot of guest rooms, because if she went to Dors—if she ever decided to—she would go with lots of friends because she imagined that there wouldn't be many people there to talk to, and she really liked to talk . . . and that immediately they should install a phone line for her, yes, a telephone . . . Of course she thought the whole thing was a fabulous idea, just fabulous, *Dad,* said Miles with enthusiasm: *healthy food, without artificial preservatives, the simple life, simple people . . . and saving the beauty of the village by buying houses to rescue them from pretentious bad taste that was deforming something so pure, so pristine,* he imagined how delightful it must be to play the flute on a sunny morning from the top two-light windows of the church tower . . . or squatting beside the river, *yes, buy it, even if Mom doesn't go, I will . . . with Irene:*

"Who's Irene?"

"A friend. You'll like her."

"In love?"

"How old-fashioned you are, Dad. She does interesting things."

"What?"

"She makes jewelry . . . and sometimes I design it for her. But we make it mostly with old things we find in Portobello or wherever . . . You should see how pretty and original it is; a boutique has exclusive rights to buy it at a high price . . ."

The last time I saw Miles he went around in sandals, with his blond hair in a pigtail, a gold ring in one earlobe, a Moroccan bag hanging on his shoulder, and the rudiments of a Viking-like blond beard falsifying his face. I imagined him in Dors, comparing him with Bartolo, the son: it would be fun to see him move about these streets. In any case, now, he seemed intensely preoccupied by the need for a simple life; fed up with London—no, Barcelona is London but worse quality and provincial, it's the same thing, I'd tired of big cities—he wanted a simple life, silence, nature, where nobody would notice him . . . Dors, with its starched Sunday suits and ties; I imagined him strolling on the bridge with the other young people on a Sunday morning. We agreed, in any case, that from tomorrow onward, or the following day to give it more time, I'd have a big account in the Central Bank of Dors, to buy immediately a house for me, and a house for . . . Well, leaving the telephone office, flanked now by the two supercilious bumpkins, to buy a house for me, and perhaps the big one, the one with the double stone staircases and the grand entrance, for . . . well, for my son Miles. Bartolomé asked me:

"You have children?"

"Yes, two."

"I have one, and does he give me problems!"

And the secretary:

"I didn't know you were married."

"Well, divorced, a long time ago."

The faces froze again. I explained:

"She's English; we're very good friends."

They both made a gesture of relieved clarification:

"Aha, an Englishwoman."

Nothing had arrived at the bank the next day, but the following it did, and so I immediately bought both houses, to the delight of the secretary and Bartolo, and that afternoon, in La Flor del Ebro, the waiter congratulated me, and the lady who owned the inn congratulated me, and the telephone operator congratulated me, since the news had spread all over town when, right after signing the contracts, I went to the telephone office to call Luisa.

When I told her, she too congratulated me. But I noticed she was down, sad on the phone.

"What's the matter?"

"Lidia."

"What's going on with Lidia?"

She was her daughter.

"A suicide attempt."

"Suicide attempt? How?"

"You can't imagine what a week this has been."

"What happened?"

"I didn't know it, but during the holidays, in Sotogrande, she fell in love with some guy on the Argentine polo team, one of those who plays with her husband, and he, of course, was amusing himself with her during the summer and then good-bye I don't remember you . . . one of those totally banal things, but Lidia wasn't prepared for something like that, the world she's been living in . . ."

The usual song and dance about the children and how they steal your life away: Lidia had abandoned her mother at the age of fifteen, when she found out about her affair with me, and she went to live in Madrid with her father the polo and golf player, and married a man like her father, polo and golf player, in a world apparently very free but still tied hand and foot to the old prejudices and the old necessities. Then the classic good-looking Argentine guy, a flirtation she thought was much more . . . and *wham,* suicide. Banal, so banal. But this only made it sadder. And Lidia was disillusioned with the world of her husband and her father, and had rushed back, again, after eight years, to her mother. Luisa said:

"I'm afraid it will happen again."

"Why?"

"She promised it would."

"You can't leave her alone, then."

"No. Why?"

"Well, I would have liked you to come here this weekend to Dors if you don't have anything better to do . . ."

"I'm sorry but I've got plans."

"Of course . . ."

"Wait . . . wait a minute . . . Lidia is telling me something . . ."

I waited. Then Luisa's voice:

"Lidia says she'd like to see you."

"Me?"

I had been public enemy number one eight years ago.

"Yes."

"Why don't you come together, then, to spend the weekend?"

Luisa spoke with her daughter.

"She says fine . . ."

"Warn her that the inn is not wonderful . . ."

"It doesn't matter, she says . . ."

"After Sotogrande and Marbella and all that?"

"Exactly, precisely . . ."

"I need you, Luisa. I bought these two big old houses here, you know, and I haven't any idea what to do with them, how to renovate them, and mine at least is urgent, the other one isn't, and you have to help me; without you I'm lost, completely lost, and I'm sure they're going to swindle me if you don't watch over things . . ."

We agreed that they would come on the weekend, and as Lidia felt like resting and not hearing noise—especially not hearing noise—they might even stay the whole week. Today was Thursday, tomorrow, Friday, she would take care of all her business and they'd leave Barcelona on Saturday morning to arrive in time for lunch. Could I reserve two rooms for them?

I did, at the inn. Aside from mine, there was only one other that had a little terrace facing the river. The only other one available was small and with only one high window, on the street. So I said Lidia would sleep there, and have more independence. But when they finally arrived on Saturday at lunch time, I realized that Lidia would not compromise on anything, and that Luisa, for the first time persecuted by guilt feelings, gave in, and gave in because she wanted to safeguard her daughter, expiating goodness knows what guilt.

I saw Lidia for the first time—I insist it was for the first time although it's true that at some point, as her grandparents say, I held this daughter of my cousin in my arms when she was a little girl—under the arch of the bridge, going toward the bridge, and with her hand horizontal to cover her eyes from the sun, looking at the countryside, looking at everything. She was alone, with her long dark hair in the breeze, and her dress, equally long, but daringly opened on one side up to her thigh, very loose and light colored, waving identically in the wind. At first she looked like a medieval figure, totally in tune with the ambience of the bridge and the village, a pilgrim like the Santiago that adorned the façade of the village entrance, with her long dress made as if from bits and pieces, like patches of a very pale cloth which someone, out of poverty, had pieced together. Then I saw, of course, that in her hand there were enormous sunglasses, ultramodern, and instantly thought, how terribly expensive; and suddenly that figure from the Middle Ages conformed to the present, and I saw her in the polo fields of Sotogrande, or dancing at Pepe Moreno's in Marbella, or wearing those fancy sunglasses looking at some blindingly whitewashed Andalusian town under a blue sun, with some man on horseback you'd see in the movies and which I hadn't seen in years, with his hair carefully combed, wearing an elegant and tasteful scarf around his neck, at the unbuttoned top of his shirt. When she put on those glasses, tinted a smoky purple color, darker above, paler below, she was no longer the pilgrim wearing a patched dress, doing penitence, but rather an elegant young woman with her face almost completely covered by the big sunglasses.

Luisa rushed over to introduce us, right there on the windy bridge, I watched her do it anxiously without her usual composure, as if she wanted everything to go well and had little hope that things would be anything but sinister, totally lacking confidence. Lidia shook my hand—I was going to kiss her—but she didn't even smile, not with sadness but with indifference, as if nothing mattered to her, as if it were futile, if not impossible, to communicate with anyone or anything, alone in her medieval pilgrim's habit, separate from us, suspended in a century different than ours. She didn't say anything to me. She walked along the bridge toward the inn between us, and Luisa, contrary to her usual self, spoke too much, terrified that something might happen, the catastrophe of silence, of a silence that could lead to confiding, to the memory of pain, to anything that might place her daughter in danger. In the inn, she said it didn't matter which room they gave her. But Luisa was so insistent about her taking the room next to mine, the good room with the view of the bridge and the river, that while the innkeeper waited for us to come to an agreement, and with a hostile tone of voice, Lidia finally said:

"But aren't you two lovers? Don't you want to sleep next to each other?"

"Shush up . . ."

"Shush . . ."

"It's not true . . ."

The innkeeper's face had darkened, filled with anger as if he had been deceived, as if these patrons, more distinguished than the usual fare, had suddenly become, with Lidia's statement, personae non gratae, pariahs, unreliable, people who lived a lie because for him, primitive as he was, "distinguished" people should also be distinguished and totally untouchable from the moral point of view. Then, as if taking the matter definitively into his own hands, and as if saying "my house is for honorable people," he took Lidia's suitcase into the room next to mine, and Luisa's to the room facing on to the street. When he served us lunch, he didn't say one word to us. In some way the conversation between Luisa and myself—Lidia remained distanced, leafing through a magazine while she ate in silence—had a hysterically insecure tenor as we talked about the houses I had bought, for me, for Diana, how excited she was to see them, we had already spoken with Bartolomé and the secretary to go see them at three thirty after lunch, we would meet at the door of my house at three thirty, yes, yes, it was all set, for sure. When we finished lunch, Luisa, with her most seductive smile, said to her daughter:

"Shall we go?"

"No. I'm staying here."

"You don't want to go see the fascinating house your uncle bought?"

"No. Perhaps later, or another day . . ."

Luisa could not give in, even though I would have advised her to let her be in her hostile detachment:

"But aren't you curious to see the village, Lidia, you yourself wanted to come . . . ?"

"That was yesterday . . . now I really don't care. Bye."

The innkeeper witnessed this dialogue, and upon seeing his preachy disapproving face, Luisa felt obliged to explain, or to offer some reason for her daughter's hostility:

"She's been ill."

"Ah . . . the poor thing."

But the innkeeper didn't understand a thing. And he refused to understand this kind of interaction between parents and children which didn't end with a good thrashing. Lidia went to her room and we left, leisurely walking uphill to arrive at the appointed time, toward my house; she wanted to unburden her heart, to tell me all about it, the guilt, the instability she felt, her daughter's pain, the disillusionment with everything and everyone, and now she chose her world but she felt she had no world to offer her daughter, no shelter to provide. After all, she didn't even own a house: she was renting an apartment, furnishing and living in it one month, a few months, or a year, then she'd sell it or rent it furnished and beautifully decorated. It was all nothing, temporary, transitory, and she, Lidia, wanted something definitive, a point of reference. She had married at the age of eighteen, still a child really, and now, twenty-two years old, her life was over, without faith in anything, no training to do anything.

We reached my house. Luisa was so ecstatic about the façade, about the almost 360-degree view from the sun porch dominating the mountainous but distant and wide horizon, that she forgot to talk about how to redo the interior, all its problems—yes, a huge library/dining room just beneath the sun porch, which looked over the entire village, and the entire bend of the river. It was perfect, and up above the sun porch, like a patio or covered living room for the summer, and get rid of this partition wall, and change those beams, and here the kitchen, and here another bathroom, no, it's better to keep the wooden beams in the bathroom, so that it would be clean, aseptic, comfortable . . . She was enthusiastic, so much so that she didn't remember, afterwards, at what point Bartolomé joined the group, and she was giving him instructions, save this vaulted niche, save this plaster arch, clean the stucco on the lower part of the façade . . .

"But this supports and makes it secure."

"Doesn't matter, that will be done in another way, we'll see . . ."

In brief, he had to begin by cleaning everything, and I saw that a current of friendly affinity, of understanding, was established between Luisa and Bartolomé, the ugly fat man, and as we left the house he promised that that very afternoon his men would get rid of the designated partitions in order to see the space, or the essential spaces, they had to work with, and to begin from there, after cleaning it all out.

Downstairs, closing the door, we met up with Lidia, who was slowly climbing the hill. As she approached, we realized she was very upset; she was like an antenna, anything upset her, any breeze could break her. Now, obviously, she was torn up by something:

"Unbelievable . . ." she said.

We asked:

"What's the matter?"

"This calm, wonderful village . . . How they've ruined it!"

"But not as much as others, it seems to me, Lidia."

"Well, Mom, you notice less in the others because they've been whores for years with all the pandering to tourists. But this harsh rough village of stone, without whitewashed walls and with only its stone presence, the things they've done are a veritable insult . . . The balcony in the square . . . criminal . . . a real crime . . . They should put those who did it and those who allowed it to be done in jail . . . These ignorant, stupid country bumpkins, they should kill them all . . ."

Bartolomé listened to her up to this point and then said:

"Watch your language, young lady . . ."

She asked her mother:

"Who's this?"

"I'm the builder."

"You? You're the one to blame for all those monstrous façades? They should put you in jail . . . You stupid, ignorant rube, you're ruining the face of this divine village . . . You're the ones to blame for everything—for a handful of coins you're capable of selling your soul to the devil . . ."

"Miss . . ."

"I'm a married woman, and don't come butting in here."

Luisa, horrified, and I both remained mute.

"Lidia . . ."

Then Bartolomé turned toward us and said:

"I'm going. I'm not working for you. You should be kicked out of Dors, because you people are corruption personified, with no respect whatsoever for human beings. I have done nothing to make this lady insult me: if you don't like my houses, well, I won't do it if you consider me to have poor taste; I won't die of hunger because of this. I don't know who you think you are to come here with such airs . . . but you'd better be careful, we don't like to be insulted here. Now you know. I might be a peasant, but as long as I live, neither you nor any of your people are going to come here to live . . ."

And Bartolomé turned on his heels indignantly and almost ran down the hill, disappearing beyond a curve of the winding street. Luisa looked at her daughter. She asked her, very calmly:

"Did you take your medicine after lunch?"

"No, you have it in your purse."

Luisa turned red as she looked for it and said at the same time:

"And you had too much wine at lunch, Lidia, you know very well that there's nothing wrong with drinking, but when you are taking tranquilizers, any little bit of wine becomes stronger . . . Here it is, take it."

Lidia took a reddish pill, threw her head and hair back, and swallowed it. Then, as if nothing had happened, she said:

"Stupid old fart. Let's go up to the castle. I want to see it."

Right then and there I got furious: I had just made a big purchase of a house that needed to be renovated, and not only had she set me against the whole town—though it was true that everyone in the village hated Bartolomé—but she had left me without a good builder to take charge of the work and change that medieval house into a livable home, and Diana's as well. In any case this left me in such a disturbed state, in which, as if in one blow, all my previous failures and mistakes—or cowardice?—came raining down upon me, that I thought for a moment to tell Luisa she had to put all the suitcases in her car and leave Dors forever. No, I wanted to go up to the castle. But I wanted to be alone, not with Lidia, sophisticated spoiled brat, who had nothing to do with the peace I had come to find in Dors, and was its exact opposite. I told her not to go up there. That I had to go alone and I wanted to regain my peace of mind; she and her mother should arrange to go up later.

Suddenly, when she heard my rejection, Lidia's eyes took on a deeper dimension, and her whole face softened and became more feminine, and the joint between her jaw and her neck softened, and her neck also became more tender, very young and fragile and soft. I would have wanted my hands, ready just before to strangle her, to move down her neck to caress it, that neck was the young Luisa, everything young, it was La Garriga with its garden now dead from which I could not disengage myself, it was that body that trembled thinking of mine, it was the shame of mine, no longer young, no longer always ready, no longer moved by emotion to respond to the emotion in hers. I said to Luisa:

"I'm going to talk to the stonecutter, and I want to go alone. We can go up to the castle together later."

Luisa had already taken her daughter by the arm, and turning her back to me, headed down the narrow little street; it was as if she wanted to help her to remain whole, not to crumble into pieces, convalescent, fragile, vulnerable; her back confidently disguised as a pilgrim's sagged, and her hand fallen to her side, dropped, for lack of will and pressure, the cigarette. I ascended slowly, calmly, as if seeking to breathe purer air. Suddenly the whole Dors project had collapsed, and I saw myself, a pilgrim seeking a refuge that was not this one which, after a couple of weeks, had become part of me, and as I went up these narrow streets, like now, ascending the steps and stone staircases and winding alleyways, it was like traveling inside myself, my self turned into an abandoned stone village which needed to be infused with new life. But Lidia also traveled inside me, destructively and desperately; and the possibility of fleeing Dors because she was poisoning the atmosphere was also like running away from myself, leaving my own empty body to rot alone in the bend of a river—and this could not be.

What I needed to do now was to speak with the stonecutter. I remember his face aged by the white dust, and I found myself wondering what his face was really like under that white Pierrot Lunaire clown mask. As I approached the church, I heard the hammer blows on the chisel and stone, which became more precise and louder the closer I got, like a call to prayer, to meditation, to the mandala, to the eye that looked at me from the middle of the façade. I pushed open the church door, but the great golden-gray stone nave was not the place of prayer; prayer came from elsewhere, from behind the small open door in the temporary stone wall, which I pushed. In the farthest corner was my friend Salvador, bent over a block of stone, chisel and hammer in hand. I realized that he knew I had arrived but this didn't stop his hammering, and I came closer and closer: he was carving a gargoyle, intensely, sharply concentrated, as if he wanted to extract from within the block of stone the figure that had always been there. But it appears that my silent presence disturbed him, because the blows were less accurate, not as strong or frequent, and little by little the hands stopped working. Then Salvador greeted me saying:

"I know why you've come."

His voice caught me strangely off guard.

"I know that you all had a fight with Bartolomé. Be careful. He has a nasty streak and can be dangerous."

I laughed.

"No, don't laugh. Things are the way they are, and if he and the secretary want to, well, they can make your life in this village miserable. Go—you and your friends should go before it's too late."

It was almost as if he were begging me to leave, and I asked him:

"But you've been putting up a fight, haven't you?"

"Me, a fight? No, there's a battle inside me, not outside. What do I get out of it? I'm poor, I don't have forces that come to my aid . . . and the secretary and Bartolomé do whatever they like; he has all the power and exerts all the pressure, and of course, next door to my house they were raising pigs, which is forbidden, and the stench made life impossible for the neighbors, but with the gift of a piglet to the secretary when the time was right, he looked the other way and no amount of protests from any neighbor will ever have an effect . . . No, no, you'd better go . . ."

Salvador's protest seemed disappointingly trivial, and the magician who was bringing forth the essential figure that had always been enclosed deep in the stone turned into a banal village neighbor annoyed by flies and unpleasant odors. This itself, I suppose, made me resist his plea for me to leave, to abandon Dors just when it was coming to life inside me, and to consider that his fears were petty and provincial compared with my hopes to civilize, my aspirations to enlighten. I smiled and simply said to him that Bartolomé had rejected the possibility of taking charge of the renovations of my houses. And that he, Salvador, should take charge, that he had better judgment and taste, and he hadn't sold out to the prevailing bad taste like Bartolomé, nor sold himself to the consumer society, which was what I was trying to avoid by coming to live in Dors.

"I don't think that Bartolomé's anger will last long. He sees that you are classy, well-educated people, who, besides, have money . . ."

I laughed at the part about money.

". . . and he's not going to fight against you much longer. He can't stand it when someone has something he doesn't have; if he has a 700 series, and someone else buys himself a 700, he'll sell it to buy a better one yet. He's not going to let others be friends with you and with other illustrious people, if he's not . . . don't worry about it, Bartolomé will do your house."

"But I don't want him to do it, Salvador. I don't want him. I want you to do mine and Diana's."

"Don't you realize that if I do it, I'll take on as my mortal enemy forever the chief leader of the village?"

"If you say so."

He thought about it a while, and then said:

"It doesn't matter. As I am already on bad terms with him, it makes no difference. Very well, then, we will fight him . . ."

Luisa had come up to meet me and told me she had left Lidia in the hotel, reading on the terrace facing the river. And the three of us, Luisa, Salvador, and I—calmer without Lidia—went to see the houses, and for three or four hours, covered with dust, spiderwebs and dirt, we completely forgot our existence, engaged in the fascinating task of rebuilding a house, of recreating something alive, starting with a ruin and our imaginations playing with walls we knock down and spaces and possibilities, building on something, creating. Finally, covered with spiderwebs, we went to see four extremely small houses belonging to Salvador, all along the top of the hill, which he sold to Luisa for ten thousand pesetas. And then we parted.

Below, in the square, in La Flor del Ebro, when Luisa and I went back down before dinner to have a drink, the waiter greeted us with a smile, and said to Luisa:

"Congratulations on your daughter."

Luisa didn't know why. The waiter said:

"Bartolomé is furious, up in arms, and goes around saying that he's going to throw you all out of the village. With the police in tow. He and the secretary are running around like chickens with their heads cut off . . . And the townspeople are happy with your daughter, because we all hate him; he's the most evil man in the region."

"The most evil but you all believe him and follow him and employ him and buy from him . . ."

"Well nobody has shown us anything else, there have not been other possibilities . . ."

We went to bed early, tired. The next morning we met up with Salvador, who had gathered a troop of eight young workers and country boys—he had even stolen two from Bartolomé and was licking his chops imagining how Bartolomé was going to react, and how he was going to go after him—to get the three houses going, mine first, Diana's, and Luisa's. Bartolomé vanished from town, or at least neither he nor the secretary were seen for quite a long time, and we spent a whole week tearing down walls and measuring and making plans, covered with dirt and happy; especially, surprisingly, Luisa, who said she didn't know why she had bought that house, that the whole thing was silly, but that something had compelled her, that she, as did I, had fallen in love with Dors, and though she thought it quite improbable that she would come more than two or three times a year to her house in Dors—mine was there, and would be opened, and it wouldn't be worth the trouble opening hers—she was going to spend very little on it, on fixing and decorating it, but that little was a little that she didn't have.

Lidia, meanwhile, had not left her room and the terrace next to her room, in the inn. She'd eat in her room, and spend the whole day in a white djellaba with her hair falling in dark cascades down her back. She read a lot—I didn't have a clear idea what—and during the moments we were together she almost didn't speak.

Luisa told me the banal story of her daughter, who rejected her at age fifteen when she saw her having an affair with me, and went to live with her rich handsome father—a good horseback rider, Catholic, comme il faut—in Madrid. There she lived the life of the Madrid debutante and she married as soon as she could, when she was eighteen, and was one of those ladies who appear in fashion magazines, with a perfect apartment and having a wonderful time, that first period of discos, trips, yachts, totally and absolutely sure of her husband, who was unsatisfying as a man, that is, as a macho, as well as a tender caretaker, a security that was destroyed when, in Sotogrande, she met an Argentine polo player who played with her husband, and on one night the whole edifice of her false conjugal security collapsed. She fell madly in love with the good looks and real security of Carlos Miguez and—too soon—she told her husband, who rejected her, and abandoned her. Miguez did so as well, as he was not prepared to saddle himself with a divorcée, especially having in Buenos Aires his wife the millionairess, an intolerable blue blood but also the owner of the vast ranch that allowed him the luxury of playing polo and taking trips.

"You know, Lidia, I just can't . . . and the kids . . ."

The usual excuse: the kids, the children—luckily she didn't have them nor did she want them, and this, she suddenly realized, gave her enormous freedom. Her husband set her up in an apartment in Madrid, they separated, she stopped using her husband's last name, her father went back to supporting her as if she were a single girl, and at the age of twenty she embarked on a career of sleeping around in Madrid: no longer in her narrow circle, but with anyone, people with reputations that were a bit soiled or frankly blackened, and she ready to go off confidently with one man for a time and with another for another period of time, without falling in love, until it was no longer a matter of relationships, but rather of weeks, simply days in which she went to bed with one after the other, tirelessly; the social circle she had left behind seemed more or less the same as the one she now frequented, with the difference that there were more foreigners now and it was less boring, but the men were all the same, and something started to wear down and die inside her forever, forever. Until, about a month ago, after some party where she got quite drunk and several men went after her, knowing she was easy, she woke up in the morning in the room in an unfamiliar hotel. She had a headache and remembered the party the night before and the repulsion she felt for all the men she met, or who courted her. She was alone in the bed, but, she realized in the dark of the noisy morning on the street, floors below filled with cars, she had slept with someone. And she told Luisa:

". . . And then, suddenly, I heard the water running in the shower in the bathroom and there was someone, a man in the shower, humming something, I don't remember what, but he was singing . . . and I couldn't remember, Mama, who I'd spent the night with, who was it, who, and I began to cry and cry, and to pray to heaven or whomever that it wasn't that unbearable Venezuelan. Dancing with him breathing heavily into my ear, smelling of that expensive cologne I couldn't stand because they all smelled the same . . . I prayed to God it wasn't the Venezuelan . . ."

And when it was, she couldn't take it any longer and Lidia packed her bags and took a plane and came to Barcelona to see her mother with whom she had cut off all communication for the past five years, ever since the moment she became the fiancée of Martin, her husband, when it seemed necessary to cut all ties with a sinful mother, who had fallen down definitely into another social class, who worked, who had a bad reputation, who was seen with painters, psychoanalysts, writers, movie actors, and a bunch of fun people as long as one had peers to gossip with about those people. But now, of course, she was like her mother, and she didn't want to be maintained by either her father or her husband, or her paternal grandmother, or anybody, anybody at all . . . She wanted to rest, rest, without anybody sticking their noses into her business or asking her about her life; she wanted only to be maintained until she could get back on her feet, and forget about that last guy, that disgusting Venezuelan with his expensive ties and his shoes that creaked, and then she would do something . . . who knows what, *I don't know, Mama, I had never thought of dealing with the problem of "doing" something, outside of going to parties, or having children and bringing them up with finesse, giving them a classy education . . . those things, but no, I don't have children nor am I ever going to have them, never; the only thing is that after the psychiatrist you took me to, and the pills he gave me, I feel good, but if I stop taking those pills and the Venezuelan moves toward me from the darkness and stands naked facing me, as he came out of the shower, with his big black mustache, and upon seeing that I was awake bent over the bed to kiss me, and at that moment, at that precise moment I had always been waiting for, ready and waiting, at that unstoppable moment I bit him on the nose and I think I must have ripped off a piece, so violent was my bite, and he whipped me and whipped me with his belt and I don't like to be whipped,* and then Lidia came to her mother in Barcelona with a nervous breakdown: she couldn't take it any longer, she had had it, and a week passed during which a psychiatrist was telling her again and again that she had to seek another way of life, another focus in life, but she was still too hurt, too fragile to take any initiative, this had happened barely two weeks ago, and she wanted to rest, she wanted no one to ask anything of her or insinuate anything, only rest, and now of course Luisa thought that there was nothing like Dors for a rest cure, nothing like this village, these stones, these simple people to ease her pain. But no . . .

The week passed amid carpenters, budgets, plans drawn on the paper napkins in La Flor del Ebro, amid conversations and discussions with Salvador, and I watched a curious relationship grow between him and Luisa, a companionship, the self-sufficiency of a couple, a mutual admiration that excluded me, their chance-yet-assured encounter with each other the whole day which could only be qualified as worthy of admiration. The price of the nails, the semigloss paint, or the bleach, the clearing of the façade and removing the whitish-blue stucco to uncover the beautiful pink and ocher and gray stone, the return to the hotel exhausted—I saw that all this rejuvenated and protected her from any other worry or relationship, since her relationship with Salvador turned into something exclusive. Nevertheless she respected the priorities, and Salvador with his band of eight committed to renovating the three houses that winter—it was also possible that the recruits preceding those who had just left after the bonfires of San Juan might return and augment the ranks with three or four more young chaps— and my house came first. Salvador and she were the ones who decided everything, consulting me along the general lines, and that's it, we spent the entire week tearing down partition walls and taking measurements.

But Lidia didn't leave the hotel. She'd spend the whole day like a ghost on the balcony of her room at the inn with two cats who had become her friends, purring on her lap, and a basket of fruit on the floor. She'd throw the skins of the pears and peaches into the river, which seemed dirty and disorderly to me, and she wasn't reading anything, as I had thought in the beginning, but only read or leafed through the magazines, since she ordered every magazine that came out, the women's weekly magazines, which in one week became a big pile next to her wicker chair on the balcony. I had the impression she read and leafed through them over and over again, which was only an excuse not to do anything, not to commit to anything, a defense, something that kept her from thinking and looking, because she rarely looked, even, at the landscape, or the people on the bridge coming into town when, in the late afternoon, on the bridge, before sunset, the couples of boys and girls would usually take a stroll on the bridge that leaned against the worn-down stone parapet, looking at and greeting their friends. Watching the people on the bridge from my section of the terrace in front of my room—without talking to Lidia, who continued to reject me just as she had rejected me when she was fifteen, and would not even raise her eyes when I'd come in—I'd often greet them: Salvador, the waiter with his girlfriend, the secretary, the owner of the newsstand, the mailman, they were all now friends, familiar faces, and I imagined that they would slowly but surely become close friends during the winter I proposed to spend in that room at the inn, watching over the work on the three houses until they were completely rebuilt, and when I moved into my own space. I would continue making friends with the townspeople, exploring and tempting them, and especially trying to control them by convincing them that I and Luisa and Salvador were right, that renovating the village was the way to restore it to its former stone splendor, and not covering the façades with color cement and stucco, so lumpen, worthy only of ignorant peasants. Now I needed to be careful and proceed with caution: this was a delicate job of bending wills, of exercising power to see if I did or didn't have charisma, to see if my knowledge and taste were capable of penetrating the hard shell of provincial pride and ignorance and convincing whoever was on my side and against Bartolomé that I was right, and what it all meant was a kind of salvation, reaching a mystical state. Could I infuse a sense of mysticism in the hearts of these rough-hewn peasants who thought only of the next day's meal, who, because they thought only of the next day and didn't know how to project or enlarge their concepts, would destroy the hope of greater things? Perhaps I couldn't . . .

In the late afternoon, sitting in La Flor del Ebro, Luisa and I discussed this endlessly. Yes, yes, she said, the fiasco of my public intervention in the case of informalist painting, had left me not only disgusted but also empty; here, then, was my raison d'être and the new me, projecting myself toward the world, constructive and constructing things, toward this village which needed to be saved and civilized in the name of aesthetics, which could also be considered, Luisa argued, an ethics. Here, she said, my task was completely outside the vile labor of making money. Here it was only a matter of an ideal, of falling in love with a place, a bridge and a castle which had to be preserved. Talking to the people—the town was small enough to quickly get to know most of the characters—and perhaps even giving a public lecture, predicating by example . . . a marvelous, evangelical task, giving oneself completely over to the outside, and moreover inserting oneself in a total way in community life, understanding and respecting, not bending to it but rather raising the standards of a still-untouched primitive way of life.

This conversation took place the evening before Luisa and Lidia left, before their return to Barcelona. The light in the square was remarkable: ripe, transparent, a faintly golden light that made the inn, even La Flor del Ebro, seem like the skin of a ripe peach ready to be picked. The waiter, who served us more cheerfully than usual, told us he would have a surprise for us when we came down for coffee after dinner. Luisa said it was probably about his engagement to be married, which he broadcasted to everyone—we had met his fiancée in our first days in Dors, introduced to us pompously and officially. Perhaps, Luisa thought, she had something in her bag, some little thing, some cheap trinket to give to the girl, as the waiter had always been friendly and cheerful with us, favoring us, and perhaps such a spontaneous gesture—she thought she had a very pretty pair of earrings she hadn't worn yet and which she might never wear—really could win us as in an election, more than any self-interested, calculated gesture, not only the waiter who already had been won over, but the fiancée's whole family, for example, and other groups submerged for now in the mostly anonymous village population, which in the long run could be useful to us.

Upon entering my room, I went toward the windows to open them, and to enjoy what was left of the evening light that was dying so splendidly upon the old stone heraldry of the bridge and on the bastions of the castle. But I didn't do it and instead silently opened the door. There was Lidia, in white, as if in her usual funk but this time leaning against the balustrade of the terrace. She didn't have that lost gaze: her eyes, clear, transparent as if full of water, were staring, staring in a straight line that went to other eyes, black ones, that looked at her from the bridge and responded to her look. I had the overwhelming sensation, in that golden light cleansed by the water of the river and refreshed by the leaves of the plane trees on the other bank, that by chance I had intruded upon a scene of shameful intimacy, that I had caught by surprise such a private scene to which I shouldn't have access, which I could not enter, that I should withdraw immediately. The eyes fixed upon Lidia's eyes were those of the black cat man, evidently back in town wearing his flimsy light-blue shirt, strolling along the bridge with that self-assurance his perfectly defined muscles gave him; I tried to step back; my presence was unwanted; I tried to leave but Lidia called to me without turning her head to acknowledge that she had heard me come out on the terrace, and asked me who he was, without even greeting me before. I said:

"I don't know."

"Is he from here?"

"No."

"How do you know he's not from here if you don't know who he is?"

I stammered a bit upon answering that, well, I had seen him once before, about fifteen days ago, wandering around town, but I didn't think he would return.

"But who is he?"

"I'm telling you I don't know."

She looked at the bridge again. Now I didn't leave, but only stepped back, slightly hiding my presence. I didn't go because I felt that Lidia and the black cat man were shameless, as if my watching them look at each other with that barefaced intimacy, my very presence, my body itself, did not matter in the slightest, and could not change anything at all—my poor insufficient body in the face of youth and this relationship that was in the making. The man now leaned against the worn parapet, his hands crossed in front of him, looking directly at Lidia, who had let go of the cats and, instead, was biting into a big yellow apple.

I didn't want to witness the end of the scene, and little by little I stepped back into my room so as not to witness something which, for sure, and at that distance, was going to turn into something bold, obscene. In the safety of my room, washing up and getting ready to go down to dinner, I imagined God knows what gross scenes of sensuality, produced by those two and at that distance: Had Lidia exposed a perfect breast, small and fragile, to reveal to him from her balcony, both of them excited by the possibility that other people passing by could see it? And what was his answer, what in him had responded to her gesture? Everything was flesh, the evening air had the quality of skin, of Lidia's softly golden flesh, and now the abundant night of her hair came down, and I had been caressing that skin, and now I would have license to, in the dark and in private, caress the public hair of the night, not Lidia's particular private hair, reserved for that man. What did he know of La Garriga, where Lidia had been born? Of the park, of the spacious empty rooms filled with clutter under the mansard roof, of the accident-prone chipped Venuses and Apollos covered with moss, upon which Luisa and I as children—with a retinue of cousins, the masquerade which at that time afforded us a false security, a safe and sound context—painted pubic hair on the statues? Time had erased our disrespect, duly punished by those who were then the authorities—perhaps the French mademoiselle, or perhaps it was the year we had an English "Miss"—but the intimacy endured. Lidia, Luisa told me, upon arriving in Barcelona, had wanted to visit, before anything, La Garriga, and Luisa drove her there when mother and daughter made up and were reconciled. Lidia told her she had abandoned her when she was fifteen because she had thought she was a whore, and now she returned because she herself was a whore, for the two of them to live or survive together, and she wanted to see that house where she had been born, when, she recalled, there had been no need for the extreme attitudes we had now. *What pushes us to extremes, Mama, I don't like to go to bed with men all the time, I would prefer not to have to do it, but something compels me—I must be frigid, I guess, and that's why I do it. Don't the psychiatrists say that's why nymphomaniacs do it?* In La Garriga when she was born—when tea was served under the chestnut tree in the garden and the children wore clean starched clothes and had porcelain, not plastic, dolls with individual faces, not all identical as if designed by the vulgar taste of María Pascual—there was no need for extremes, *never again, I would never again meet anyone who would take me to such extremes, never again. Can't we buy La Garriga, have servants as people did before, have lots of children and cousins to shore up a sense of security, a microcosmic world that would teach us how to live? Mama, are you a nymphomaniac? No, you're not, I know, you've never done what I did. My psychiatrist in Madrid when I went to him because I was rolling out of one bed into another and wasn't finding satisfaction in any of them, told me no, nymphomaniacs did not exist, that my upbringing . . . or my lack of education . . . my empty frivolous life . . . my desire for revenge . . . hating that Argentine man who didn't love me . . . To do something . . . something, have a world of my own, different from my husband's, different from yours, Mama, but my relationship of dependency has been impressed upon me ever since I was little, Mama, don't say no, that I don't have the right to depend, that I have been made to depend on someone to take charge of me . . . Yes, yes, Mama. Men are better than women . . . oh, not in the sexual sense only; yes, I also looked for sexual experiences with women but they soon bored me, I'm not made for that, and it's too bad because it would be so much easier, but men are better because they know they can't depend on anything or anyone. Right, Mama? I remember when I went to the psychiatrist in Madrid, an eight-year-old boy was waiting to have a session with the psychiatrist who shared an office with mine. I wanted to be his friend and I asked him what he was going to be when he grew up. And he replied that he was going to be something, he didn't know yet, but something very important, which he was going to know when they gave him his vocational psychological test . . . Yes, don't laugh, Mama: they give men vocational psycho-tests and not us—they only ask us if we're nymphomaniacs or not and that's all, and how are we in bed and if we reach vaginal orgasm or only clitoral orgasm, and the only thing one can do is to look back at the past, at teatime in the wicker chairs under the chestnut trees in La Garriga, when every-thing was secure and when we hadn't yet begun to paint pubic hairs on the statues in the park.* Now Lidia said, Luisa told me, that she was dreaming of returning to La Garriga to live there per-haps forever, but no, La Garriga had to be sold, the estate had to be transformed into a development that would squeeze the maximum out of each handful of terrain so that we, those of us who played there when we were children, wouldn't die of hunger. Luisa already told me that the blueprints, the plans for the development of the estate, were already almost fin-ished, that some money was already coming in, she knew this from very good sources, that the trip with Lidia had served the purpose of finding out about this, from the supervisor, about how things were going, if good or bad, and she, she told me at the table in La Flor del Ebro where we were having our after-dinner coffee, that she and Lidia were going to leave the next morning and would return—she at least if she managed to get Lidia back on track in some way during that week—she hoped with good economic news. We clicked our cognac glasses, toast-ing the definitive end of La Garriga and its whole heavy load of memories and related incapacities.

I saw that man, the black cat, walk away from the bridge directly toward us across the square, as if something had ended and he was ready to begin something new: for this he needed to speak directly to us. But he didn't greet us. He sat right down at the table next to ours and also ordered a coffee with a cognac, good-naturedly greeting the waiter with whom he began chatting when the coffee and brandy were served. After a while the waiter asked him:

"Shall we tell them, then?"

The cat man shook his head no, no, don't tell them yet. But the waiter served himself a cognac, knocked it against his friend's, raised it in our direction and we raised ours to his, and toasted. Luisa asked:

"What are we toasting?"

The waiter answered:

"Bruno won't let me say anything yet."

Bruno. His name was Bruno—black—and he said:

"Later, in a while . . ."

His Spanish was perfect, though with an Andalusian lilt and a strong Italian accent. When he changed to our table he said that he was in fact Italian, but that he had worked in a restaurant in Torremolinos, when Torremolinos really was Torremolinos, not as it was now, ordinary and horrendous: he had gone there, been there three days, had returned in disgust, and would never return again. He was fed up with Italy and had come to Spain thinking that he might still find some virgin land, some opportunity, but nothing, and tomorrow he would leave again, in the morning, back to Italy to look for things elsewhere. How old was Bruno, I wondered, to be wandering about as he did? Perhaps thirty-eight, thirty-seven, forty, at least, in this light and close up. I had thought he was younger from afar, but no, the wrinkles around his thick-lashed eyes were not only the wrinkles of the sportsman, the man in perpetual contact with sea and wind, but rather more doubtful, subtle wrinkles that neither affirm nor negate character, that do not affirm the flesh but rather undermine it and make it droop. Nevertheless his fine Italian face, so perfectly chiseled even in its roughness, his lean physique, his well-defined muscles under the cloth of his shirt were impressive. Why was he drifting? He answered:

"I don't like the Spain of today, I like how it was before."

We also loved it before, the Spain of La Garriga, of El Ensanche. But he only "liked" it as a gourmet devouring a delicious dish, hence his relationship was frivolous, with a global

Spain, excluding him from the true Spain. We, on the other hand, liked the Spain of the past but also hated it and that's why we were her prisoners. He was leaving. We couldn't leave, even if La Garriga's park of chestnut trees was being developed. We talked about Cinecittà, where he had worked several years in small roles—he named some roles in some important movies, but those roles were so insignificant that we had to lie claiming to remember but we didn't remember anything—a Cinecittà that was no longer what it had been ten or fifteen years ago. Nothing was like ten or fifteen years ago, I thought to myself, not even you, old man, especially you, yourself—and I, I myself, though lesser, I have more resources—you're not what you were fifteen years ago when you were young. He said:

"Well. I'm off. I want to make it to Barcelona to spend the night there."

And he stood up to say good-bye. At the moment he was getting into his car—he had the top down—Lidia, in her long djellaba with her hair tied back, and long jingling earrings, walked out of the inn, and came toward our table. She didn't sit, but stood watching the man who shut the car door at that moment and started the car.

"Who's he?" she asked.

"Bruno," Luisa, I, and the waiter said in unison.

"And he's leaving?"

The car backed up: Luisa, I, and the waiter waved good-bye and the car headed for the bridge to the road. Lidia did not wave good-bye. The waiter said:

"But he'll be back."

We all looked at him, surprised. Lidia asked:

"Tomorrow?"

The waiter answered:

"No, next year."

We asked him how he knew. Tourists always say they're coming back and they never return, which he, the waiter, didn't know, because he was not used to tourism, but a man like

114

Bruno never returns, his kind says he does but he doesn't. But the waiter insisted:

"He'll be back."

We laughed and made fun of his insistence, declaring that it was naïve on his part, until Lidia vivaciously also persisted in teasing him, perhaps to get the truth out of him, good-naturedly calling him rube, ignorant bumpkin, accusing him of falling in love with Bruno, which the waiter did not like and said:

"Miss . . . one doesn't talk about such things here . . ."

As Lidia continued to make fun of him, the waiter blurted out the truth:

"You see that house across the way, the one I offered to you here on the square, and which you said you didn't like because even if it was very pretty, it didn't have a view? Well, that house is mine, that is, my mother's and my uncles', and I just sold it officially to Bruno: two hundred thousand pesetas . . . that is, one hundred thousand, and now we're partners."

We all asked in a chorus, partners in what?

"Partners in a bar, a restaurant. Maybe a discotheque. Next year in the spring, he said, we would begin to work, and then, if it works well in the summer, well, then in the fall I can buy my apartment and get married . . ."

We were stunned. This was the end of everything. Torremolinos, Cinecittà, every loser, every has-been would be coming here to settle in Dors, the most remote village in the world with its mystical castle of Calatrava crowning the hill for all the centuries as a symbol of the eternal: Montsegur. This man, however, a symbol of the transitory, of everything that's fleeting, of what the bourgeoisie makes a fashion one day and deflates the next, this victim who wanted to take revenge on the passage of time that was leaving him behind, was going to come, perhaps with a retinue, all of them like him, who would cut off at its roots the ancestral reality of life in Dors, and install discos and noise in this peaceful haven, and the vulgarity of everything common and thus, perhaps because one is conscious that it will last very little, and then why build anything of quality if one knows all this, that everything one does will be obsolete in four, five, six years at the most, and then people will want other things not yet known at this time, and meanwhile, let's go on with things that can be replaced like the human beings in Bruno's bed, no doubt, one human being the same as the next, consume, consume, and that's it, the discarded skins left scattered on the ground and our beautiful dream of peace and tranquility completely destroyed.

Of course it was necessary to act. Salvador, perhaps, would help. The waiter said that the secretary and Bartolomé had served as witnesses to the sale and that Bartolomé would help to renovate the house or what parts needed to be renovated. And they planned to advertise . . . on the highway to Valencia thirty-five kilometers away and therefore, if they advertised the Onassis, which would be the name of the disco and restaurant, well, this would bring a lot of people to the village. It would be a beautiful restaurant, very typical, said Bruno, who understood these things and he didn't, and would probably bring singers and shows, if this became fashionable in the region, and people began to come from Tortosa, Gandesa, Mora, Tivisa, and Falset, aside from people from the highway. Besides, he said, he would renovate the first floor for guests, and even though Bruno suggested making the first floor for him and his wife, she didn't want it, she wanted a modern apartment on the main road, small, easy to manage for her alone with her mother, not an apartment in these enormous houses, with huge rooms, which they'd never finish cleaning.

Lidia listened to the entire dream of the waiter in La Flor del Ebro in complete silence. When he finished talking and we said good night, the three of us went to the bridge to enjoy the warm night breeze, stunned in silence, and as we leaned on the parapet she said:

"He was here when I saw him."

"Who?"

"Bruno."

She didn't understand a thing because she was too preoccupied. And we talked and talked, saying there was only one
solution: bring more and more people to Dors, but people
chosen by us responding to our taste and our way of life, colo-
nize Dors with more or less prominent people, more or less
famous, with power, so that they wouldn't continue to ruin the
village, and so that, eventually, a junta of neighbors, all with
good taste and all of them seeking tranquility, could put up a
united front against the devastation that a Bartolomé, leader
of the ignorant bosses, could wreak upon Dors, and against
his will also oppose the malevolent influence of a Bruno who
would bring "civilization," that is, tourism, like a golden marvelous mirage: those who wouldn't "come back" and saw what
we precisely did not want for the village, that what we were
fleeing was "tourism" and "civilization" when poorly or insuf-
ficiently understood, a way to sacrifice it to all the horrifying
demands of a consumer society that wants to consume more
and more because it has still not reached its plenitude, envi-
ously contemplating the "progress" of other places that have
"progressed" more. Lidia said:

"Mama . . ."

"My dear?"

"I want to stay here."

"What?"

"Well, until next week."

"Why?"

"I don't know. Aren't you yourself saying that we are enjoying the last era of peace in a marvelous village like this? Well I
would like to really enjoy it . . . alone . . . I don't even know the
castle, but I feel as if the church, or the castle, has some answer
or solution for my problems . . . I'd like to stay. He can take
care of me . . ."

She pointed at me. It was the first time she referred to me.

"He can make sure I'm happy, make sure I'm not alone
. . . I'd like to see the house you bought, Mama, I don't know
why not before . . . He can make sure I take my pills when I

should, and not forget and end up like a bundle of rags hanging over the railing of the balcony in the inn as I have been
all these days . . . and I don't feel like leaving the cats, which I
like, unlike those big terrible dogs, black dogs with yellow eyes
whose barking he liked and didn't let me sleep at night, but
not the cats—I want to stay with the cats. Does this matter to
you, Mama, one way or the other?"

No, she didn't care, as long as Lidia promised to obey and
behave, and not drink cognac and wine when she was taking
tranquilizers—and she shouldn't stop taking them—as she
already knew how she could get.

Then began that curious, terrible week. How to win her
over? It wasn't only a matter of seducing her, which was not of
immediate importance. It was something else: how to make her
see me differently, not like the "uncle" who takes care of her,
not like the grown-up responsible for her physical and spiri-
tual welfare, but something else . . . How to get her to let me
in? It was difficult. Too much unfamiliarity, on the one hand,
and on the other, too much familiarity. How to make, or to create between us a relationship similar to the one that existed
between her and Bruno, even without knowing each other, and
that wasn't pure sensuality but something else, part sensuality,
part prior recognition, part attraction and interest? After all,
he wasn't that much younger than me. Eight, six years? Close
up, I already said, his face looked wrinkled and old, six years
younger, at the most. Forty-one. He wasn't that young. And
nevertheless . . . sitting there on that terrace after Luisa left,
with our books on our knees, and she with her cats, I looked
for forms, formulas, weapons with which to knock down that
tremendous wall that separated us, which wasn't a hostile wall,
but rather a wall of years, of lack of interest, a feeling that she
didn't think of me as a man but rather as a relative, and that I
didn't produce any interest in her whatsoever. Was it love that
I wanted from her? No, no. It was recognition, that's all, reac-
ceptance into a charmed circle whose shape was still unknown
to me.

I asked her:

"Have you read this?"

She turned the page of her magazine. She looked:

"No, I read very little."

"It's very interesting."

"What is it?"

"Lévy-Bruhl."

"Oh, Mama and I spent a whole afternoon trying to find this book to bring it to you."

"Yes, I needed it."

"Why?"

"To explain to myself, in some way, my relationship with Dors."

She laughed, biting into an apple.

"And what do you need to explain yourself for? Isn't the relationship itself sufficient?"

"No."

"It would be enough for me."

"But this can help me deepen the relationship."

She yawned. I had to win her over in some way.

"Have you ever heard of the 'mystic law of participation'?"

"No."

"And the primitive soul?"

"Nope."

"In some way I feel like I've found my primitive soul here in Dors. In primitive societies they believed that part of a man's soul could inhabit an object—a tree, for example, or a stone— and that the life of that man was profoundly tied to that object, tree, stone, house, animal, whatever; that a part of him deep down *was* that tree, stone, house, animal, and it shares with him the same destiny, and they possess the same soul and same voice; and any harm that happens to that object which incarnates his primitive soul is a harm that the man himself feels, any disturbance or oppression to the stone or the tree, is a disturbance to the individual too. We have here, together, a mystic law of participation . . ."

119

"Can there be a mystic law of participation with two things?"

"Yes, with many. The primitive soul lacks unity and connects with a part of its environment, with things."

"Well then, my primitive souls are these cats."

And she laughed. Did she not understand? Wasn't she interested? How to make her interested?

"There are many people who spend their lives seeking their primitive soul and are miserable because they don't find that lost piece of themselves. After coming to Dors I feel that Dors, this village, these streets, the castle and the church, are my primitive soul, to put it that way, which finally I have found. I feel so close to this village that leaving it fills me with fear . . . fear that something will happen to it, and often, walking along its streets, I feel as if the locals, the storekeepers, you yourselves were walking over a piece of my body, and the streets were mapped in my inner self."

Lidia had dropped the magazine. Something at least, I said to myself. And she hugged the kittens. She looked at the bridge, empty at this hour on a Monday morning, and her gaze floated, as if flying over a branch, descending upon her and stopping in midair. I had to continue. I've never been a professional seducer, those who wisely know how to progress gradually in their flirtation finally to take their prey, and I didn't know what would be my next step. I covered my face with my hands, my arms leaning on my knees. I almost moaned at the same time, fearfully, at the truth I was improvising.

"But I haven't reached the end. I have found this village, that's true, and its mystic law of participation in my soul exists, but something in it, something essential, evades me, hides from me and the mystical marriage cannot be consummated. It's as if my essence had been taken from me and I've remained here because I want to gather or participate in it."

I felt her hand caressing the back of my neck. My fraudulence—was it fraudulent?—was producing results. She drew near me. Before I had been pure thought and she, of course, also like a primitive being, didn't know how to think abstractly.

Now however, when emotion emerged, the historical custom of generations of women during millennia had made her fall; emotion is easier than thought. And her hand had caressed my neck. I felt that the cats, perhaps jealous, leapt from her lap and began to play softly, aggressively, in a corner. Then I raised my face toward the castle that crowned the village.

"Like the castle, for example."

"What about the castle?"

"One can't enter."

"Why?"

"It's forbidden. There is only one door. The walls are impregnable. The key is in the hands of someone in Madrid, and you have to make your way through a formidable bureaucracy in order to get permission to enter. They say they don't grant permission to enter because the floors are not secure and there exist legends in the town that people have fallen into holes—remember that the grandparents told their grandchildren, grandparents of the old people now—and they're afraid that parts of arches will come down, and stones and loose blocks will fall, I don't know. That's the excuse. The fact is that nobody has entered . . ."

Upon saying this I remembered, fleetingly, two presences seen one night, or glimpsed or imagined, in the bushes inhabiting the interior of the fantasy castle, two elastic animal forms . . . or perhaps it was only a dream, it seemed so remote now, those two figures glimpsed from a bell tower, one very clear night.

". . . Nobody has entered, and I feel that nothing of mine will be complete until I enter the castle, you know?"

"What?"

". . . One night, when the moon is out, let's go climb the church tower and from there let's look at the empty interior of the castle, the abandoned corridors and broken arches, and the great staircases overgrown with thyme and rosemary bushes."

She clapped her hands.

"Yes . . . yes, let's, I'd love to go."

"It would be easy, perhaps, using influences in Madrid, people I know at Bellas Artes, to get them to lend me the key and give me permission to enter. But doing it that way would always somehow be like remaining an outsider, like acknowledging my impotence with the castle. And it would also mean never recovering the essence of my primitive soul. I have to do it another way, like an affair, through love . . ."

"Don't start up with this love business."

"Oh well, I know, you young people don't believe in love."

"How are we going to believe in it seeing you people and your example?"

". . . Well, love *c'est une façon de parler* . . ."

In some way, as I spoke to Lidia, I had hit upon something: I had stayed in Dors to enter the castle, to enter in a specific way—as I had remembered those two that night, which now, just now, I recalled—to take possession, become one with it. Luisa should never find this out, because she would immediately call the director of Bellas Artes and the whole thing would be taken care of in the blink of an eye, and then I would be just an authoritarian old man, and would not gain entrance to the castle; not only that, but I would put an end to the castle, violating its secret without—as it should be and as I wanted it—becoming part of it. The magic would be broken. I continued:

"I am sure that everyone in the village has entered the castle and doesn't admit it. I am sure they have a secret they keep and don't tell anyone, but there is some ancient tradition that gives them the right to enter the castle—who knows, not all the time, but at some point—because for them, as for me, their primitive souls are inside the castle, a tree, a stone perhaps, which they must recognize. They don't speak about the matter amongst themselves, they don't plan their comings and goings inside the castle, but they go . . . yes, they know the secret I would like so much to know."

"Ask them."

Now it was my turn to laugh at her feminine pragmatism. She blushed when she realized her simplicity, and looked at me for the first time and said:

"No, of course not . . ."

And for a second I felt I held her in my power. She was so young; it was easy to possess her. But, I knew it was difficult, so impossible, because there's something in the soul of the young that only gives into others like them, a language, a look in the eyes—like the one on the bridge—an irrationality and anti-intellectualism that would always leave me outside, behind, alone. Now, for a minute at least, now I had her, she was mine. I said to her:

"Come with me."

"Where . . . ?"

"I'm going to buy some clothes."

"Here?"

"Yes, one must begin by wearing a disguise . . ."

We went out, she dressed in her white djellaba, people turning around in the streets to look at her. I continued:

"Yes, a disguise is important. It's also a mystical participation. Primitive man wore lion masks to attack his enemies especially because he wanted to be a lion, he wanted to have the courage and have the ferocity of a lion. Now I am going to disguise myself . . ."

We entered a clothing store: it was dark, with dark shelves, an old-fashioned counter from the turn of the century, with oval-shaped glass display windows. I asked for black corduroy pants—and a jacket, also black corduroy. Lidia said:

"Yes . . . now I understand: you're going to dress like those your age here, in black corduroy like those who have always been rooted here, in the earth, to thus acquire their powers and unravel the secret of the castle . . ."

I smiled. She had understood, in effect, she was entering what her generation knew as "my wavelength." I tried on the trousers. She said:

"Awful, they look terrible on you!"

"But it's my size."

"But it's awful. Look how wide the legs are, how big the backside is . . . the way they hang . . ."

"That's how they wear them. You wouldn't want me to put on blue jeans at my age, no? Those tight ones that boys wear . . ."

"Of course . . . that's how they wear them here. You look awful."

"It doesn't matter. I'll wear them, miss."

We left and I said:

"When they're washed and shrink, when they begin to lose their jet-black sheen and the black corduroy fades, turning greenish, is like a second skin, ceases to be a disguise, forms part of one's self, and there are people who have had only one pair of black corduroy pants and only one black corduroy jacket which has served them their whole life . . . that's when perhaps they learn the secret . . ."

"Yes, but then it will be too late."

"Too late for what?"

"To enter the castle."

"They won't care. They will already have entered, in some way."

"But these pants, no, no, I can't stand them, so inflexible, so stiff. Let's go to the inn and wash them, yes, yes, don't make me beg you, I'm going to wash them immediately for you to begin to tame them, soften them, so that they form what you call your true disguise, so that they won't even be a disguise any longer . . ."

At the inn she requested a basin, hot water, soap; she made me take off everything and put it in the basin, I in my underwear, she with her sleeves rolled up, both of us laughing, I pouring more hot water from a teapot, both of us terrified of ruining the articles of clothing I just bought, as she had never washed anything remotely like this black corduroy, nothing more than a pair of stockings, underpants, or some delicate blouse, the kind that is hung out to dry on a shower curtain bar, and gives an air of intimacy, of sexuality to a woman's bathroom . . . How to do it! Oh no, the black corduroy was swelling, getting very heavy, and the black dye was coming out in thick streams . . .

"But that's what we want . . ."

"But so much!?"

"It's what washerwomen call 'the first water.' "

"Oh."

Then, between the two of us we wrung out the jacket and pants as much as we could and hung them on the railing of the terrace. Black water was dripping.

"Look, I wet my djellaba and it might be stained."

"Change."

"OK. Let's go out."

A few minutes later we left the inn arm in arm. She was humming something and feeling happy. I asked her:

"Are you happy?"

"Yes."

"Why?"

"I don't know. Why do people like you have to analyze everything to death? I want to see my mother's house and the castle . . ."

I took her to see the four houses with stone buttresses and arches over the doors which Luisa had bought with the intention of connecting them.

"Yes, like Dali in Cadaqués."

"Of course, like Dali in Cadaqués."

We went through the four small houses, recently cleaned, with the partition walls torn down and on the ground. I examined windows and floors and differences in levels, and said no, this wasn't the house they had to demolish to leave a space for a courtyard between the houses, but rather the other one, over there, she would tell her mother, that they shouldn't do anything further until her mother arrived . . . No, no, on the contrary, she changed her mind: they should do it right now so that things would be totally irreversible and just as she wanted. We climbed the church tower; the sun was setting, one of those heartrending Dors sunsets, all gold, all silver, all green and the great amphitheater of graded planted hills, and below, in the foreground near us the arches, two-light windows, staircases covered with pasture grass, lianas hanging from destroyed windows, bristling with swallow nests, moist like a jungle, growing in some mysterious way as if inhabited by presences that did not reveal their names. I was about to say that one night here I saw . . . yes, I saw Bartolomé with Bruno in this jungle, sharing the magic . . . but no: I didn't need to say anything but rather be silent, because if not, the possibilities of entering someday would diminish.

Every day we went out for a while, or later, for longer excursions in the hills: we'd sit under an olive tree, or lie down in the pasture under a hazelnut tree, or look at the pine trees, farther up, and how the gray basalt rocks wrinkled like rhinoceros skin, as if we were living on the back of an immense sleeping animal. Sometimes we also slept. And she'd tell me that for her, too, Dors was becoming her primitive soul. Perhaps, she said, perhaps from the very beginning when she just arrived, and without being able to contain herself she insulted Bartolomé for having destroyed, and for continuing to destroy, the beauty of the village. Perhaps, she said, she had taken part in the matter of her mother's house because she wanted it to be her house, her first house in her whole life, and even though she was only twenty-two, it didn't matter. She had the sensation that all that she had lived before was false, that only this, the rose-colored castle we saw below on its hill as if protected by the embrace of the river, that only this hard stone village, only this was her reality, and the rest had left no trace in her.

One afternoon, under a hazelnut tree, we were talking quite a while about Luisa, and she asked me with great curiosity and detail about her mother. She said:

"I barely know her."

"And she, you."

"Yes, and she barely knows me."

"But you're both very close."

"Not as close as I feel to you."

Turning to look closely at her, I raised my head over my hand and arm leaning on the grass. She opened her eyes, realized something was going on inside me, and said:

"No, not that. Don't be silly. How could you think that! But the fact of being able to tell you things . . . I don't know . . . The fact of being able to ask you if my mother had real vaginal orgasms or clitoral orgasms . . . the fact that both of us are connected in the primitive soul we have found in Dors . . . yes, that."

I let my head drop again down to the grass and I looked at the leaves of the hazelnut, not very high up; we were on the last terrace marking the hill like a stone tray, just before the wrinkly basalt beginnings of the skin of the hill and of the pines like hairy fuzz on this immense animal; a tray that sustained us alone, tranquil, looking at the big valley, the river, the village below. Now she leaned on her shoulders. Through my closed eyelids I guessed the contours of her face.

"If you want to make love with me, well . . . I don't care."

I opened my eyes.

"Just like that, coldly?"

"What other way?"

"I don't know . . ."

"And it wouldn't be coldly. I love you, yes, I love you a lot . . ."

"But it's not enough."

"Not for me."

"Not for me either."

"But that is what I want, what's missing."

She lay down again, and then immediately she stood up and stretched out her hand to me:

"Let's go?"

I stood up.

"And what you're missing?"

"Let's not talk about that. It so happens . . ."

"But if you don't talk you don't understand."

"And if one understands one kills it."

"That's an absurd prejudice of you young people, that if one talks one kills the heart of things; it's not like that, it's the opposite: I'm an intelligent man and you're an intelligent girl and we must talk . . ."

"Yes, but in another way."

That night Lidia, naked, when I had already turned off my light, opened my door and came into my bed. We made love, once. Then she got up in the darkness to leave.

"Don't go."

"What more do you want?"

"That you stay to spend the night with me."

"No, you're not my man."

"Why did you come then?"

"Why am I going to limit myself to making love only when I am in love, and only with my man? No. There are many reasons to make love, without needing you to be my man and without having to be in love."

I said nothing.

"Why? Out of affection? Out of curiosity? Out of identification with your mother? Out of pity? . . . That's it . . ."

"You're already trying to analyze."

"Why not?"

She remained silent, naked, sitting at the foot of my bed, and in the light of the match with which she lit her cigarette, I saw her caress the cat in a way that she had never caressed me. I saw, also, that she was thinking.

"You're right. Why not think? It's fun to think. I had never thought before: I had only done things, followed impulses."

". . . tropisms . . ."

"What?"

"It doesn't matter. Continue."

"Thinking not about big complicated things like you and your castle and your primitive soul, which I don't deny is a lot of fun and therefore quite compelling. No. Thinking about oneself . . . about Mama, La Garriga . . . how things happened with Gerardo, and then with Diego . . . and then how things didn't happen with all the others until the point of exhaustion."

"Until being totally *fed-up?*"

I underlined the word. She perceived the irony. And kept thinking, I saw her thinking in the dark.

"No, I've seen too many movies about elegant ladies becoming totally fed-up. That's out of fashion now. It's entirely another wavelength."

"What was it then?"

She kept thinking, yes, I saw her think; at least it was something she had done only for me; that part of her like part of her body was mine alone. She answered after a while:

"I don't know. Perhaps I slept with you tonight to know what it was then . . . so different than what happened tonight. So different too from what it should be. Good-bye."

And she disappeared from my room.

The next day I didn't see Lidia all morning, because I went to work in my house. When I woke up I felt the imperative need to finish it soon, not to delay any longer, I wanted to have my retreat, my own castle that I would decorate with my own mysteries to confront that other castle impossible to scale, seen only from the outside. And at lunch time I ran into Lidia who was coming down from her house, doing exactly what I'd been doing in mine, compelled by the urgency to finish it, to settle in her house. At the table in La Flor del Ebro we talked about ceilings, roofs, and beams, and how to know if they were rotting—the white paint begins to peel off, and they get cracked and greenish, that was the secret—about craftsman furniture, about Salvador, she especially talked about Salvador, who intrigued her, that quiet man who seemed to know everything, his little wise blue eyes, all that he didn't say was so enormous, the entire history of the region, the entire history of an era embodied in his hard face, in his hostility without arrogance or violence, which only seemed to tell them to leave him alone with his hatred, that his hatred was so vast that it could feed off itself and didn't even require revenge, and because his

129

hatred was so vast and so self-sufficient, his love too could be enormous.

I said to her:

"You're analyzing."

"Or imagining."

"Can't they be the same?"

"I suppose."

"Do you like Salvador?"

"No, he's old."

"He's four years younger than me."

She didn't respond to my attack. She didn't want to talk. I saw, immediately, that more than anything she had gone to bed with me last night to leave behind a stage and enter another with respect to herself and our relationship. She had digested and eliminated me. Now I had a precise place in her constellation, and she had placed me on a precise path I couldn't veer from because it was the only way in which I was of interest to her, and she knew that I knew I wanted to remain interesting to her.

That night Luisa returned. She brought with her Patricio de Bes, her gynecologist: he was a handsome young man, elegant and worldly; he was the one who had recently extracted her left breast and the one who, periodically, gave her checkups for cancer. Suddenly, when I saw him, two questions arose: How was it possible that during the time I was in Dors not once did I remember that Luisa, my ex-love, my lifelong friend, my cousin, my confidante, my sister, had recently suffered the trauma of a dramatic operation, and who during five years— yes, the horrible period of five years—was never completely sure that the next day some cruel metastasis wouldn't turn into a tumor in any part of her body and the cancer would kill her? Not once did I remember it, my poor cheerful good friend. And two: How was it possible that during all these days I spent alone in Dors with her daughter, Lidia, the latter did not once even allude to the fact that her mother was in danger? Was she so selfish as to forget it completely because it was something that annoyed her? Or was I always a bit sentimental? But in someone as anti-intellectual as Lidia it was also possible that her brain, terrified at this possible loss, might reject the idea and bury it in oblivion.

In any case, Luisa was in top form. Patricio de Bes immediately went all over the village with us, we showed it to him so that he'd admire it, so that he'd love it, and he said yes, that he too would buy a house.

We were in the square. I saw that Luisa didn't want anything to be bought, by the way she said *yes, well, we'll look for something for you, let's see, and what kind of house do you want, tell us and we'll definitely look,* and I saw that Lidia didn't want it just as I didn't, but he didn't realize. He was charming, Patricio, with a very pretty wife and four sons in high school, but no . . . what was it? We had once asked the same question regarding him, Luisa and I, and she had said: "He has no pathos." He has no pathos, no depth, nothing beyond himself and his experiences and he'd always resolve everything without tragedy or joy but as some form of happiness, even if it seemed like dissatisfaction. He was a man with a lot of fight in him, a perfect unsinkable individual, and all his artistic frenzies—he had been one of the great buyers of my paintings and had a good collection of Spanish painters of the informalist school— were legitimate, his tastes and judgments correct, but in some way all this was not rooted in his personality, but rather gave the impression that he could disengage from his preferences easily and would continue to function perfectly, without any disturbance, in what people usually call "the world of the living." Why did we reject him so? We hadn't agreed upon it, but we did reject him, at least at this moment. I said:

"Look, Luisa, there goes Bartolomé."

"Where?"

"To the other side of the square."

"Ah, there he is, coming out of Bruno's house."

"What's he doing there?"

The waiter supplied the explanation:

"He's going to fix that house. Bruno wrote to me, and we're now in agreement: he's going to do it."

We raised a ruckus: what monstrosity will he create? And right here in the square, after the secretary's balcony, now Bruno's house, perhaps painted green in this ambience of golden-gray stone. Luisa said to me:

"Call to him."

"He's angry."

"Call him over: he's seen Patricio's Mercedes, and since nothing fascinates him more than cars, he'll come . . . you'll see."

I called to him. He looked at us and somehow, because of what we wore—my black corduroy was still not dry—and the way we looked as a group different than what one normally saw in Dors, he decided to come over. We greeted him cordially, even Lidia, and we invited him to sit down with us. We introduced him to Patricio. The fame was familiar to him, not only the last name, he said, but more than anything he believed that he had operated on the wife of the provincial governor, the chief authority, who went to him for the births of all his children, which Patricio confirmed. And then, with great pride, Bartolomé invited us all to a drink in honor of the doctor, saying:

"You should buy a house around here."

"There is nothing else that I want."

"But that's very easy."

"But you have apartments, Bartolomé."

"No, also two or three old palaces on the hill. You're married and have children, right?"

We answered yes and that he had to go, and we too if we wanted to get to Barcelona in time, and we were leaving the order with him, and he, obsequiously saying yes and without fail, that it would be an honor for the village to have an eminence like Dr. Bes, that doubtlessly this would be published in the local papers, that he should return soon and that it was a pity, really, they hadn't met before because that way he could have bought a house already before leaving today.

"We'll leave it for the next time," said Patricio.

"Come back soon."

We put all the bags in Patricio's car, Lidia got in without saying good-bye to me, along with Luisa and Patricio, and off they went, leaving by the bridge. Bartolomé and I returned to La Flor del Ebro and sat down. He made it clear to me that Dr. Bes was the kind of person we should attract to Dors, as it would give the village a lift. A silence followed: obviously we, Luisa and Diana and I, did not seem sufficient to him. I said this to see how he reacted. He had no problem responding.

"You're sort of arty types, and artists are dangerous, and the people, even the priest, are beginning to get alarmed. I'm telling you this without any ill intentions. For example, you're divorced. Señora Noyà is divorced. Your daughter is divorced. And how is it possible that your ex-wife would come live here, in the same town as you, being divorced?"

I said we were very good friends, and aside from having a lot in common, we had two children who kept us very connected, and a few little grandchildren—I wasn't sure if two or three, nor if they were boys or girls—and that our relationship wasn't anything out of the ordinary. Bartolomé hesitated a bit before continuing:

"The priest is not happy. And the Caritas committee, the ladies, are positively terrified. And not without reason, you already saw how that girl, Lidia . . ."

"What's so special about Lidia?"

"Well . . . I don't know, several boys mentioned it: the look in her eyes, so insinuating, and then the clothes she wears, that white djellaba. Sometimes it seems she has nothing on underneath, strolling around town for everyone to see."

"Some make a fuss because they wear skirts that are too short . . . now because they're too long. Silly old ladies . . . they should let people live in peace."

Bartolomé stood up.

"My wife is the president of Caritas. She was the one who pushed for the building of the new temple, there below in town, so that people wouldn't have to climb up to the castle to church every Sunday . . . or on the evenings for novenas. That church, which you and those like you have so much contempt for, has meant progress for the town."

"Well, then, if we're so contemptible, how is it possible that Dr. Bes is such a good friend of ours?"

"He won't be such a friend when he wants a house, and when you folks—who know perfectly well what houses there are and how many there are and which they are—don't give him any help whatsoever. I'll bet because he's married, as God wishes, and you don't like normal people and normal things. Old houses . . . filthy stone houses! I mean really, let me tell you, do you know what the big problem is I'm finding, working on Señor Bruno's house?"

I was surprised that he now was "Señor" Bruno.

"What?"

"That the boys, the young workers, don't like to renovate houses, they find this . . . well, even shameful; it's almost impossible to find people and, like Salvador, I'm going to have to bring people from outside and this is going to be expensive."

"And you're also going to charge us a lot."

He thought about it for a moment.

"Not Dr. Bes."

"And Bruno?"

"Not him either."

"Why?"

"Haven't you heard the latest news?"

"No."

"Well, he has written a lot of letters to the waiter in the café and to me. He wants us to tear down all the walls and partitions on the ground floor and in the basement, because he's going to set up a discotheque. Yes, it will be fabulous for the village. It's going to be called 'Onassis.'"

"Onassis!"

"Yes, Onassis. Don't you think it's a good name?"

"Yes, yes, very good."

"And as I am going to be his partner—all three of us will be partners, he, the waiter, and I—I'm not going to charge a lot; at the beginning the partnership has to be protected, especially if it's for the good of the village."

"And what does your wife say? She's not horrified?"

Bartolomé barely hesitated this time.

"No."

Then after a silence he said:

"Not yet. Later, when it's done, you'll see, she'll like it. Rosa Mary is not hardheaded. A bit pious that's all, for having been a novice and all . . ."

"You too had religious training . . . ?"

"Yes."

"And nonetheless . . . Bruno's partner in a discotheque?"

"What's so special about that? Recreation for the youth, the dances, there's nothing bad about that, I don't think it's a sin."

"And Padre Carmelo, what does he say?"

"He doesn't know yet. One shouldn't spread any rumors until things are finally settled."

He got up and left; he was a new Bartolomé, with projects much larger than his apartments in the New Quarter, now that he was going to have a discotheque and had met Dr. Bes, who had brought into the world the four children of the governor of the province. I saw his eyes shining with his dream of grandeur and power, his whole dream that did not reach beyond the most minimal frontier, his desire to leap beyond his shadow guided by cheap magazines and television, the desire for greatness, finally, the romanticism that nested in his ignoble heart, so easy to buy was the heart of the village rich man.

The year following my move to Dors was a year committed to work and to relating: I was completely possessed by getting to know both the most primitive and most superficial roots of this village with which I was totally identified; not only the village but also its landscape—an experience I discovered for the first time in my life—formed part of my very being. What I had said

135

somewhat flirtatiously to attract Lidia, referring to Lévy-Bruhl, was true: Dors and its environs had constituted my primitive soul; any offense against the "mystic law of participation," any vilification was, in short, an insult to me and I participated profoundly in the destiny of those age-old stones whose existence transcended my life span. Trying to communicate in a more or less civilized way with those people I knew was impossible, that is, impossible to impose my values, my ways of thinking, my way of life. Communication, in any case, was brought about at the level of mystery, of mute participation in the same activity, as with Salvador and some other peasant, choosing the tiles for a floor and our parallel feelings upon knocking down a piece of the house that was de trop and where I wanted to make a bit of patio out of two perfect Roman arches—the mortar that connected them was mixed with bits of brick, hence we were sure this was a Roman construction. My excitement and their excitement were so parallel, so similar that we went to celebrate in the square with the waiter and the owner of the bar by dispatching several bottles of wine, the good stuff, the house vintage, which I made them take out and serve to all the noisy partakers who joined in. Going by one street I saw a curtain open slightly and a woman's face, old or young, looked at me and then dropped the veil again upon her intimacy by the brazier table. Women didn't exist in Dors. When they married they became cloistered as wives—and even as human beings— from everything that wasn't simply the tight-knit nuclear family. In the square the secretary introduced me to his young beautiful wife, who, for that instant, put up with the annoying comments, quietly smiling, but who soon left without saying anything—asking the most trivial questions like, "Have you been living here long? And your wife, when is she coming? Do you have children? And what work do you do? Oh, you were a painter, you must be retired by now; yes retired, well, I have to go make dinner, see you"—and she didn't leave even a trace in the waters of the male conversation, like a stone that falls and doesn't even make ripples.

Autumn was coming and people were beginning to prepare for the wine harvest and the Feast of Pilar, gathering mushrooms in the hills, and I smelled with delight the transition from one season to the next as my house progressed, along with Patricio de Bes's, and Bruno's—after Luisa had just left on her way back to Barcelona, after giving me good but vague news and greetings from Lidia, who wanted to return but was trying to get back on her feet, perhaps find work, perhaps meet people and make her way into a new network. One Sunday night in the square—Luisa hadn't left yet—we saw Bartolomé stroll by with his wife on his arm, tall, good-looking, much younger than him, dressed in the latest fashion, all shiny and as radiant and new as if she were one of those polished electrical artifacts, one of those automobiles Bartolomé's heart coveted. I was surprised by the shock of realizing that this beauty was Bartolomé's wife, and Luisa and I commented, wondering how could it be that this common loud-mouthed ambitious presumptuous toad with his utter lack of humanity had been capable of conquering such prey. Luisa said:

"Here, of course, she looks like a radiant beauty . . ."

"Anywhere, Luisa . . ."

"But she has no class, so common, so normal-looking."

"She's a pretty woman, wherever you put her."

"Not in Barcelona. In our world she'd looked like a country bumpkin, very ordinary . . ."

"I don't know: look how long her legs and arms are, her neck . . ."

"Her neck, the neck . . . you always with the neck. Well, I'm going, it's late already and I don't want to be too tired when I get to Barcelona; I have a lot to do tomorrow."

We kissed each other good-bye affectionately, and I sent her back with messages for Patricio about his house. When the car left, I sat down again in the café, to write letters and postcards: to Diana, telling her how the houses were going, and to my son, telling him to come visit me. Also to some galleries to send me the paintings they hadn't sold, to me here, in Dors, so that

137

I could store them here. Bartolomé and his wife reappeared in the square arm in arm and in their Sunday best—I didn't believe that anybody got dressed up anymore for Sunday; this was one of the most charming customs, giving the town its local color—looking almost furtively toward my table. Upon seeing me alone, Bartolomé raised a hand in the air greeting me with an exaggerated gesture of friendship and cordiality, and I gestured to him to come over to my table. He introduced me to his wife, who smiled sweetly, without saying anything—it was obvious that she had absolutely nothing inside her stupendously well-coiffed head to say—and they both sat down with me. I made them order whatever they wanted and I began a conversation with Rosa Mary. I asked after her health, her family, what she knew about how her son was doing in the service, and she answered with completely empty monosyllables, totally lacking content, interest, feeling. But after each of my questions, and after the monosyllabic answer, Bartolomé interrupted, asking me about the new car Luisa had bought—a green Renault—about when Dr. Bes would be coming, about our houses . . . about my house. I told him about the discovery of the Roman arches on my patio, and he laughed, saying to me, *you with your Roman arches, here all the houses have Roman arches, that doesn't mean anything here, here other things have value.* I said to him that if he wished we could go up to my house, they had finished installing the electricity on Saturday, and if we hurried we could still manage to see the view from my window. We began to walk up the hill, amid the rich man's protests about how uncomfortable it was to have to climb so much, about how narrow these streets were without any pavement except old stones worn down by the wheels of carts that surely had rolled over them for many centuries, that not even a lousy SEAT 600 would fit in these streets—how was it possible that people like us would choose, for the pleasure of it, to live there? We passed in front of Luisa's house. I noticed an ironic smile on Rosa Mary's mouth, the first sign of having something inside, of being alive, that she had given. I asked her:

"Do you like it?"

She laughed.

"I don't like these things."

I asked her:

"What do you like?"

"I'd like to live in an apartment in Tarragona."

"Ah, yes? I didn't know. Tarragona is very beautiful. The old part of town and the Roman remains . . ."

"Yes, and very progressive. Many foreigners. But I got married and came to live here, and here my children were born, that is, my daughters and my one son, Bartolomé. I think you know him. They're already the age to get married, my daughters. There's nothing like marriage . . ."

I added:

"Of course, when one has had a happy experience with it, I suppose there is nothing like marriage, when there's understanding . . ."

Then Bartolomé interrupted:

"Happy marriage? Bah . . . humbug, understanding . . . Women are useless, they're a burden. I'd be happy with a washing machine, an electric stove, and a cookbook."

I looked at Rosa Mary to see if at least she blushed at her husband's bad manners. Nothing: the only little sign of life I had caught a glimpse of went out suddenly like the light of a candle, and during the rest of the walk until we reached my house, she'd say yes or no to something unexpectedly, as if a weak thread of smoke were rising from the wick of a candle for a few seconds after it's been brutally put out.

We went up to my house. We looked at the rooms, the view from the living room and library, from my office and my bedroom overlooking the whole valley in its plenitude and part of the castle. Rosa Mary and Bartolomé peered out a window. She said:

"The view is very pretty from here. Too bad you see all those old roofs and ugly streets . . . but farther away the view is pretty . . . Look, there's the house of . . . that lady who's a friend of yours whose name is Luisa . . . I think she's your cousin, they say."

"Yes, my cousin. We spent our whole childhood together."

"And she's married?"

"No, she's been divorced for a long time . . ."

There was a moment of uncomfortable silence. Then Rosa Mary said:

"There are no divorced people here."

"Of course: there is no divorce in Spain. But they were married in France, and got divorced. Like me: I was married in England and also am divorced . . . but we're still very good friends."

I was referring to Diana. But Rosa Mary said:

"How nice. There's nothing like family."

I preferred to pass over that point and not dwell on it as I was of a diametrically opposed opinion. These people who lived three and four generations in the same house—as in the past, as in the times of the summers spent in La Garriga—seemed horrible to me, and this empty shell of a woman was the result of all that family life.

We parted ways again in the square, I waiting for them to invite me to dinner as people do in the city, but I had already realized that in the village social life didn't exist as we understand it, only family life, cousins, relatives, meeting in the street, outside the church after Mass, but never the delightful six o'clock meal, for example, in which the civilized arts of conversation and friendship are cultivated.

The waiter in the café was my main source of information. He had the greatest contempt in the world for Bartolomé and Rosa Mary: she, he said, was the daughter of an ice cream salesman in Tarragona, and took on the airs of a great lady and never greeted anyone. Yes, all the money was hers, all of it, and Bartolomé, of course, was a hard worker, earned money with his construction company and selling apartments and building lots, but the money was hers, say what they might, and came from the working-class origins of a chain of ice cream vendors—

not even a factory—on the coast, from Tarragona to Sitges. No, she wasn't shy, she was swollen with pride, and didn't allow her daughters, who were very pretty by the way, when they came back for vacations from the nuns' school in Tarragona, to dance at the dances with the local boys, who were not fit, according to her, to be their partners.

Many things happened that year: my fight with the secretary and with the mayor because he was financing a pool and ball courts, but the town didn't have a garbage dump or a garbage man, and it was horrible and not at all sanitary, the belt of filth that grew day by day, month by month, in plain view, around the village. But I got nowhere; that's how they were and how they'd always be; it was more important for Dors, like some larger towns, to have a pool and sports field, but the smell of garbage piling up in a circle around the village, rotting and invading the streets and fields, didn't matter one bit. The secretary asked me:

"Aren't you a big fan of local color?"

But it was possible to forget all this, the aggression, the bosses giving me the cold shoulder and gossiping and making aesthetic decisions without consulting me. I had offered them my advice—humbly because I knew it couldn't be done any other way—saying that as they knew about olive trees, cultivating fields, and agro-industry, I would never try to influence them in that sense, but that I understood aesthetics because it was my profession, because I had traveled and I had seen, and this would contribute to the town's welfare, which was what I was trying to do. It was possible to forget all this because of the broad passage of the seasons sweeping by like classical mythological figures, almost totally personified by their individual features, because of the figs and grapes of the last days of summer, the old Mediterranean vintage, the search for mushrooms in autumn, and the start of winter with its bitter cold—which I experienced for the first time starkly, pleasurably—and the ritual slaughter of a pig on the village streets, when one would hear at twilight or in the morning

141

the desperate cries, and the blood running in the old stone gutters and the children and old people participating in the naïve violence of this old savage ritual, and the trees bursting with olives, and the gypsies who would sleep under the portals even if it was snowing outside, among their animals and children and rags, and who earned their keep as day laborers and on payday would celebrate with drunken orgies, banging their tambourines with sticks, and flamenco dancing and fighting in this austere, cobblestoned Aragonese village as long as the olive harvest lasted; and as the afternoons got shorter and the outdoor work in the fields was reduced to a minimum in the winter until there was none and everything was indoors, everything in winter was beside the hearth and now presided over by the wife who became, briefly during the winter, queen of stews, of thick garlic garbanzo bean soups in her pots: she was spinner of destinies and of clichés as she crocheted—one couldn't understand how she had time for this pastime with all the hard work she had to do—on the brazier table behind the window curtains, or while she watched incomprehensible movies from other remote worlds on television, and dreamed of things she didn't say and cultivated and deepened her power, her prejudices, her loathings in the conniving circle of the other wives whose husbands, as Bartolomé put it, would have liked to replace them with washing machines, cookbooks, or other artifacts, while the men were playing cards with the priest, in La Flor del Ebro, closed now behind its windows, without outdoor tables, filled with smoke and black corduroy and yelling at the soccer on television and bullfights from past fiestas.

Luisa would come from time to time. More than anything, I suppose, to see me, not to see her house, which interested her but not that much. How was I? What was I doing? Nothing, I'd tell her, I was doing nothing for the first time in my life, and barely speaking with anybody. In silence and living at a snail's pace I began to feel that my spirit was being reborn again. I would think a lot—but didn't want to tell Luisa—about Lidia

142

with the pain of not knowing how to see her, and I'd ask how she was doing:

"OK. Fine. She's fallen in with this clichéd fast crowd in Barcelona, but you could see that coming: she's pretty, they're sophisticated and free, and they enjoy her company. I don't know if she's fallen in love, but I see her going out a lot, buying a lot of clothes, reading very little or nothing. From time to time, she certainly remembers Dors. Sometimes, too, she doesn't go out, decides not to answer the telephone and stays home and doesn't get dressed for days as if she wanted to recuperate, recover—and that's when she most asks about Dors. Especially about those famous cats she is desperate about . . . Have you seen them?"

I explained that they now slept in a basket in a corner of my room, curled around one another or on a corner of my double bed where they'd move to in the morning usually, and that I myself fed them—meat, milk—and they had become very attached to me. One was named Tàpies, the other, Cuixart; explaining to the townsfolk, especially the innkeeper, why I had given them those unpronounceable names was a task I soon abandoned. Now, at the inn, I no longer ate with the other customers in the dining room where mostly truck drivers passed through, but rather I ate in the kitchen itself, warm, filled with smells and smoke and aromas and the comings and goings of the innkeeper's wife and her assistants. I'd sit in a corner, near the fire, as if I were waiting, with the cats on my knees. The silence made up my conversations with her, the silence that was everything, the naked winter landscape and the silent locked castle I didn't even think about but which existed there, above—without floodlights now, as there wasn't any hope of even one miserable tourist in a low season for all of Spain, and even lower from that point of view for Dors—watching over the passage of time.

Sometimes I did go up there to take some sun on cold sunny Sunday mornings and look at the clarity everywhere. I would pass my hand over the stones, and on the masonry I'd see the marks of ancient medieval stonecutters, a Star of David, a compass, a cross, a circle, an S with which they counted the ashlars they had completed and for which they charged; more than anything, these personal signs of individual traces submerged in time—of dark lives in their time and even more obscure now—kept me company and were my friends and extended their hands to me across the centuries. The greatest pleasure was to find out that some of the building stones of my house also bore the mark of the compass I saw on some of the stones on the castle; that same stonecutter who had worked on the high and mighty castle somehow had worked in the same century on my house, and even if his name or his face or his circumstances were not known to me, well, he was a friendly presence who hung around me.

On one occasion my son Miguel came from Barcelona and said to me:

"I like to see you this way. I've never seen you better. No . . . I don't want to buy a house. What are you turning into, a real estate agent? No, you have a house and my mother has a house, I don't see why I should buy a house."

I explained to him the need to save the village. I explained that if left in the hands of "progress" as they understood it, it would soon be destroyed, and would be one more town like so many in Spain:

"Yes, with their renovated modern houses, without style, without a sense of ensemble, where the inhabitants are proud of their unnecessary four-story apartment buildings and appliance stores, but when it comes to producing a postcard, for example, they take a photo of the only corner or only house they haven't destroyed and which, given the slightest occasion, they would be totally set to destroy."

But I felt a warmth in Miguel toward me I had not felt before. He was a serious, rather solitary boy, and hadn't inherited his mother's charm or beauty, or imagination; I knew he disapproved of her as much as he did of me. He was interested in the social sciences, always talking about Durkheim (wouldn't it be better to make him a philologist? I think so, but philology not in its relationship with literature, but rather, as a science, as a discipline), and he'd spend long hours alone in his apartment, studying. He had never understood my paintings, which he had always told me he frankly considered insignificant, a passing fad. I am not sure of how much my reaction against the media in Barcelona, and against the informalist school, were actually the fault or result of my conversations with my son. I never saw his mother and Miles, and didn't even talk to them on the telephone more than twice or three times a week, cordially, amiably, with a touch of irony, though not superior or distant, which did not secure further intimacy or contact. He said:

"We'll have the whole family back together in Dors, then."

"You won't be coming much, I assume . . ."

"I don't know: I like this. If it doesn't go downhill too rapidly, I wouldn't be surprised if I came to see you more here, even to spend vacations here with you, more than when we lived only six blocks from each other in Barcelona."

"I like your honesty."

"You're a more interesting man, and have more integrity here than in Barcelona with all your colors . . ."

"But I'm doing absolutely nothing . . ."

"It is more honest than to do what you were doing."

I was silent for a moment.

"You never liked Luisa."

"I never thought about her."

"But the world she involved me in."

"No. But anyway, it was none of my business."

"Yes, it was."

"Here, anyway, do make sure I can have a nice room in your house, with good light, calm and quiet . . ."

I laughed.

"Noise in Dors!"

He laughed too, with me this time, not at me.

"No, there won't be any noise. But nice and calm. I'll bring my books and spend time here, keeping you company, and studying . . ."

I didn't say anything, but as I watched him leave, so serious, so stiff, so alone, I felt a deep tenderness toward that little boy whose childhood and adolescence Diana and I had stolen, to the point that—perhaps as a reaction against our aestheticism and cosmopolitanism—he dressed, almost vengefully for his age, in a tie and stiff white shirt and dark suit like a provincial notary public, and everything about him was precise and emphatic; anyway, at least he didn't have, though he did lack a sense of humor, the stiff mien of a professor or a notary public. He was loveable: the little 600, identical to the millions of anonymous SEAT 600s (you couldn't distinguish one of those cars from another in the city) was taking my son away, who now that I was, as he said, a dropout, no longer in the horrible competitive career, now he could love and understand me and would be a calm and benevolent presence keeping me company in Dors.

When Luisa came the next time, I told her, and I told her how happy I was with this news from my son. The houses were almost ready. Mine, especially, was already waiting to dry so that it could be given a coat or two of paint, then we'd begin to bring the furniture, which Luisa had ordered by messenger, to Dors. Spring was starting to burst out all over, and in the riverbed the watercress grew potent and fresh, and the erect poplars were beginning to be covered with a downy fuzz that in the reflected light of dusk was scarlet, but which upon unfolding in the form of leaves, fabricated the freshest green. I thought I wouldn't like spring: too many blooming almond trees, too much of a cliché in places like this, like the blossoming almond trees in the slightly corny last scene from some Jeanette MacDonald movie of my youth. But there was a breeze, in any case, and if there was a breeze the whitewashed walls would dry quicker, and if the walls dried, the paint would dry. Luisa promised me a weeklong visit to help me move in, find me a housekeeper who would take care of me, decorate my house, and the other things in which a woman is inevitably more handy than a man. She told me:

146

"I'll bring Lidia."

"I would like that."

"She's doing badly again."

"What's the matter?"

"She's going out at night too much."

"I don't see why that's a problem . . ."

"You know . . ."

"The people . . . ?"

"Yes."

"Oh well, it doesn't matter."

"You know what I mean. She's jumping from bed to bed again, and that's not good . . ."

"You seem restless . . . You're not doing well."

On the café table she took my hand.

"No, I'm afraid."

"What's the matter?"

"It will have been a year . . . Pap test next week."

"You're afraid."

"Yes, a lot."

"Want me to go with you to Barcelona to keep you company?"

"No."

"Lidia can keep you company."

"She doesn't know anything."

"What do you mean, she knows nothing?"

"I haven't dared to tell her that I had a breast cancer operation. I feel ashamed. Illness is humiliating, and cancer, when one still has it inside, is the most shameful of all. Do you realize that in this moment mortal metastases might be reproducing in my body? I'm ashamed for Lidia to know that every minute—every second, every step of my life for the next five years—is under the reign of terror, and shame."

"Why shame?"

"All illness is shameful."

I sat there looking at her, she, the source of life itself, self-sufficient, the song of glory to herself, nobility, the lily: total lack of self-awareness, her courage, her lack of cowardice. I took her hand. I understood that I should say nothing to her daughter, that she was ashamed to admit it. In that square, closed to the outside like a living room of high walls, with the peacock-blue sky in which some stars shone brightly, I felt the heat of intimacy, the transition from holding hands to the bed, to the embrace, to the kiss, to love, was banal, and if we had been lying in the same bed perhaps it would have been the necessary and natural corollary of these joined hands. But intimacy, outside of love—and even inside it—is impossible. An exclusively feminine connection, another name women—strong and controlling women—give to everyday sticky domination . . . No, intimacy doesn't exist, only friendship, so different, faith and trust, or on the other hand, the ferocious night, love's clarity beyond and close by, night in which moments happen, encounters in which the body is transcended as body and connects to a body alone and transcended—either as matter or as spirit—in order not to know each other, as my body now did not know hers and wouldn't have touched it for anything in the world, and being mutually faithful once concluded that brief material encounter. I saw her absolutely alone, much lonelier than I, but it was impossible to sympathize with her because she rejected sympathy with all her might. I could have spoken to her perhaps about La Garriga and the dewy park, and the golden parterres amid the voracity of the ivy, and the pubic hair on the statues and the glasses painted on the Venuses, and the creaking of the white wicker chairs, and the heat in the summer in my attic room . . . All that, which for me was present and alive, and which is why I was such a compassionate sentimentalist, for her was over and discarded and she was seeking other forms of life. I saw that her hand was covered with little sores.

"What's the matter with you?" I asked.

She pulled her hand away, hiding it.

"I went to the dermatologist. My hands were beginning to be covered with those old-age liver spots. Horrendous. I went to the dermatologist to burn at least the larger ones, but he says that he thinks they won't go away, nothing can be done about them."

After that she left. Diana's house was all finished, also, and I didn't call her on the phone because it seemed to me so impossible and so disagreeable, deep down, for her to come intrude upon my solitude, my peace, my silent union with this village, and with my primitive soul.

And the landscape changed again and one day I saw Bruno's white car parked in the square and all the shutters of his house opened on to the square. Spring, then, had a golden cheekiness filled with the sugary buzzing of insects, which was almost intolerable, and it was hot at night and the clouds piled up and it rained at night and the next day dawned clear and freshly washed, renewed. I had no desire to talk to Bruno. I greeted him from afar, but made no gesture to come over to him or for him to come over to me. The waiter at the café had left his post and was with Bruno and Bartolomé, on the opposite side of the square, looking at the façade and discussing. I trembled over what was going on. Sunday, at least, I didn't see him in the almost-deserted square—I imagined him taking long energetic hikes in the mountains, in the glade, like a dark stealthy animal wandering around the jungle to return in a calmer state after having devoured his prey, back to the square and to work on Monday. His eyes met mine from afar, a slight bow, nothing more, but in those eyes—perhaps his eyes meeting anyone's produced a similar quantity of emotional reactions?—there was such intensity and even intimacy, in a negative sense, like that look I saw in Bruno's and Lidia's eyes when one afternoon I intruded upon the terrace at the inn, and sensed the obscenity of having caught them looking at each other. No, we couldn't speak to one another: we knew we couldn't, nor feign a friendship or even a camaraderie, not yet anyway. He was with my enemies and he knew it, and he knew I felt he was on the opposing team among those who believe in progress and have a poor understanding of civilization, and that they were my enemies. Nonetheless, that calm early summer evening—I reflected that it was almost a year since I had come to Dors and that I had never been so calm, so content—I would have wished there not to be even one stain from that civilization I had discarded in such a total way when I went native and didn't leave Dors again. There were pigeons pecking in the sun in the square, and no car frightened them away. I had the delicious sensation that I had witnessed changes in Dors for a whole year, that the waiter at the café was someone else, and I could talk about "when the other waiter was there . . . ," and long for other times when the service was better.

Suddenly a peasant in his Sunday best came out from watching the bullfights on TV at La Flor del Ebro, greeted me. I greeted him, we had never exchanged a word and I only knew some trivial details about him—he was the one whose dog was killed during the winter hunting season, and his daughter got married last Sunday—which when I learned of them, there was no need to know more; but the tables were outside again, under the portals of La Flor del Ebro, and in the most remote corner of the square some little girls also dressed in their Sunday best were playing jump rope. Next Saturday Luisa and Lidia would come and I would be able to move into my house; I had told the wife of the innkeeper and she had cried, and me too. Aunt Cinta was truly an aunt and promised to find me a good housekeeper: she would speak with Señora Luisa to give her instructions next week. I threw some breadcrumbs to the pigeons vaguely pecking about in the empty square.

Suddenly I heard a racket of loud car horns, not only one car, but many at the same time: strident horns, horns in various absurdly harmonious notes, and curses from a farmer with his cart loaded with vine shoots going over the bridge to the square, blocking the narrow entrance. The people from the café came out from under the portico to look, the curtains in the windows raised and female faces glimpsed, and when the peasant with his cart left room for them to pass, we watched, bewildered, an enormous yellow truck that said TRANSPORTES KWONI enter the plaza, immediately followed by an enormous Volvo pulling a *roulotte*, and then a Hillman, a Mercedes-Benz, and an Italian car of unknown make. It looked like a circus entering town with that enormous yellow truck and the *roulotte*, also enormous, the passengers shouting directions in unrecognizable languages in order to be able to park in a certain order in the square which suddenly got very crowded. People were coming, getting out, arriving from God knows where and notified by who knows whom to witness what at first looked doubtlessly like some foreign circus. But after listening for a while I realized that the strange language I didn't think I understood was English. And the voices were familiar. I saw doors open and a cloud of people come out, young men with long hair and sandals, women in shorts or djellabas carrying babies on their backs like Indians, slightly plump older women with disheveled long blond hair, a black man as shiny as a telephone, all of them making a colossal racket, shouting about the beauty of the village, the marvelous bridge, beginning now an ascent toward the castle, toward the church, toward the streets, but stopping because they obviously wanted to get organized, and the mother with the twins on her back stepped into the *roulotte* to heat up milk on the stove, and the black man started playing the flute, and nobody seemed to be paying any attention to anybody and the whole life of that gang, of those rope dancers, went on as usual, laughing, admiring themselves, and a long-haired, slightly husky woman with gray streaks in her hair, disheveled and loose down to her back, and wearing a long dress obviously designed by Liberty of London, which dragged along the ground, in rainbow velvet with a tail like a peacock, who took out a mirror and hastily combed her disheveled tresses. When I saw her, electrified I stood up and shouted:

"Diana!"

She looked everywhere, electrified, dropping her mirror and squinting at the figures of the peasants in their Sunday best or dressed in black corduroy, who looked at us stunned from the shadows of the portico. I felt paralyzed with terror: is this what Diana had become? And then I saw a skinny blond boy jump out of the big yellow truck, with a hint of blond beard on his chin and long straight blond hair falling on his shoulders, who went to open the back doors of the truck: feeling as if I feared that, when he opened them, a retinue of tigers and lions and panthers would leap out, I recognized him against my will and shouted:

"Miles!"

But I still didn't move, and the boy also stood there petri-fied, squinting at us, the country folk in black corduroy, with his hand on the lock to the truck door. Behind me I heard Bruno's voice:

"We'll do well at Onassis if we begin like this!"

Furiously I turned toward him as if he had insulted me and turning back I said:

"It's my ex-wife . . . and my son . . ."

And I leaped over the ledge of the arch, and ran across the square—among the pigeons which some of the troupe were beginning to feed, and which incredibly perched on their shoulders and heads as they laughed—shouting, Diana, Miles, and all of them, upon seeing me run toward them at top speed they shouted my name, and opened their arms and we all embraced, Diana, Miles, I laughing amid a flurry of pigeons and shouting from the troupe who all wanted to kiss me, look at me how great I looked all dressed in black corduroy. It was very important that they all immediately buy black corduroy garments and rustic espadrilles: they wanted them now, but no, no, it's Sunday; *you look great, you look like the troupe in one of those music hall zarzuelas we would go to, to laugh at the fat sopra-nos when we lived in Barcelona, how wonderful, what a wonderful village, how sunny, spring in London was* aw-ful, *simply awful, so we suddenly thought of coming to Spain and giving you a little sur-prise, to move here, and see how it goes and how's this village that you had invented, yes, Dad, don't deny it, you invented this village, you, you, don't lie, before it didn't exist and it's simply marvelous, much better than what we dared to hope, so primitive—so unspoiled. Isn't it wonderful, it's incredible—real countryside around, the road here was sensational, real country, not like in England where everything is perfectly manicured and looks green to play golf, but here this is rough, wild, truly virile, marvelous, you have such good taste, how proud we are and how excited to see the house, we want to move in immediately, it doesn't matter, even if it's a bit damp, let's wait a few days before we take the piano out until it's totally dry, when do you think it will be all dry?*

"Maybe in a week."

Miles said:

"Then the hotel . . ."

I said:

"The inn . . . of course there's not enough room for so many people . . ."

Diana said:

"We passed a wonderful hotel."

I said:

"Well, Diana . . . I don't know how wonderful."

"Well, if one doesn't take it too seriously, quite kitsch, with the whole façade covered with broken tiles of every color . . . very primitive; it could be fun."

They were ready to find everything fun. Miles and Diana hugged and kissed me incessantly, as if they had found a long-lost loved one and meanwhile the others took out suitcases, pots, plaid blankets from the cars; and the African, lying facing the sun on the parapet, playing a flute, and I realized that he was playing Mozart, which—for some reason at that moment I couldn't manage to articulate—gave me a sensation of calm, a feeling of restfulness. Miles introduced me to his wife, Bridget, with her blond twins on her back, as if introducing his maidservant; and when I, in classic Spanish mode, was going to make a big tender grandfatherly scene with my blond granddaughters peeking around her Indian-style back, she went back to the *roulotte* to finish making their dinner. On the other hand, when he introduced me to a boy who was almost the exact copy of himself—tall, thin, emaciated, smiling—except dark-haired and with more of a beard, he did it with an affection he didn't have when he introduced me to his wife:

"This is Bill, my accompanist."

"Your accompanist?"

"Yes . . . you know I play the violin. I have to have someone who accompanies me, right? That's why I married his sister . . . she's a good kid. And here in the truck, among other things, we're bringing the grand piano, Bill's, a fabulous Blüthner—wait till you hear its sound. Will it fit in the house?"

I would have liked to have said no just to see, to test how they'd react, but Bill immediately provided the answer for me:

"Because if it doesn't fit . . . perhaps we could buy another house, a house in which it fits . . . ?"

And Miles suggested:

"And why not buy a big house, with good acoustics, that will be only a music salon?"

"Not a bad idea . . ."

Then they introduced me to the African, also an accompanist:

"Umbi, from Kenya."

And Diana said:

"I'm dying of thirst. Later we'll introduce you to everyone else; right now they're busy with their children and luggage. Come, come everyone, let's have something cool to drink . . . I'm dying of the heat . . . I had forgotten how hot it can get in Spain . . ."

I said:

"We're barely beginning."

"How wonderful—that's exactly what we want."

When the whole troupe had settled down under the portals, before the stunned eyes of those gathered around, the gathering seemed so large to me that it filled the tables; the women around one of them, with crying children whom they were trying to convince to drink from some small bottles, telling them that it was good English tea; and Umbi, Bill, Miles, Diana, and I grouped together at a table we sat around.

Bill said to the waiter:

"Coca-Cola."

Diana immediately got furious. "You come to Spain, a pure, primitive country, to drink Coca-Cola and poison yourself with preservatives?" That was okay for degenerate countries like England; after all, they had come to Spain tired of London's pseudocivilized life, to live close to the earth, to have pure nutrition. Then Diana called to the waiter again:

"Make us a big pitcher of fresh lemonade, for all of us."

The waiter looked at me, as if asking me what she was saying despite the fact that Diana spoke perfect Spanish, with a slightly comic English accent, like that of a comedian imitating an Englishwoman. I repeated her order. He was speechless, but I asked him to do it right away. Diana said:

"I am absolutely *dis-gus-ted* with this matter of Kissinger and Thieu. I refuse to put up with it. We have done nothing but spend the whole trip from London discussing Vietnam. That Nixon, in order to win the election is going to end the war in Vietnam just like that seems to me immoral . . ."

"Mom would like Vietnam to go on and on."

"It's not that, but I find it disgusting."

Bill chimed in:

"Everything's disgusting, Diana, you know very well. Just think. When they asked Mr. Fulbright if the USA wasn't ending the war in Vietnam because it couldn't betray the high ideals of President Thieu, he responded: 'Well, we put Thieu where he is. What's the big deal, then, with removing him?'"

Diana said this was nihilistic. She belonged to a generation for whom things still mattered, and she thought it was the absolute last straw that they were sitting here in a stupid restaurant, in horrible Formica chairs—*why don't you do something?* She said to me, *so that they don't use Formica in such a beautiful place, they're ruining it.* Meanwhile *look at the marvelous sunlight on that amazing castle on top of the hill* and she asked me if I was a friend of the owners of the castle and I said no, that it was a ruin, that here we weren't in England where one went country-house visiting, but this castle was important to her, just as Nixon's immorality mattered to her—it had to do with her generation. Umbi interrupted:

"Let's not talk about generations."

Miles explained to me that Umbi was fuming because he was in total rebellion against his parents who had been Mau Maus when it was fashionable to be Mau Mau, and had eaten who knows how many whites. But he was so disgusted with the atmosphere of his country that he went to London and devoted himself to the flute and nobody played Mozart like him in all of London . . . and he dared to say all of Europe.

At that moment the waiter returned looking desolate:

"There are no lemons."

Diana looked at him with disbelief:

"There are no lemons in Spain?"

I explained:

"It's not the season."

"What does that have to do with it . . . ? In London we have them all year-round."

Then began a huge argument between Bill and Diana, who seemed about to throw plates at each other's heads, regarding refrigerated fruit, the loss of vitamins, the dependence of the northern countries on the southern countries for citrus, what people were saying about the Common Market, and that the whole thing was a horrendous scandal, that in Spain, the country of sun, there were no lemons . . . I suggested sangria.

"Sangria!"

"Sangria!"

"Sangria!"

The word spread enthusiastically from table to table, from face to smiling face—it was the perfect solution, marvelous after such a long hot journey and then we would go up to see the house and the castle—and spread even to the women feeding their children at the end of the table, until two little indistinguishable English boys who formed part of that strange retinue began to say with their incredible accent, and banging the table with their little freckled hands:

"San-gri-a . . . san-gri-a . . . san-gri-a . . ."
Until Diana shouted at them:
"*Shut up now . . .*"

And they quieted down laughing, and came running over to her and kissed her and she kissed them, without ceasing for a second to talk about Kissinger, with whom she was evidently obsessed, and Thieu, and the general immorality. And I watched my ex-wife, talking at an ear-splitting volume and laughing loudly at the other side of the table, that soft white woman with the wild hair, her face powdered, with a little band of Pitimini roses tied around her head, looking for a hint—not because I was interested in her, but out of curiosity—of intimacy or of a past between her and me, which an allusion or a glance could have revived, and could have connected me to her in another way than simply with a supercivilized being who continued to amuse me, but no sign: she was a slightly plump lady who said words and words and got excited about abstract topics, and who didn't even look at me or at the castle, who didn't even sense how, as we dispatched pitcher after pitcher of sangria, the light in the square was fading while the shadows of the inn's old battlements slanted across the pavement, and not one moment did she draw near or give me the opportunity not only to remember the past and to resume our bond, but also to explain my presence and my experience here and they their sudden presence and unexpected voyage to Dors. I felt that they were infinitely more modern than me: I needed explanations and motivations for such spontaneous actions and sudden impulses as was, obviously, the arrival of this whole troupe in Dors, with a grand piano and all, and without even knowing if it would fit in the house I had made for them. Diana said:

"They have to take out my chaise longue."

"Mom, it's too late now."

"What time is it?"

"Almost nine."

"We've spent the whole evening here drinking cider—no, sangria it's called, it was delicious—without going to see the house and the castle? That's the last straw—and where, pray tell, am I going to sleep?"

I suggested that tonight those who could would move into the inn. She asked me to make the arrangements for her, and she asked Miles to take her chaise longue out of the truck. She could not even think of spending a night, or sleeping in a room without her chaise longue being there. Yes, they were to take it out immediately and bring it up to her room that I had chosen for her at the inn.

I arranged things so that Diana would get the room next to mine which Luisa or Lidia usually had, and which had the pretty view from the terrace of the bridge, the black poplars and the river. She congratulated the innkeeper's wife for not having modernized anything, and the latter laughed, as if saying she were crazy and God willing she would redo the whole inn next year. But luckily Diana didn't listen to her, because she was watching over Bill and Miles and Umbi bringing the immense chaise longue and putting it in the room. The innkeeper's wife said:

"Maybe put it here, to see the view . . ."

Diana laughed saying:

"Yes, but with my back to it. I'm like Gertrude Stein, I love a pretty view, but I prefer to sit or recline with my back to it."

Before the wide-eyed stare of the innkeeper's wife, trying to have a friendly and pleasant conversation she asked:

"Have you read Gertrude Stein? One must read Gertrude Stein. It's impossible to understand today's world without having read Gertrude Stein. There's the chaise longue."

And while they installed the luxurious artifact, upholstered with faded pale-pink silk and lighter aquamarine cushions, numerous cushions in every shape and dimension which over twenty characters seemed to be going downstairs to look for, coming back up hidden behind a tower of these soft comfortable artifacts which Diana arranged on her chaise longue, feeling more comfortable according to her taste and habits. We all went down to dinner—it had been arranged for all of them to sleep there, on cots or in sleeping bags, some in the rooms of others without being hampered by this inconvenience, saying it was fine for one night—and they said they were all tired. Afterwards I went upstairs to Diana's room where she was reclining on her chaise longue with its back to the magnificent open window through which the cool night air entered, and I settled at the foot on cushions while we talked—and now she did ask me about my life in Dors, exclaiming *wonderful, wonderful, exactly what we want, although I don't know how long I'll be able to put up with all this, perhaps a short time, but it's wonderful all the same, and I'm dying to see the house, and that castle, do you think it might be possible to buy that castle if it belongs to no one? It would be fun, to have it, for the hell of it, perhaps to give concerts* . . . And Umbi was playing the flute in a corner and the children were crawling over the cushions and her and she hugged and kissed them from time to time. Until we got tired and the sangria and later the good table wine at the inn had made us sleepy and relaxed, and then the women went to their room, and Umbi climbed into his sleeping bag at the foot of Diana's bed and the conversation continued a while longer amid the snores of Umbi, until Diana fell asleep, and Miles covered her, and went into his bed, and Bill took the children to another room, and I went to mine.

But I didn't go to bed. I was afraid to. I went down to the square, as if to take the pulse of the townspeople after the arrival of such an extraordinary troupe. I was a bit ashamed to say that Diana was—had been—my wife: she was flabby and had aged, and in her old age, cheerful and vivacious, and contrary to my defeated melancholy, I saw my own years reflected, as if in the eyes of the village, I had declared myself defeated, forever, irrevocably, no longer with any rights to life. I sat at a table outside. But my friends, the usual folks, didn't come over, not even the waiter; I heard them whispering but they didn't ask the usual captious questions of the peasant intended to penetrate the truth—*how young your wife is, how old is she? I thought the other one was your wife; and they speak Spanish, how curious that they speak Spanish; and are they musicians?* I couldn't bear that silence solely because they were so amazed at what had happened that they didn't even know where to begin to ask. And I stood up again before the waiter came over, and started my slow ascent, very slowly up the hill to the castle that Diana wanted to buy to give concerts, which they still hadn't begun to illuminate in celebration of the annual tourist season, which in Dors existed only in their ambition and imagination.

There was a gentle breeze, above, on the esplanade that surrounded the castle, and the sky was clear and filled with stars. It was useless to try to think of another place more beautiful than this, this bend of the river there below and this fistful of stone houses, barely glimpsed, at this hour, from here. Nonetheless, everything was real, magnificently real, nothing was magical, nor transcendent; around me the houses, and even the sky, offered themselves as a counterpoint to fear, to the unknown: this little parcel of the still-pure world, was mine, and I was going to know this little parcel well, connect with it in all its aspects. Only behind the walls of the castle—irredeemably locked with a key that doubtlessly lay numbered in some public stockroom in Madrid, where some employee, not one of the most brilliant, was in charge of hundreds or thousands of keys to castles, fortresses, churches in a state of infinite deterioration, waiting, in turn, for the moment to arrive for him to retire, and to be classified among the other ruins there, behind the walls—began the mystery, or at least the unknown, or the magical, a magic that had been quite diminished this evening when Diana, who had always had what she wanted because she had always had lots of money, and because she knew her money tripled or quadrupled its power being in Spain, proposed, prosaically, to buy it. To buy it not to inhabit it; from below it looked at least in part like a ruin; but yes, perhaps, like Tintern Abbey, for only the personally invited to see sunsets from there, and to organize concerts beneath its heralds, its ceremonious doorways, its architraves, its arches, its two-light windows. To transform that castle—the property of myth, and my not-yet-explored primitive soul—into her private property and with her pragmatic and hedonistic mind, preparing to enjoy what that demystified castle would procure for her, and that extension of herself, an almost corporeal and material extension, those who lived in a circle around her, loving her, from Umbi to her twin granddaughters and, it seemed, I myself. Perhaps the presence of these Brits, so healthy, so free—she knew, and she'd say, that her health and balance and realism were due more than anything to the very prosaic fact of having and always having received rent in sterling pounds that might experience slight fluctuations, but that was secure and always had procured her freedom and security. It didn't give any aspect of nobility or metaphysics to her possibility of free will—countering or counterbalancing our existence, that is, I, Lidia, Luisa, as intense and slightly hysterical Spaniards, still persisting in these ancient anguishing tasks of finding ourselves and a meaning to life. Her grandmother had sat upon Darwin's lap. Her mother had an affair with Bertrand Russell. What was left for her to do, then, but to be profoundly ironic about everything related to angst, cosmic or not? Or with mystery, religious or lay, with white or black or red magic, or whatever color it was?

Perhaps as if responding to my thoughts, and while I was sitting on a little hill overlooking the village and the valley at the edge of the esplanade, I saw a stealthy figure appear along the edge, turning the emphatic corner of the castle. It was Bruno. He was walking directly toward me, and in the time that it took him to walk from the walls of the castle to where I was, I had time to wonder if Bruno had been observing my movements on the esplanade, possibly for quite a while, simply for the pleasure of observing them, like an entomologist, who from the movements of the coleopteron can deduce its behavior. Yes, it was possible; it was almost certain, really. And what was he doing here, at this hour, alone, like the owner of the castle without the necessity of having bought it, belonging to him, to the world of beauty and myth and fear, like the high priest of some dark religion, so ancient that it has already lost all its connections with the present, and nobody no longer remembers what it is, and what gods it worships: only the rites remain, void of piety, the priests, like Bruno, emptied of functions, without powers or attributes, wandering around the ruins of the old places of their cult like the castle and the church of Dors. Perhaps, I thought, seeking with a trace of hope still the remains of the ancient gods silenced by time. He said to me as he approached:

"Good evening."

"Good . . ."

"What are you doing around here?"

"I can ask you the same."

Bruno laughed and said:

"And you have more right to do so. In this year you have lived here you have become proprietor and lord of the village. Everyone loves and respects you . . ."

"I don't know how long the respect will last after the arrival of today's theatrical troupe."

"Who are they?"

"My family . . . my wife—ex-wife—my son and daughter-in-law, my grandchildren—horrors!—and some friends . . ."

"Umbi."

"Yes, Umbi. How do you know?"

"He was up here, just a few minutes before you arrived, and was playing the flute. Classical music. Interesting this boy, Umbi."

"I haven't talked much with him. I am really confused today, with this cascade of events . . . I hadn't seen them for eight years and I was just fine . . ."

And he completed my unformulated thought:

"And you don't know what place they're going to take in your life and how it will be affected . . ."

"I don't know."

"And they're coming to stay here, to live?"

"I don't think so. For a vacation, I suppose . . ."

"It would appear as if the vacation in Dòrs will be rather lively, not to say dazzling, from now on, what with the team your family brought, with what Luisa and Lidia bring to the table . . . and with what I can humbly contribute . . ."

His sarcastic tone bothered me. And I said:

"I am sure that what you contribute will be the liveliest—as you say—in these here parts."

"That's possible, though not this year: no, this year we're going to inaugurate the Onassis in a month, more or less, but this year it will only be a typical little restaurant, done tastefully and with a slightly pricier menu than the usual fare around these parts, but more civilized, more European . . . But next year it will be a lively scene because then the discotheque will be up and running, and a bar, of course . . ."

I was tense with fury.

"So why wait a year?"

"This year there are not enough people. You, the eight people who arrived this afternoon, me, Dr. Bes, his wife, Lidia and Luisa, and the count stops there, because the locals won't come."

"And what makes you think that next year, next summer, Dòrs will be a happening tourist center?"

"Once the ball starts rolling, it won't stop: Lidia, Dr. Bes, the English people, me, even you will attract more people, and this will become a colony . . . a very particular colony, quite chichi, chosen, somewhere between elegant and artsy, and this place will soon have an impressive reputation. In four or five years it will be in all the tourist guidebooks to Spain, I assure you, with five-star restaurants, luxury hotels, and all."

The vision Bruno presented me with was terrifying, a dark perspective, but I couldn't deny that it was true. He continued talking: at the beginning the visitors would be a select group, like me, like Luisa and Lidia, like my English family, but little by little it would deteriorate until becoming a place that was more or less popular, with high prices and new hotels. The vision of the New Quarter—bristling with skyscrapers inhabited by Dutch and French people who wouldn't have the faintest idea why they came to Dors, vulgar spenders and spoilers of the streets and the square and the stone arches of La Flor del Ebro with its rickety tables turned into "typical" things—made me shudder with horror. Bruno continued his sermon:

"What you have to do is buy."

I looked at him.

"Buy what?"

"Houses. Houses and plots of land. All you can. In three years the value will have multiplied by one hundred. Don't you realize? If one had a little nest egg . . ."

But I didn't. He continued, enthralled, Mephistopheles trying to promote his projects, trying to involve Faust in infernal schemes.

"The houses on the hill, for example. These houses on the hill you love so much and for which you have fought so fiercely . . ."

"How do you know how much I've fought?"

"Bartolomé told me. That the locals laugh at you. But let them wait, he who laughs last laughs best. Now, while they're laughing, we have to buy them at a low price, for next to nothing, so that later we can laugh even better . . ."

"We . . . ?"

"Well . . . I mean, those of us who understand the artistic merit and character of this village and its value from the aesthetic—and touristic—point of view, this mass of stone houses from the seventeenth century and even older, piled up half in ruins on this hill. We need to buy them. Almost all the locals are ready to sell, and they will sell them for a 'steep price,' thinking that with that price—laughable on the other hand for those of us who know what a masonry house in a medieval village is worth, and especially what it can be worth—they're taking advantage of us . . ."

I looked at the valley, growing dark. Bruno was dreaming awake:

"Then, renovate them. Join partners with someone, with your Salvador, for example, who has feeling and taste for these things, and fix up the houses . . . or even bring more people—people, yes, important, who have pull, who can bring other important or prestigious or famous people, or just simply elegant types—and sell the houses at a lower price to these elegant artsy people, so that the unwary ones who will come later will be sold houses already renovated, but not to the first ones, so that they will feel like they are lords of Dors, discoverers; we will know that they are not the owners but rather that we are the real owners. And people will start talking about Dors; it will be 'in fashion' and the property will go up in value but it doesn't matter because we will own the houses, and people will pay to live in an atmosphere that is so 'unspoiled' by tourism . . . All those snobs who flee spoiled places as if there were, ultimately, any possibility whatsoever that any place or person would not be spoiled . . . thus is life after all . . . And then, meanwhile, we will have gone on buying land on the other side, lots in the New Quarter, or partnering with Bartolomé who is owner, or his wife is owner, of almost all those lots; and there, where it doesn't matter, where the view won't be destroyed, go on building more and more apartment buildings, expanding horizontally, and the Americans and the French and the Dutch will come and buy and buy until all of Dors is covered with foreigners and rich people who won't know really what to do, how to amuse themselves because, let's be clear, here there is no amusement, the village, that's all, no sea, no reservoir, no . . . well, hills, yes, ruins, yes, but that's not enough for those people, and souvenir stores will be put in, the local cuisine will be inviting and we will give a big impetus to the local crafts, and folkloric music and those things, and then, of course, this will be hell for you and me, for us, and we will sell and get rich, and with our pockets filled we will leave here because life will have become intolerable . . ."

"Where will we go?"

"I don't know . . . To hell, I suppose . . ."

And he laughed. He patted me on the back, and left his arm around my shoulders with that lack of inhibition for touching that I've observed so much among the Italians and which is in a certain way repulsive, though only because it reminds us of our own prejudices when we react to a sweaty arm for a second, a bond of flesh that connected me to Bruno, that associated me with him, a thin, dark, hard, muscular arm and a fleshy hand also with a muscular palm, as if in the palm of his hand Bruno had the greatest fleshiness of his whole body concentrated and I felt its heat on my back. He continued:

"We will all go to hell. The whole world, I presume, is going to hell, but going to hell doesn't matter, as long as one knows where and when one is going, and out of one's own free will and harvesting the largest number of possible pleasures . . . The terrible thing is that others control one without one knowing and without having pleasure . . ."

"The largest number of pleasures?"

"Yes. Don't look at me with such fear. I have done everything, absolutely everything in my life, except kill someone . . . and perhaps, some day I will do that . . . I hope for pleasure."

He wanted to shock me. Tempt me. Make me react. But he was not going to dominate me. The heat of his compact body, near mine, surrounded me. He lit a cigarette. I asked him tentatively:

"Isn't hedonism a little out of fashion?"

"It might be. But I belong to that generation for whom seeking pleasure . . . 'la dolce vita' . . . has been important: I belong to 'la dolce vita' generation."

"But you are very young."

"I'm the same age as you."

I asked him, offended, frankly annoyed or vexed:

"How do you know my age?"

"I found it out."

"How?"

"Ah . . ."

That was his answer, and he exhaled a mouthful of smoke after a long suck on the cigarette, which I felt would burn such a strong point of light that he was going to devour the whole cigarette. He was incredibly youthful. Could we be the same age, this elastic black cat, and me? We could be from the same generation; Bruno and I could be from the same stage of life, but it seemed totally impossible, me with all my life done, behind me, and him, without anything behind him, nothing, a period in Cinecittà, a restaurant in Torremolinos, maybe a period when he was a pimp in Rome, or in Venice . . . Yeah, nothing more. He had everything ahead of him and he wanted to do it, and here was Dors and here I was, and he was planning to play games with all of us, he wanted to implicate me in his dangerous and dirty game with that "we," with that "being the same age," in his goddamn game of destruction and prostitution which implicated not only me, but the whole village, and all of civilization.

My mission at the beginning with Luisa had been to save Dors, to bring more and more people, but only chosen by us, who shared our taste and our way of life, colonizing Dors with more or less prominent, more or less famous people with power, so that the village wouldn't continue to be spoiled. We felt that the village had to be saved and civilized in the name of aesthetics but also ethics, which we believed, in some deep way, were one and the same.

Bartolo had returned from military service and had formed a partnership, like his father, with Bruno Fantoni in order to open the discotheque in the square, providing his manual labor as payment for his participation in the business. Together, Bartolomé's son and the black cat strolled along the cobblestoned streets, sat in La Flor del Ebro, could be seen on the bridge looking at the river. When I passed in front of them, they gave me a side glance, distrustfully, intuiting that in some way I knew their secret, their meetings sheltered by the night inside the castle impenetrable to everyone except them, for their clandestine trysts.

The first year after the arrival of the English everything went smoothly, but then the friends of friends started coming to the village, then relatives of the friends of friends and thus an endless chain turned Dors into a center of tourist attraction, with all the consequences that I had wanted to avoid. Since the arrival of Diana, Miles, and his retinue everything changed: the "chosen" people seeking an atmosphere of beautiful stones little by little attracted people who were less peaceful, and those people brought people who were even less tranquil and with tastes less and less similar to ours—instead of rose-colored stucco there appeared the horror of the souvenir stores, the village living a postcard destiny of inhabitants who in time were strangers in their own town, who would be exiled without changing place. Snack bars, hotels, nightclubs, arts and crafts stores, lots of alcohol, marijuana, prostitution, madness, crime, blood spilled. One life kills another, one death revives another. Six years after I arrived, I was the one to blame—the one who had initiated the irrevocable process of corruption.

Part Three

As THE LIGHT FADES—IN MY NARROW INNER COURTYARD it is always dim—everything grows unwelcoming: I observe how each object changes its expression hypocritically, conspiring with the enemy, until when the dark swallows all the light I'm left alone on one side, and all the rest—my cane and my slippers, the armchair I sit in to squint at the dirty hole this courtyard is, my faithful Shetland cardigan, and sometimes Tàpies himself—has passed into the hands of the enemy on the other side, preparing to attack me. This daily wrestling match that exhausts me every day is completely ineffectual; I sweat so as not to give in one millimeter, my muscles tensed and teeth clenched with the final effort before I collapse panting, defeated, and with the whole weight of night upon me. But I know it is useless to fight; fear is something that emerges like the chills in old people, from the depths of their bones, not something that attacks from outside.

Tàpies, however, is not my enemy. We understand each other because he doesn't require intimacy, and rarely caresses, only when he feels like it; I get up from my armchair, pour a little milk in the blue plastic plate, and leave the door of the little kitchen terrace ajar so that he can go in and have milk whenever he wants. When I arrived a little over a year ago, Luisa left me here after swearing that in this apartment she made available to me they would never manage to find me if they decided to come looking for me in Barcelona, something which, according to her, was completely improbable. Nonetheless as soon as Luisa left, I locked both locks on the front door. I put the coleus out on the kitchen terrace—Luisa brought it here to humanize the apartment, I imagine, but I don't like it because indoor plants bring bad luck—and called to Tàpies, who came over. I caressed his back and said to him:

"Tàpies."

He meowed. His yellow eyes looked at me for a second to mark me and then he walked away, climbing along the terraces and cornices until disappearing several stories up, on the roof covered with television antennas, abandoned boxes, broken bikes and foul-smelling ventilators. If Luisa hadn't organized my life so that the concierge in this building was obliged to buy food for me—I never leave the apartment, and since the first time she included a bottle of milk without knowing that I hate milk—I would have never bought it and Tàpies would not have food.

The typical symptom that the hour of fear approaches is my maniacal urgency to repeat the last rituals of the day: Before my wasteful twilight struggle resolves in nocturnal immobility procured by tranquilizers and sleep inducers, I get up from the chair in my study, and in the kitchen I see that Tàpies has entered, has drunk his milk, and has gone away again without even rewarding me with a meow; it's no longer necessary for that door to remain open. But before closing it I go out on the balcony to pour a little water on the coleus choked by pollution and, after this shallow act of compassion, I close the kitchen door with a latch. I begin to pace around the apartment, making certain that the windows that face the street and which I never open are securely shut, turning on the lights, even the most useless one, with the goal of eliminating my fear of the slight transition of the usual penumbra to the darkness of twilight. The last thing to protect myself is to lower the metallic shutter of the kitchen. But even so—even though the inner courtyard is so narrow and is at the back of the house and this is the sixth floor—before the shutter is tightly shut, I bring my eyes close to a crack to scrutinize the courtyard in case those outlaws somehow might have discovered the way in, scrambling onto the roofs of neighboring buildings, walking along the edges like cats—they're bricklayers, and in Dors I'd admire the agility with which they'd clamber onto scaffolds and slide down pipings—from ledge to ledge and from balcony to balcony until finding mine. Upon recognizing it was mine, those brutes would bang their pickaxes, hammers, wood-carving tools, keys, fists, feet, until busting open the shutter, breaking the windows, and entering to destroy me, as they swore upon banishing me from Dors under the rain of stones and bludgeons that dented the car, Luisa stepping on the gas to cross the San Roque bridge, to take me away and hide me from the village.

They say that during the recent night of San Juan fiestas they sacked my stone house—tall, medieval, erected beside the church at the top of the village—and just as with other years, the recruits leaving around that date organized the ritual bonfire next to the castle, this time feeding it rancorously with my books, my papers, my paintings, with the furniture and wood carvings I bought from them when they still laughed at me because I paid a "fortune" for things which they considered useless. Why, then, wouldn't they carry out to its final consequences their revenge against my corrupt and corrupting person? Yes, they will come and drag me out of this apartment that shelters me, and will drag me back to Dors to kill me by stoning in the Plaza de España, while the faces I knew and loved so well, now transfigured by hatred, revenge, rancor observe my lapidation from their glass lookouts which, against my most passionate advice, Eustaquio had installed to affront the façades of the square, intact since the Renaissance.

Luisa visits me, nonetheless, almost every evening, assuring me that they won't come. That I should calm down. Open the windows. Go out. If I returned to Dors, she says, then maybe

173

my life would be in danger. But only maybe: pain over the death of a boy is gradually cured over the course of a year, especially during a year when things have changed so much that the inhabitants of Dors, who thanks to that death "thank God" got rid of so many "strange people" who disturbed them, are now delighted with the "progress" signaled by tourists snooping around the church, and inside the castle recently opened to the public—an interior I still don't know—emptying the brand-new souvenir stores, filling the snack bar, restaurants, discotheques. Yes, they're delighted with the foreigners who from the San Roque bridge take photos of the fortified parapet and through it, the steep hill of streets and masonry houses, crowned by the ruin of the castle of the lords of Calatrava right next to the Gothic tower of the church. They've "discovered" Dors, and have turned it into a postcard cliché. From London Miles writes to me that in the new edition of the "Guide Bleu" they indicate Dors with several stars, even mentioning the landscape of hundreds of stone terraces that gut the craggy mountains all around, where in the spare meters of land they harvest the peasants' know-how to revive age-old olive trees, rows of vineyards, almond and hazelnut trees. Before I arrived in Dors, the village was only a name in the "Guide Bleu."

Yes. They say my books, my paintings, my papers, my studded and patched old doors and windows wrought laboriously over centuries, that the "I" incarnating my house has disappeared. Everything into the fire. It hurts me. I thought that nothing could hurt me any longer, hurt me as much as the loss of those modest objects I meticulously collected around me to find consolation in my intimacy with them after my many failures in other ways. But I am surprised to see that it doesn't destroy me. This solitary man remains standing, knowing that he cannot return to Dors, beaten down by the gnawing old pain of exile. I'll never know the interior of the ruins of the castle, of which I only caught a glimpse in the nights, from the church tower. I will not see again—as I saw from the sun terrace of my tall stone house, according to which way the wind was blowing—that velvety landscape of gray or green olive trees. I will not see it again, for a single moment passing a window without even acknowledging what I have seen. I will not go up to the hills to spend afternoons lying underneath a hazelnut tree, reading or not reading, with the village sheltered in a narrow bend of the river and the whole valley at my feet, giving form to that . . . that what? Contentment? Happiness? What were those six years in Dors? Postponement of the punishment I deserved after publishing my diatribe against the commercialization of the galleries and the stale, static informalists? Or were they simply the renewed possibility of feeling pleasure, such as that first vision of Lidia as medieval pilgrim walking barefoot along the San Roque bridge, the breeze tracing in her long patchwork dress that body I got to know so well? My son Miles, with his tanned torso and golden Viking beard, sitting in a meadow of poppies, alone in the sun, playing Mozart on his vertical flute, outside of time, able to do without everything, except Mozart and the sun? Or the classical aroma of thyme and of rosemary in my hikes in the hills with Bruno, during which I asked myself why Bruno, who wasn't much younger, had access to the exclusive rites of youth that were closed off to me. What did this man have, thin and cruel like a black cat, but also with that silky voice and manner that attracted them? Or were those years simply the security provided by those sturdy golden stone houses, perhaps not particularly beautiful, but with a quality that marks me and causes me pains, like the sturdiness in the village of men's faces and women's fertile hips?

Now I've locked myself up in this apartment because I refuse to see anything that is not the hills of Dors. It's curious because never before Dors was I vulnerable to landscape, so much so that my memory discarded all those I had known and now I cannot comfort myself with the reconstitution in memory of previous landscapes. When I was little they'd take me to Blanes to bathe in the sea but instead of beach and horizon and pine trees, which I imagine would have existed, I remember instead the inside of the house, the wallpaper of dark modernist digits on a purple background, a place I later had no problems disliking, because of the noise, dirt, vulgarity of the coast. I could rescue, perhaps, the park at La Garriga where I played with Luisa and my other cousins during almost every summer of my adolescence, but with its broken statues, its urns with agave plants on the balustrades, its wicker armchairs under the chestnut trees, it wasn't landscape but rather an extension of the drawing rooms of my great-grandmother's house. I have been, and I was until Dors, an urban being, a pavement weed as it were, a café, newspaper, movies, bookstore intellectual, and the silence I'd associate with the notion of "landscape" before Dors produced in me a malaise. I actually couldn't sleep without the hum of cars and buses below in the street. No exterior ever left traces in my paintings. During the years I dedicated to the challenge of painting, I burned all my vitality on the efforts of the imagination, of discipline, of calculation, of emotion, eliminating from my canvases any suggestion of an object or a landscape. It was a kind of painting that could be done without ever leaving this apartment or knowing anything else beyond the detested comforts provided by Luisa.

Luisa wants me to return to painting. But I refuse. Maybe it's because of this hope Luisa tries to insert into my life when I have accepted that I am nothing but a crumbling ruin, that I feel a certain repulsion toward her visits. It's not rejection. If I would lock the door she would understand as she has always understood everything. Only this she doesn't understand, my denial of hope. She doesn't understand it because Luisa has lost her flexibility and can no longer be different than what she now is, let's face it, an old woman. I try not to touch the objects in this apartment she prepared for me—knowing, as she knows, all my tastes and manias—as it would now repel me to touch her mutilated body, which, before, I would touch with love, tenderness, passion, thirst, friendship, compassion, affection, curiosity in a thousand ways in a thousand different stages of our lives, but which now I refuse to desecrate by touching it with repulsion. In Dors, walking around her bedroom naked, hiding with a towel hanging from her shoulder the scar of her extracted breast—a scar I kissed a thousand times to assure her that it didn't disgust me, and this was true—she'd stop abruptly in front of the mirror and say:

"Look."

"What?"

"Am I so despicable?"

I looked at her, thinking for the first time, with a frozen cramp of recognition: you are no longer made for love. You have withered. The disease that didn't kill you, killed your flesh, and I don't want to touch you again. Of course if one takes in account her almost fifty years, Luisa is still a fine woman. Even in Dors itself I have seen my son Miles go nuts over her when, tall, dark, cheeky, she danced slowly in the dark against him, a little high, laughing, in her Dior miniskirt sassily showing off her fabulous legs under see-through black stockings, and wearing a branch of bay leaves behind her ear like a gypsy. But Miles did not realize that the penumbra, the dress, the black stockings were not mere attributes but necessities of her seduction. Naked before me, standing in the crude spotlight under which, so as not to ruin the effect, she wore makeup, her flesh seemed to me slightly but horribly withered, her aged skin, her admirably thin arms without firmness, wrinkled at her elbows so that they no longer served to be bitten, the same with her knees now hidden under very fine stockings or by a suntan. Sad. The farewell to our mutual flesh. Impossible to touch each other again because it would mean deceiving with a consolation, not imposing standards as with everything, because if subjectively we remained worthy of love as objects—and this was important—we didn't continue to be so: I aspired shamefully to push my stomach in, and Luisa, here was Luisa, naked, crying. To distract her I asked:

"Did you remember to take the Pap test this year?"

"Yes, a while ago. I'm fine."

"How many to go?"

"One. They're five altogether. Pass me that stocking."

And she dressed quickly, as if ashamed. She was never going to acknowledge that her flesh was defeated. She, who swore never to throw in the towel and who was the champion of looking at everything with detachment, now didn't have the fortitude to look at herself. In devaluing this magnificent, almost fifty-year-old woman I felt a horrendous sensation, a pleasure in my cruelty refusing to be Luisa's partner because it was now humiliating, as if willfully relegating myself to the territory untouched by the young and desirable, what one who has lived knows belongs to a type of experience that is neither moving nor exciting, as when people don't even look at me when passing me on the street. Luisa doesn't feel my need for youth, this thirst to invade their exclusive freedom, to penetrate and possess what is no longer within reach except through the fantasy of love. How not to feel the excitement of being young in Dors, if during the last two summers an ever-growing colony of youths gathered to make music with Miles and Bill, and later, when the news spread that that paradise no longer existed, Dors filled with young people who gathered there to participate in the rituals that excluded me? How they walked . . . how they dressed . . . how they danced . . . the way they talked and what they said, disconnected, incomprehensible allusions to beings and values so distant from our world . . . their indifference, their freedom . . . the incredible varieties of nongenital sex they surrendered to and which they proclaimed, yes, pleasure for pleasure's sake that excluded us older people, who understood those practices because we had read Marcuse, for example, but we had not transcended our "liberated" sexualities in the clichéd sense of the word.

Rituals. Were there rituals, properly speaking, in Dors? They talked a lot about Jung, mandalas, the lingam, his and hers, sex with religious impersonal transcendence, ideas that would lead almost inevitably to orgiastic rites. If there were such rites, naturally they did not include me. At night, from the church tower, posted in the highest two-light window I would often contemplate the interior of the Calatrava castle, overgrown and in ruins like a painting by Claude Lorrain. The doors were walled over with bricks and the windows were too high to scale. But as powerful as my obsession to discover and finally participate in those rites was—an obsession that led me frequently to scramble up to the bell tower to spy—I couldn't do it every night, and it was probably on one of those nights when they celebrated my exclusion and their triumph with their rites. Around the village rumors began to spread: One girl was not in bed in her parents' house precisely the night I went up to the tower, and her father gave her a beating when she arrived at dawn. One boy hooked up with an English girl and vanished. His parents went everywhere with keys and bludgeons in their hands the last summer. The mothers in mourning saying novenas, praying for God's protection. Until they found Bartolo dead inside the castle, the castle whose key was finally sent by the Administration of National Monuments in Madrid, and which they still refused to give Luisa and me access to, with all our influence.

And if Luisa were right and I should start painting again? Though it might only be to avoid feeling totally economically dependent. But that's a problem I still don't have the strength to face. She says I should go out on the street, to take walks. That Barcelona is lively, prosperous, beautiful. But, what happens if I'm recognized? Not only by my current enemies but by those from before who want me to paint again so that they can leap at me like wolves to demolish my exhibit, in revenge. Now that certain hints of landscape would inevitably appear in my work, they'll say "romantic," "old hat?" and they'll fixate on the fact that I can't tear myself away from Dors, with the goal of destroying me. If I don't paint—and as much as Luisa insists, I don't intend to—I will continue to be comfortably forgotten. Besides, those enemies with whom I could meet up in a bar or on the street and who could recognize and remember me no longer matter. They are to be feared, but the new enemies are worse, those who at this hour are beginning to produce noises in the courtyard below. I go over to the metallic shutter in the kitchen. I make sure it's tightly shut. I return to my armchair to sink once again, as if into an abyss, into the depths of my obsessions, but I hear another sound outside as if there were people in the courtyard and then I can't stand the tension any longer: I go over to the shutter and open it just a bit. I look. Shadows of legs: it's them. They're coming to take revenge for the death of Bartolo. I grab my cane to defend myself from that army of peasants dressed in black corduroy suits. I go over to the shelf, fill a glass of water, and take my first Valium 10. I walk around the apartment a bit for the tranquilizer to take effect; meanwhile the courtyard is populated with the hanging legs of men who have come from Dors to murder me. I go over to the kitchen shutters again and look, firmly grabbing the cane to defend myself: the shadows of the legs move as if they were marching in a row along the peeling wall. A window opens and sheds light on the courtyard: someone is gathering those pants that had been hung on the line to dry. The pants are empty: there are no legs to fear. The Valium is taking effect. I'll prepare an egg. I don't feel like anything else. Tonight I don't want coffee. Instead, before going to sleep, I will take a sleeping pill to shield myself in darkness until morning, although everything will begin the same again, again ending in this same fear.

Part Four

WHEN THE DOORMAN PHONED ME TO ASK IF HE COULD let Miguel come up I should have said no. A good kid, he was used to his strange father, and never ceases to show me an affection I don't deserve, especially since he knows that I don't have much love for him, he, the second born who was born when he shouldn't have been born; from the beginning he lacked the qualities I fell in love with in his mother, he was always the ugly one, the shy one, the diligent one. His visits fill me with guilt, especially because abjectly, as if conscious that they cannot be a source of joy, he never forgets to bring, like a safe-conduct, a gift: a fresh pineapple, a cheese, a magazine he knows is too expensive for my pocket, a publicity pen from the engineering firm where he works. However his visits bring me a modicum of pleasure: he remains awhile with me placing his presence between me and nightfall, and later, when we run out of things to talk about, which happens very soon, he leaves. But on this occasion I was already forewarned that something unpleasant was going to happen because Miguel had called to tell me:

"I want to talk to you this afternoon; I have something pretty interesting to propose to you."

The idea that someone at this point had "something interesting" to propose to me seemed at first laughable and, after hanging up the receiver, I was frankly disturbed that Miguel was the bearer of this proposition. It's true that outside of Luisa he's the only person who "worries" about me. But perhaps he worries too much; the solicitude of his somewhat dull sensibility only reiterates to me that I'm no good at anything, something I already know but that I hate to see underscored. Luisa claims that it isn't that I don't love Miguel, but that I'm afraid of him. Whatever it is, I realize that my feelings toward him are unfair. When he was old enough to choose between his father and his mother, and despite knowing that he was taking a risk, he chose to leave London in the heyday of Carnaby Street and the Beatles, and to rebel against the luxury of Diana's house to turn to a father he barely knew but who he knew was a failure, and with whom, after a couple of weeks, it was very clear that he would never get along. Luisa said that with his short hair and white shirts he looked like the only son of a mother who was a widow. I remember how I used to laugh at him with Luisa, who asked him one day:

"And does your mother have lovers?"

Miguel blushed, looking at his textbooks:

"No . . . I don't think so . . ."

"Then she must like women."

"That's a lie!"

Luisa sighed, revealing that she was fed up with his prejudices.

"How could such a good-looking woman not have a lover?"

Triumphantly Miguel raised his head from his books on differential calculus from which he believed he got the right answer, burning and vengeful:

"She's too old."

"What do you mean she's too old? She's the same age I am and I'm your father's lover."

Miguel, blushing, defeated, left the room where Luisa and I remained, laughing. We knew perfectly well Diana didn't have lovers. Once when Luisa asked her in front of me, Diana answered her:

"Look, Luisa, at the age of forty-three I no longer have any interest left in licking some guy from head to toe. I've done it too often. I now leave that to the girlfriends who go to bed with my sons."

And without taking note of the slight blush of defeat in Luisa's cheeks, she asked with her usual vehemence:

"But do you realize the things that son of a bitch Johnson is doing in Vietnam?"

From the clutter of newspapers in every language covering the silk rococo chaise longue from which she rose only on extreme occasions, she picked out *Le Monde* and passed it to Luisa, pointing to a paragraph with her finger loaded with rings. Luisa didn't care a fig about Johnson and Vietnam, though she acted indignant to please her interlocutor, since (from what I can tell) Diana is the only woman Luisa respects and even fears. Diana—who had gotten a bit fat and soft with the same years that had regaled Luisa with firmness, activity, and chic—nevertheless preserved the radiance of her dirty-blond tresses gathered with a shell-shaped comb in an enormously unruly tuft at the back of her neck. If Luisa is only capable of having a private interior vision, Diana's vision, instead, is ample, directed solely toward things and events on the outside, to the point of exhaustion. She was used to discussing until five in the morning with the friends gathered around her divan, writing letters to the *Times,* phoning her female relatives married to members of Parliament, to peers married to her cousins. She'd send her two terrified sons, then children, to demonstrate with peace posters in Trafalgar Square, ordering them to call her from the nearest telephone if there were street riots and discreetly to offer her house in Bloomsbury—immense, luxurious, untidy—to shelter anyone who needed to hide from those pigs, the English police. Relations with his mother became intolerable for Miguel when he reached the age of wanting to be an individual. The lack of an organized education, the total disorder or absence of meals, the inexhaustible money that was running out and later, suddenly, would increase because certain investments that had not been moving were beginning to reproduce in an obscene manner, the unbearable music and musicians all over the place, the constant invasion by Diana's protégés in Miguel's modest private quarters—all this determined his wish to move to Barcelona where, as I understood, he could study for his engineering career in peace as Spain was an orderly country where strikes were not widespread. Besides, he confided to me upon arrival, he really wanted to live alone but he lived for a time with me, however, not in an apartment which his mother, from her telephone misplaced among the newspapers on the divan, could call at all hours, asking him to sign protest letters or to use the tickets for the Oistrakh concert which nobody else could take, or if the first narcissus of the season—with which she was filling her apartment, bought from the most expensive florist in London—had not brought joy to his heart. No, Miguel wasn't inclined to see himself deprived of a private life, nor jeered at for his faith in the exact sciences, nor for his incapacity to distinguish between Telemann and Buxtehude, nor for his lack of vocation for political causes. In Barcelona he had a private life. So private that not even I knew when he married an inconsequential university classmate whom I hadn't seen more than four or five times in my life and who showed no interest whatsoever in seeing me more frequently than I her. When Diana learned about the marriage she phoned me from London to ask me what Nury, the bride, was like:

"Is she beautiful? Dark and beautiful and Spanish, like Luisa?"

Her interrogation began with that familiar and cruel requirement of beauty. My negative response cut short the questions: Diana immediately seemed depressed, and nothing I could say brought back her curiosity. I also no longer ask Miguel anything. I only know that they don't plan to have children until Nury finishes her engineering degree, but I don't know when that will be. I tell Miguel:

"You're going to get too old."

"You're too afraid of old age."

"What do you expect . . . with my fifty years?"

He then asserts heatedly that a fifty-year-old man is not an old man who is all washed up, look at his uncle Bertie Russell for example, who must be close to a thousand years old. These are things I know very well. But when Miguel assures me of them I am painfully bitten by the certainty that indeed I am all washed up.

That Miguel's surreptitious arrival with Luisa signified the existence of a conspiracy put me in such a state of agitation that as soon as they presented the purpose of their visit I tried to send them away with mockery and violence. Huelva? Me, paint a mural in the Huelva airport? Were they crazy? Did they perhaps not know that I was never going to paint again, that I had cut off my own hands and when hands are cut off they don't grow back again like the tail of an ophidian? What was the point of returning to the subject? Proposing this to me was aggravating. It meant that not only did they not care how I felt, but they didn't respect the pain and clarity with which my already old decision had been made. Didn't Luisa remember? Wasn't she the principal instigator of my attitude in that era? It was true that Luisa, after I left Dors, had suggested at some point that I should take up the brushes again, but a mere word loaded with sinister memories was enough to silence her. Now the two of them, Miguel and Luisa, oil and water, were tightly linked in a common plan. Why this insistence on cornering me in this way? Did they perhaps not know what kind of artists paint murals in airports, that official mafia that distributes shares of the pie without taking into consideration aesthetic rigor? Besides, I was no longer interested in painting. I didn't even know what the young people were doing. And why Huelva? Wasn't it an unimportant airport, a kind of consolation prize, this mural they were offering me? Luisa replied, passing me a Valium and a glass of water:

"Yes, Huelva is small."

"You have to begin somewhere, Dad."

"I'm not beginning anywhere, Miguel."

"But why?"

"Ask Luisa, she's your ally and she knows."

Luisa didn't want to talk. Obviously she had already talked it over with Miguel who, with his lumbering sensibility, insisted and insisted and insisted. Why did I refuse to paint, which was the only thing I knew how to do, and sit here rotting in this apartment, living off Diana's, Luisa's, his charity? And since I refused to paint "seriously," why not take advantage of this commission which Luisa, with her friends in what Manolo called "the upper echelons," had scored for him? Didn't I realize that this didn't mean only Huelva, which really was a small place, but rather it was a way into a group of painters who shared the profits earned from official murals? My attitude seemed negative from all points of view. After all, what happened seven years ago, well, the truth is nobody remembered. It no longer mattered at all. I listened to Miguel's aggression with my eyes and teeth clenched as if I had to accept being boxed into a corner of the ring. Until I managed to say:

"Luisa."

She realized I was calling upon her to help me and she brought the coffee and served three cups. Then, regretting having served me, she drank mine in one gulp and sat down to sip hers. She crossed her legs and began talking. She had wanted to tell me before, she warned me, but her situation was getting desperate: she might even have to sell this apartment.

"Why?"

"I haven't heard from Lidia in three months."

"You've been lying to me, then."

"I didn't want you to worry, unnecessarily. Not even a letter. Nor a postcard. As if the megalopolis of Los Angeles had swallowed her up, her and her lover."

"The guy who was dedicated to making sandals?"

"No, another one. I have to go the United States to look for my daughter, I don't know for how long . . . and private detectives are very expensive there. We could be dealing with the worst possible scenario . . ."

"You know that Lidia doesn't do drugs."

"No, but . . ."

"But what?"

Luisa served herself more coffee before being able to answer:

"Lidia is almost thirty now."

Luisa, for the first time acknowledging the pain of being fifty, placed the onus on her daughter, who from time immemorial had been approaching the experience of her own aging. It was so incredible that so much time had passed since the pilgrim on San Roque bridge had been transformed from a static image of medieval art through the simple artifice of wearing big modern sunglasses, a garment of patches, her haversack bag, her straight hair, her slim body, her bare feet, into a living modern being who crossed the bridge, entered the parapet gate and sat at a table under the arches of La Flor del Ebro in the square, to drink something refreshing and await her confrontation with me at twenty-two years of age, as she had already faced me at the age of fourteen.

I said to Luisa:

"It can't be."

"Anyway, she'll be twenty-nine, which is the same thing."

I crossed over toward Luisa's chair. I made her lean her head against my side and I empathized with her, thinking of this anonymous Luisa mixed in with thousands of identical beings, moving along the turbulent streets of Los Angeles in her thirties, forties, fifties, in the impersonal solitude of apartments like this one, disappointed by new friendships that are not enough, rejected by a land where one cannot sink roots, her initial nonchalance turned into caution, then economy, then into a fear she cannot resist because I know that with the years one forgets the ways to resist vulnerability and that's when one crumbles and can no longer paint. All I wanted was for Luisa, for just one moment, to stop thinking about the same thing I was thinking and I said to her:

"Luisa."

"What?"

"What did you do to convince them?"

"What do you care if you're not going to paint the mural?"

"Who knows."

Perking up again she looked at me with dry eyes and looked at Miguel who was heading into the other room where he had taken refuge so as not to witness the scene. It didn't cost anything to lie for a while, perhaps for a few days.

"You know that I've been friends for a long time with the general manager of Iberia. Despite the slightly louche reputation I have in his world, he still sees me as the wife of the owner of Banco Tenreiro, and he's a bit servile. He was then an ordinary employee who would let his cigarette burn his yellowish fingers while he'd look at me in fascination when I'd enter my husband's sanctum sanctorum without asking permission. Imagine how easy it was to convince him."

"That's not what I want to know."

"What, then?"

"What credentials of mine did you present?"

"Your name, Antonio Muñoz-Roa."

"I don't have a name."

"But Lisandro Pastor does what I ask him to do."

"Yes, but his advisors?"

"What do they know about art?"

"It's not about that."

"What then?"

"How did the committee decide?"

A few very long seconds passed in which Miguel, who was staring at Luisa, was getting more and more nervous. But it didn't matter because Luisa was no longer thinking about Lidia; later she could betray the hope I gave her but I rescued her for the moment, and that was enough. Miguel couldn't resist any longer.

"Tell him, Luisa."

"Don't get involved in this. You don't know your father."

"Tell me, Luisa. If I accept I am going to have to know it."

The three of us continued to say nothing until finally Luisa began very slowly to tell the truth I had been fearing:

"I showed them your paintings. Not only the two I own but I went through a list we made with René Metrás of the people who had bought your paintings in your good times and I went to see all of them. And I asked them to lend me the six best ones. They, of course, with the hope of a revival of Antonio Muñoz-Roa that will make the prices go up, didn't hesitate. And I showed them to the dignitaries . . ."

"Which ones?"

"You don't know the dignitaries nowadays."

"No. Paintings."

"Ah, well, in the first place that immense blue one, in which it seems there were hues of the same color until you begin to discover other colors as if disguised by the blue . . . and that other big one that is like a marvelously well-organized spider-web of graphs made in fresh paint with a spatula . . . and then that smaller one, remember, a bit Vasarely, half-red and half-green, with green openings in the red and red openings in the green . . ."

Miguel and Luisa faded away. I covered my ears, refusing to hear anything further, never again, to lock myself away forever, to close my eyes so as never to see anything again, burst them asunder, tear them out, seal them . . . for the admiration for A.M.R. in the newspapers and two weeks later, the insults to A.A., the band of bearded young men jeering at A.M.R. coming out of an art film theater and the stone that brushed Luisa, who was with me . . . The familiar voices of the Dau al Set crowd gossiping in the cafés, on the telephones, in the galleries, under the trees of a corner building . . . All of them gossiping because they preferred to act through their agents and all they do is gossip to wash their hands of the matter in the eyes of "their" public, chattering as this man and woman now chatter while I cover my ears, and the shouted insults— I haven't authorized them to revive anything, they don't have the right to invade me in this way, I didn't ask anything of them, I don't care if I die of hunger on a corner or am put in an insane asylum just as long as they withdraw their obscene unauthorized expectations. *Go. You have to go, leave me alone, open the door,* and I keep on insulting and not opening my eyes or listening to their entreaties. I drop my hands that were covering my ears, and look at them. Now the others will come, the Dors gang: open the kitchen door so they'll come in to take hold of me, tie my hands, put me in a bag to take me back to Dors, where they'll make me a martyr in public amidst the howls of satisfaction of the whole village. What a relief to feel the hard rope knotted around my wrists, preventing me from moving my hands! Why didn't I suddenly move them five centimeters, enough so that Bartolomé could have cut them off with his saw, and then the miracle would have worked? A tractor had just climbed the steep slopes of those narrow streets, occluded by the first mist, to my house bringing me a load of firewood. Under the stone arches of my wine cellar an aromatic hill of logs that were too long, that didn't serve to combat the cold of Dors because they didn't fit in my stoves. I called for Bartolo who at that time still had such naïve ambitions that he would fulfill with his new electric bought with his savings. *Yes,* he said: *cut the wood in half.* A couple of hours and hundreds of pesetas, but it was work for two men and he needed me to help him. We took off our vests and set to work in the freezing cold dungeon. The furious sound of the saw immediately stopped any possible communication, at least by any means I knew. But holding down the logs on the sawhorse for Bartolo to cut them, I felt, upon seeing his beautiful profile through the smoke and the flying sawdust, that he was a powerful being suggesting that I connect with him in some way, if I dared to take to its ultimate consequences the dialogue established by the firewood I offered him again and again, and which he returned again and again to saw with his irresistible burning saw. Through the smoke I scrutinized his eyes to verify that he was sensing me the same as I was sensing him. Bartolo wasn't totally concentrated on his work: I sensed his fear that in his distracted state he'd hurt my hands, five centimeters away from the powerful blade of his saw. But immediately I realized that his margin of inattention was interior, insignificant, sufficient only to reject my person. However, the precise details of flesh that shaped his features and body, as if detained in the precise perfection of his prime, suggested something to me. To me, now—or to all men and women, always? The thunder of the saw reverberated in the ancient stone vault, I sweating, Bartolo sweating. We took off our sweaters and I continued substituting log after log on the sawhorse, Bartolo's damp shirt sticking to his chest. He knew the danger of his saw so close to my hands, but didn't warn me, not even with a glance. And how was I going to stop looking at him, if in his negligence I picked up the certainty that those two figures who from the church tower I saw sheltered one night inside the impenetrable castle were Bruno and Bartolo, who knew the secret of how to enter the castle, and that Bartolo belonged to Bruno as he belonged to Lidia, and the cluster of those three excluded me? No propositions coming from Bartolo, whose inattention was the space they occupied inside him. The sawdust flew. Sparks leapt from the saw. The vault was heating up with the friction of the blade against the logs he kept sawing clean and effortlessly, five centimeters, now three centimeters from my hand. Bartolo took off his soaking shirt. To show me the fine assemblage of his body, more powerful and different from that of a man or a woman for being so young and so perfect? Wasn't this a snare to indicate to me, mature and sedentary, that I had no right to touch him? But . . . if I moved my hands abruptly—five, three centimeters—and he cut them off? Wasn't that the necessary final consequence of the dialogue of my logs and his saw? Wouldn't this erase with the sacrifice of my hands all the other relationships of Bartolo and upon becoming his victim I would steal from them the principal role, becoming one with him, and remaining like an eternal weight on his back? Three centimeters. I felt the heat of the blade, the poison of the certainty that my blood would separate him from the rest. The arch of his torso that bent over the rearing weight of the dominated machine that kept cutting so cleanly. The shine in his eyes and the freshness of his skin and the explosion of his laugh denied me like a rejection. Three centimeters with the next log and the next, and two, perhaps, with the next: that distance separating my hands from danger was the abyss in which I would fall if I didn't employ a lucidity that was getting more and more difficult to seize with each log I replaced. The motor of the saw faded a bit. Bartolo said:

"It's running out of gasoline. I'm going to put more in."

"That's enough for now. We've already worked plenty."

"Are you tired, Don Antonio?"

I reacted only internally to the inflicted wound:

"No. But I'm thirsty and they brought me a fabulous bottle of wine. Let's try it."

I still have my hands: I'm looking at them, useless as they are, with the palms facing up, one on either knee. And Bartolo is dead: an arch of the castle crashed to pieces on top of his naked body with a thundering noise one night, and the whole village was awakened by what was supposed to have been happening inside the walled-up castle, blaming me for everything, I who had been excluded. How long is the lifeline on my palms! Between my legs, my cane falls lifelessly onto the rug. Is there not an asylum for failed painters? A space where in the misery of anonymous oblivion, hungry, frozen stiff, covered with filthy rags, I can compete with those who remain of my profession and class to see whose fantasies are the cruelest, whose envy the most omnipotent? I would be happy to take refuge in such a hospice. Diana, Miguel, Luisa are the ones who insist upon "maintaining me": this apartment, a little food, a lady who comes to do the cleaning . . . all superfluous. But they insist and here I am. Luisa knows that if she is forced to sell this apartment there won't be any problem because Diana will immediately rent another for me, since she's ready to maintain me until the end of my days without my doing anything to justify myself: she avows that existence is gratis and doesn't require

194

justification . . . just as, according to her, it is not justifiable that she enjoys the millions inherited from a grandfather she never knew: "These are not times for charity . . . ," the grandfather would have responded to his friends in the club who suggested to him that in England there perhaps existed other heiresses less ugly than his fiancée, but he, with that carefree assertion, took over mines and farmlands and blocks of houses in London and tenements in Manchester and obscure businesses managed by his lawyers, all of which she, Diana, availed herself of now. Why shouldn't I do the same, since she already had more than enough? Why shouldn't we enjoy her millions, I and all the people who touched her life? The problem, which is ultimately Luisa's and Miguel's—it pains me that he and Luisa share it—is my dignity: idleness mines the integrity of the human being; all the psychiatrists agree that not doing anything is dangerous; work lifts the spirits. Getting in touch with my former work will resurrect the competitive and arrogant man I was . . . In short, that whole stream of inadmissible clichés I allow them to repeat so that they have compassion for me, as I cannot feel it for myself. Why can't Luisa accept that I am different, infinitely more vulnerable than she is? Why make a big deal out of dignity, if the problem—if there is one—is so much darker? Why doesn't she accept that if it is impossible to defeat her, I, on the other hand, was really defeated by Dors?

The worst of all is that I'm sure that the next time she comes to visit me she'll bring brushes and paint, and behind my back she'll hide it all in some drawer so that suddenly, days later, upon opening that drawer, I will find those things casually hidden there. She refuses to recognize that inspiration is extinguishable and that I ran out of it. The curious part is that Luisa didn't admire my "genius," not by a long shot, since deep down she's a philistine who ends up appreciating everything in terms of value, of "good taste," and as a decorator she only sees a painting in its relationship to the rest of the room it's in, never the painting itself in its essence, its vocabulary, contained in the empire of its own laws. However, she was the one who organized my first show at René Metrás's, and who, already separated from Lidia's father and also from Tenreiro, introduced me to Cuixart, to Tàpies, and Tharrats. She was the one who urged me to join them, to aspire to the excitement happening in Barcelona, crazed with the certainty that informalist painting was big and the now thing. Whether figurative, concrete, or informalist, it was all the same to Luisa: what mattered—and this matters—is what's considered important. And at that time informalism was important. I had returned from London six months earlier, leaving my two sons and wife there to move into an apartment on Gracia where, because I couldn't think of anything else to do, I had started painting. Although in London and in Paris I frequented the exhibitions and galleries, my old temptation for the plastic arts had never taken the form of an activity, as I had never thought of buying a painting since doing it was to recognize that my only possible relationship with painting was the defeat demonstrated by the thirst to possess. And in Diana's house, where everything seemed to be produced by spontaneous combustion, from those delicious English breakfasts to passionate conversations and the car at the door to attend Nicholson's vernissage, all thirst for possession was superfluous, as was all activity. In the somewhat uncertain solitude of my apartment in this Barcelona from which after so many years I was completely disconnected, nevertheless, I began to draw, reluctantly at first, and then to paint, watercolors, gouache, oil, many oils, very big, very enthusiastically until after six months I was no longer leaving my apartment, discarding all possible contacts which I hadn't accepted in this different, noisy, hypertense Barcelona which neither recognized nor accepted me. There was a moment when I was vulnerable to this rejection and I decided to accept it, accepting defeat in my slightly tardy attempt to find my own being, in order to return to London and be welcomed by the charming alternative of Diana's house, and to spend the rest of my life playing happily with that golden ball of yarn that was my son Miles. Now I no longer needed contacts or reasons to remain; I could give myself the immoral luxury of not asking myself questions. And one day when I was coming out of a Mantequería Leonesa grocery store with my nostalgic packet of Twinings Orange Pekoe Tea, I met Luisa. We sat down to have a drink in an outdoor café on Diagonal. How beautiful she was! Taller—if that were possible—and more erect and slim, with all her brunette effervescence; in the ten years I hadn't seen her she seemed to have become consumed in her own slow fire becoming a daring stylization of her essential self, the kind of woman I was not attracted to. But I wasn't attracted to Diana either, with her peach skin complexion and her pre-Raphaelite head; like poor Swann I was always destined to fall in love with women I didn't like. It was easy to talk to Luisa. The subjects we shared came to us ripe like summer fruit: the people, the legion of scattered cousins after La Garriga, my Diana and her Manuel and her Tenreiro and our failures, and how difficult life was, now. Nevertheless, as both of us wanted to touch down somewhere on earth we would return again and again to our adolescence in La Garriga, circumnavigating, of course— more than anything because of a shared consciousness, as we admitted later, that this moment had been premature—the fact that we had been lovers from ages sixteen to twenty. Now was the moment to say other things, that Manuel ultimately was not a good horseman and that he hadn't even excelled in that, internationally, that Lidia was beautiful, that Miles was handsome, that we don't cut off the tail of the lizard to then keep it in a box, feeding it to see if the tail could really grow again. In the outdoor café on Diagonal, that new "first day" I maintained the opposite thesis: we wouldn't cut off the tails of lizards but rather would frighten them, to see if these little animals, when scared, really did let shed their tails, which stayed behind, dancing. She told me about the end of her marriage with Manuel, a story I knew because Manuel was from our family and the tentacles of family news, like an exceptionally lively ivy, have the capacity to cross seas and years over and over again, to come back to life in a city in the antipodes, in the encounter with a friend or a cousin, bringing one up-to-date.

And I covered my ears because I didn't want to hear more, ever again, and I closed my eyes because I didn't want to see them and didn't want them to speak to me anymore because I didn't want to hear them—they should go, I hadn't authorized them, how come they thought they had the right, that even if I were dying of hunger they should go, they should go . . . and I didn't open my eyes until they left, until I heard the door close, their voices behind the door waiting for the elevator, the sound of the elevator going down, the car starting up six floors below . . . and only then did I uncover my ears that had heard everything, and opened my eyes that had seen everything, my paintings, again, the red and green windows vibrating, so penetrating because they weren't windows, and the spiderweb that had captured the enormous blue fly from the sky . . .

They'll have to maintain me. They'll have to manage. The problem, anyway, is not serious, since Diana with her customary unconsciousness is ready to continue maintaining me to the end of my days without me doing anything to justify my existence. Because according to her human existence, life, is not explainable or justifiable, just as it is not explainable or justifiable that she has the millions inherited from a grandfather she never knew and doesn't care about. The problem for Luisa and for Miguel—it pains me that it is so for Luisa—is my dignity: "Putting him in touch with his former vocation will bring back the competitive and arrogant man he once was." A series of inadmissible clichés coming from Luisa who knows that everything is impossible, and who refuses to admit that I am different, that yes, it is possible to defeat me, as Dors defeated me, because I am a different person than she is, and because, besides, I believe that a man's greatest strength is to see himself naked, knowing and admitting defeat, while women always keep the aspidistra flying, keep reinventing themselves in other vocations and other possibilities of existence which I don't believe in. Maybe this is why women believe in God more than men do.

Only after Luisa left did I think of La Garriga. Twelve cousins and second cousins are a lot, it is true, but if they carry out the urban development they're planning—my grandmother's park converted into small houses with walls as flimsy as these, with little gardens copied pointlessly from the gardens in the Doris Day movies—it will be a thriving business, producing lots of money, or at least sufficient money so that I don't have to depend on anyone, with my modest need not to live but merely to survive. But Sergio de Noyà, the cousin who's dealing with the matters of the inheritance, says that we should wait, that not yet, that in one, or two or three years, the land will have acquired so much value, that we will all be rich. The fact is they all are rich. Not Luisa and I. That is, Luisa is and she'll be richer if she waits, as they all want to wait, since the family will probably put her in charge of the interior decoration, since that's the profession which life has led her to specialize in, and then, with Luisa at the helm, the development won't be as horrendous as all the other suburban developments in Spain. I have to wait, then, two, three years, and Luisa is begging me not to sell my part, as some cousin has tried to buy it from me, because this is an investment that will grow and the cousin knows it and hence like a bird of prey around a corpse, knowing about my failures and my poverty, she haunts me, she hangs around me, to stick her beak in when she can.

But even the problem of La Garriga causes me anguish, though only because I will have to go out, sign things, and talk to people. No, I am not afraid that those guys from Dors will come to kill me. They won't take the trouble because they know I'm a condemned man, and that little by little I will rot away cruelly in life in another way, and I will end my days more painfully than what they, with their short imaginations, would be able to provide me as death. I am afraid of the others, those in whom Luisa has awakened, in the depths of their minds, the memory of my paintings and my being, gone to awaken a dead man in their minds and who knows if they'll recognize me on the street and come over, and tell me how much they admire me, that why didn't I continue painting, that of all the first-generation informalists I doubtlessly was the most talented, why did I let Tàpies, Cuixart, Canogar, Saura, Millares, that gang take first place, which they could only take because I withdrew . . .

I withdrew? How I would like to know the truth? Luisa doubtlessly knows it, but it's an untranslatable, incommunicable truth, a truth that one must live together and die for. I withdrew? Can that be true? At the beginning, fifteen years ago, we were all the same—one animal that had the engine, and five, ten different heads, ten different talents. But the conviction existed that Spanish informalist painting was the total truth of what we could not take away, and no other form of painting existed. We were a cenacle. We barely knew one another, at least many of us, and many of us even denied that we were grouped under one category, or denomination. We were rugged individualists, who discovered at the same time something that was in the air. An air of enthusiasm, of discovery of a whole new continent that we informalists sensed, at the end of the 1950s and beginnings of the '60s! How far away today is that juicy atmosphere, that aroma, that live authentic material which was painting for us in those years. One exhibition followed another. We'd meet in cafés to chat with critics, with amateurs. And then, the group as a whole, the great exhibition Gaspar gathered together, and which he sent to all the countries of Europe, then to the United States, which was the consecration, and later the São Paulo Biennale: we had transcended our destiny, we were thrust into the whole world, our message of rigor was not a provincial whim, but rather a language the people who in the whole world knew, understood. The excitement, when the first painting by one of us was sold to the MOMA in New York. It was as if we all had sold, as if we all had triumphed equally and it signified that all of us would sell, all of us would get rich.

[Epilogue]

"You're not studying."

I was painting, like now. It was a rare occasion when many cousins got together during Holy Week at La Garriga, but they had sent Luisa for some unspecified reason saying that she had "behaved badly" at the nuns' school, and they sent me to prepare for a mathematics exam I'd have to take soon, after several shameful failures. It was raining in that park that was suddenly frozen, deserted, immense, and the house creaked with the swelling that happens to old houses, like plants, in the spring. Luisa sat near me to read on a broken-down disheveled old bed like the one in my apartment on Gracia, curled up like a cat by the fire: I was the fire, the only one lit up in that old mansion where other cousins were playing ping-pong down-stairs while their mothers were urging the telephone operator to hurry the calls to Barcelona, to beg their husbands to come join them on the weekend. I didn't want Luisa to see what I was painting. I didn't want anybody to know that I painted and didn't want Luisa to corner me, to seek me out as she had been doing despite my subterfuges to avoid her from the moment she arrived. The Jesuits in the confessional had assured me that what had happened two years earlier, when Luisa and I were fourteen, was a sin, and that we would go to hell without even the decency of being able to stop in the antechamber of purgatory. Everyone had gone on an excursion to Montseny; grandfathers, grandmothers, fathers, mothers, uncles, aunts, cousins male and female, servants had all left us convalescing from chicken pox, isolated in adjacent bedrooms precisely in this attic where I was now painting, so that we wouldn't contaminate the other cousins. Luisa and I chatted, shouting back and forth across the partition. They had warned us, expressly, not to scratch our scabs because if we did this we'd be marked forever. It was difficult to restrain oneself in those attics heated by a dense air buzzing with flies; one didn't know if what was itching so bad between one's eyebrows was that big almost-dry pimple, or a fly, and one scratched to find out and blood came out and I shouted to Luisa across the partition wall that I was bleeding. She appeared in my room barefoot and stained by the plague; she too was bleeding. She had torn off a pimple near her hairline, on her temple. She went over to the cloudy mirror over the white porcelain jug on the vanity and said:

"Look. I'm going to look like a monster with this hole here. Nobody is going to want to marry me. That's what my mother said. What do I care!"

"I too am going to be marked forever."

She came over to the bed to examine me and sat on the edge, and we began to show each other our pimples, and to compare the quantity and the appearance of the marks. Luisa opened my pajama top and touched my chest. She rolled up her nightgown to show me the pimples on her legs and hips so that I could touch them, and I touched, and then farther up I touched her belly, her new stiff pubic hair, her body stained and bleeding, and she put her hand under my sheet to seek in the sticky heat of my bed where my body was burning, and then she got completely under the sheet and everything happened with the urgency of adolescents, but with that skill, that knowledge Luisa had been born with:

"Touch me here."

And then:

"Now with your fingers there, no, lower . . . Do you like it?"

And then:

"Let me be on top for a while."

Rain fell on the chestnut trees whose branches we could glimpse through the porthole of the mansard roof crowned with shining volutes and iron lightning rods; it wasn't any old rainstorm but rather the final rainstorm at the end of the world, splitting the sky with lightning, flooding everything with the universal deluge that punished sinners but which saved a single couple, which in this case was not us because we were the most impure of all, according to the threats of our confessors at our schools in Barcelona. We knew that we were going to drown. What continued to happen every day between Luisa and me, until our convalescence ended in the isolated rooms under the mansard roof that summer, was not only the sin of impurity. Our flesh, in appearance, had been cured of its blemishes but I was left with a little hole between my thick black eyebrows, and Luisa, another one the same on her temple . . . the stains, they assured us, of incest, that tremendous sin that weakens races, so filthy that the Church forbade marriage between cousins so that not even under the Lord's protection was a union as terrible as incest permitted. Luisa would spell out the word in syllables behind me while I painted, curled up on my bed, enjoying the pleasure of the heat emanating from me, after almost two years of avoiding each other for fear that the pimples of the soul would clamor for our flesh, so clean in appearance. When I asked her, without turning around, what she was reading, she answered:

"*The Life of Lucrezia Borgia.* It's about incest."

I had already read it. It was a red book belonging to a collection of biographies all lined up on the higher shelves of my great-grandfather's library. My confessor told me that that book was there because my great-grandfather was one of the most infamous Catalan heretics, that the whole collection should be burned. But my cousins had already read those forbidden books. From the oldest to the youngest they had passed along this stock filled with a world of erudition. *The Life of Lucrezia*

Borgia was one of the favorites, a guaranteed source of tempestuous masturbations, exhausting dreams, confessions incapable of washing away sins because no penitence formulated a complete repentance, a source where new auto-erogenous zones were discovered by my older female cousins beneath their mask of modest marriageable young ladies, a source of secret silent shameful encounters among my most virile male cousins, which took place in the hasty secrecy of rooms inhabited by mannequins devoured by rats and chitchat, or under the trembling protection of bushes alive with insects and cattails during long summer sunsets in the most inaccessible zones of the park. I still smell the perfume of those yellowing pages, of their leather bindings, the broken springs of the divans we lay upon to read them, the hot air in the rooms where we were supposed to be studying, or convalescing, or taking a siesta. But Luisa and I talked only about incest: this time we were falling in love secretly but unhurriedly, talking leisurely about things that captured our imaginations, thus to pass over confessions and family, nuns and priests, and to go to forbidden movie theaters in Barcelona and to see together in the light of day parts of the city that at other hours, we knew, were infested with what they called "vice." I had stopped having friends at the Jesuit school, and Luisa at her boarding school, and as soon as we returned to our own homes on the weekends, not letting anyone else know about our relationship, we would call each other on the phone to meet, to go out together and see the city.

José Donoso (1924–96), a Chilean novelist and short-story writer, was one of the central figures in the "boom"—the transformation of Latin American literature that began in the 1960s. His fiction depicted a society undone by moral decadence. His novels include *Coronation* (1957), *The Obscene Bird of Night* (1970), and *A House in the Country* (1978), an allegory of Chile under Pinochet's dictatorship.

Suzanne Jill Levine is an award-winning translator and the author of numerous studies in Latin American literature, among them *The Subversive Scribe: Translating Latin American Fiction*. She has translated works by Adolfo Bioy Casares, Jorge Luis Borges, Guillermo Cabrera Infante, and Manuel Puig. She is a professor at the University of California, Santa Barbara.